Disciple's Quest
The Adventure Begins

Walter F. Cantrell

ISBN-10: 0692564586

ISBN-13: 978-0692564585

Cover Design by Tyson Roberts

Editing by Rebecca LuElla Miller

All Scripture verses are the Author's own wording or taken from the New King James Version. All direct quotes are listed at the back of the book.

Scripture taken from the New King James Version®. Copyright © 1982 by Thomas Nelson. Used by permission. All rights reserved.

Published in the United States by Grace and Truth Publishing

:

DEDICATION

I would like to dedicate this book to my four wonderful children; Joshua, Jonathan, Victoria, and Timothy.

TABLE OF CONTENTS

A GREAT DEBT

Doubtful Martin placed the last sack of feed on the wagon then took off his gloves.

An older man holding a clipboard called out to him. "Hey Doubtful, could you come over here?"

"Sure Mr. Brown." It still seemed a little odd to be called by his nickname, but after several years he'd gotten used to it.

Doubtful approached Mr. Brown who was standing next to the owner of the wagon.

"Jake needs someone to help him unload that feed into his barn. I told him you could go with him and take care of it. When you're done, go ahead and take your lunch break, and I'll see you after that."

"No problem," said Doubtful.

Jake stepped up into the wagon and took the reins. "Come on up and have a seat. It's not that far."

Doubtful climbed into the passenger seat and rode along. After they arrived, he unloaded all the feed, then Jake thanked him and gave him a small silver piece as a tip.

Nodding his head, Doubtful said, "Thanks."

"Do you want a ride back?"

"No thank you," said Doubtful, as he glanced over his shoulder. "It's not that far, and I like to walk."

As Doubtful strolled back into town, a few horses and buggies rumbled down the street while many of the women bustled along the walkways, shopping at the local markets. When he had gone a little further, he saw two men shaking their heads and gesturing wildly as they talked. As he came closer, he was able to overhear them.

"A great debt! How did this happen?" shouted one of the men.

"I don't know," the other one replied. "The whole thing sounds preposterous if you ask me."

Doubtful stopped and listened some more, trying to figure out what they were talking about. Had some new tax been placed on their town? What had caused these men to become so agitated?

Doubtful walked up beside them. "I'm sorry for interrupting, and I don't mean to eavesdrop, but I heard you mention a debt that all of us owe. I'm curious as to what this is all about."

One of the gentlemen took a puff from his pipe then removed it from his mouth. "A few days ago a mysterious stranger came around telling everyone who would listen that they owed a great debt to God. We weren't in town at the time to hear it for ourselves, but from what we understand he also said that if a person didn't pay this debt in full, then he would spend eternity in extreme torment when he died."

Doubtful scratched his head. "I've never heard of such a thing. How could we owe such a large debt to someone we can't even see?"

The other gentleman who was short and portly held out his hands. "That's what we're trying to figure out too."

Doubtful continued talking with the gentlemen, but after forty-five minutes of guessing and speculating, he left having more questions than answers. Realizing he had used up most of his lunch break, he headed back to the feed store. Along the way, he wondered why this mysterious stranger had come to the Town of Lost and gotten everyone so worked up about a mysterious debt they supposedly owed.

Doubtful made a quick stop at a fruit stand and purchased some berries to eat on his way back. As he neared the feed store, he shrugged off the conversation with the gentlemen and prepared to get back to work. The reason everyone had given him the nickname of Doubtful in the first place was because he was always skeptical of new information, so he wasn't about to let some wild story get to him. He worked through the afternoon and after loading the last bag of feed for the day, he said goodbye to Mr. Brown and left.

On his way home, two sisters named Lisa and Susan stepped out onto their front porch to greet him. Doubtful was a handsome young man and used to getting attention from the young ladies of the town. He was about five feet ten inches tall, well-built, but not too bulky. He had sandy brown hair, green eyes, and a pleasant smile. He didn't mind the attention from the young women, but he wasn't interested in a relationship at this time in his life either. He politely nodded toward the two sisters and continued on.

After arriving home, he made himself a sandwich then sat down to read the town newspaper. But as the evening wore on, his thoughts drifted back to his conversation with the two gentlemen. What if there was something to this debt the stranger had talked about? He had not spent much time thinking about God or what happened after death, but he always assumed everything would be okay.

He stood up from the table and headed toward his bedroom. 'Tomorrow is my day off, so I'll look into this further,' he thought.

Drifting off to sleep, Doubtful reassured himself that everything was going to be just fine.

When the next day arrived, he started by visiting his aunt and uncle. After his parents died of pneumonia when he was just two years old, they were the ones who took him in. He never really felt close to them, but still, they were the only family he ever knew.

His Aunt Mildred answered the door. "We haven't seen you in awhile. Come on in."

He stepped inside the house. "Just wanted to come by and talk to you and Uncle Bertrand about something that's on my mind."

Aunt Mildred closed the door and pointed to the couch. "Well come on in and have a seat."

Doubtful told her about his encounter with the two gentlemen the day before and his concerns about what they discussed.

Aunt Mildred shook her head. "Why are you bothering with such things? Talk of some make-believe debt is just foolishness. You need to focus on more important matters."

His Uncle Bertrand peeked over the top of the newspaper he was reading. "I'm surprised you're letting such things distract you. You need to focus on your job and getting ahead in life."

Doubtful stood up and turned toward the door. This conversation had gone just about the same as every other conversation he'd ever had with his aunt and uncle. "It was good to see you two again, but I've got to go meet some people."

Aunt Mildred stood up. "Don't be a stranger."

Uncle Bertrand set his paper down in his lap. "Tell Mr. Brown I said hello when you go into work tomorrow."

Doubtful left and talked with a few of his friends, but they weren't any more helpful. Finally, he decided to go talk to Mr. Brown, hoping he might have some answers.

Mr. Brown saw him marching toward the store and called out to him. "What are you doing here on your day off?"

"Something's on my mind, and I can't shake it."

Motioning for him to come inside, Mr. Brown said, "I've got a few minutes. Come on in, and we'll talk about it."

After sitting down on a stool, Mr. Brown said, "So what's the problem? Is it about money? Do you need an advance?"

"No, nothing like that," said Doubtful as he sat down beside him. He went on to explain the conversation he overheard the day before, and how he'd tried to find answers earlier that morning.

Mr. Brown folded his arms across his chest. "Seems like I may have heard something about this mysterious stranger you're referring to, but I don't usually pay much attention to stuff like that. And I'm surprised that you of all people are giving it any thought."

"I know," said Doubtful. "I don't understand it either. Usually, I'd never let something like this bother me."

Mr. Brown nodded. "I wouldn't get too carried away with trying to figure it out. This is not the first time a stranger has come to the Town of Lost thinking we needed someone to tell us how to live our lives. What they don't understand is that we were doing just fine before they got here, and we'll continue to be just fine once they leave."

"I guess so," said Doubtful. He then paused and sighed. "But it does seem like an important topic. If there is a God and we owe something to Him, then this would affect all of eternity."

"That's what they want you to think," said Mr. Brown. "If they can scare you into believing you've got this huge problem, then you'll have to rely on them for the answer. Religions were invented to

4

control people." Standing up, Mr. Brown said, "I'm glad you stopped by, but I've got to get back out front. I'm waiting for a shipment of feed to arrive."

Doubtful hopped off the stool. "Thanks for talking with me."

"Glad I could be of help," said Mr. Brown as he walked toward the door.

Doubtful wandered around the town, attempting to relax and enjoy his day off, but no matter how much he tried, he couldn't stop thinking about the possibility of owing a debt to God. He sat down on a bench and watched the people going by. Suddenly, he mumbled to himself, "Everything Mr. Brown said makes sense, so why is this still bothering me?"

He sat there for a few more minutes, then got up and headed over to the market. Once he arrived, he proceeded to the fruit section and began picking out some fresh apples. As he turned to leave, he overheard an older lady talking to the merchant about a stranger who had recently come to the town.

Wondering if this was the same person the two gentlemen had talked about the day before, Doubtful spoke up, "Pardon my manners, but was this stranger you're referring to by any chance talking about God?"

The lady whirled around. "Did you hear about him too?"

"Yes," said Doubtful, "but no one seems to know exactly what he said."

The lady placed some grapes in her basket. "I don't know if I can be much help because I've only heard bits and pieces."

Giving the woman an anxious look, he said, "Anything would be helpful."

The lady paused and put her hand to her chin. "As I recall, it was something about how God isn't pleased with us as we are, and something must be done to fix this. As soon as I heard that, I just ignored everything else. I don't need some foolish stranger telling me what God thinks about me. The idea that some man believes he can speak for God, if there even is such a being, is nonsense."

Doubtful thanked the lady for her time and started toward home. He'd hoped this lady was going to be able to help him, but now he felt she had actually made things worse. Why wouldn't God be pleased with him? He was a good person who always tried to live his life with respect toward others. Surely, this stranger couldn't have been talking about people like him, could he? He must have been talking about the really bad people, the criminals, or those who cheated and took advantage of others.

After arriving home, Doubtful made himself some dinner then sat down to eat. He glanced around at the small room, proud of what he had accomplished thus far in his life. When he had turned sixteen, he moved out of his aunt and uncle's place and spent the next six years staying with different friends while working odd jobs.

Now that he was twenty-two he had a steady job at Mr. Brown's Feed Store, and he even made enough money to rent this small room from the Johnsons when their daughter had gotten married and moved out. Life hadn't been easy, but he felt good about the direction things were going, or at least that was the case until today.

Still struggling with the whole dilemma about God and this debt, Doubtful tried to console himself by playing back in his head the things Mr. Brown had told him, but no matter how logical these arguments sounded at the time, they weren't very convincing right now. What he thought was going to be an easy problem to resolve, had turned out to be more complicated than he could ever have imagined.

Doubtful changed into his pajamas. 'Maybe I just need a good night's rest.'

He lay down to go to sleep, but his mind wouldn't cooperate. He tossed and turned, as he desperately tried to quiet his thoughts, but the same questions kept racing through his mind. What could he have possibly done to accumulate such a large debt, and why was there such an extreme price for not paying it? And most concerning of all, why would God not be pleased with him?

When the next day finally arrived, Doubtful decided he had to find some answers.

He quickly got dressed and headed off to the feed store. As soon as he arrived, he went around back and found Mr. Brown examining some receipts.

Mr. Brown looked up from his clipboard. "You're an hour early."

Doubtful held out his hand. "I know this is short notice, but I need another day off."

"What's wrong?" asked Mr. Brown. "I don't think you've

requested an extra day off since you started here."

"It's what we talked about yesterday, it's still bothering me," said Doubtful. "I appreciate you taking the time to discuss it with me, but I feel like I still need some more answers."

Mr. Brown looked around at the bags of feed that still needed to be organized. "Go ahead and take a day to get things sorted out, but be ready to work even harder tomorrow, so we don't get behind."

Doubtful thanked Mr. Brown and then went home to pack his backpack with enough supplies to last for the day. If no one in the town knew anything about this problem then maybe someone outside the town could help.

Doubtful hurried toward the countryside, and after hiking for an hour, he arrived at a winding dirt road. A few minutes later, he came upon a man with a cheerful look on his face, bobbing his head side to side while humming a song. The man was neatly dressed in brown trousers and a white shirt, and he wore a wide-brimmed hat to keep the sun out of his eyes. He stood at the side of the road, leaning against his staff as if he was waiting for someone.

When the man spotted Doubtful, he smiled and pushed his glasses further up on his nose. "Hello there. What brings you by this way today?"

Doubtful set down his backpack then took out a handkerchief to wipe the sweat from his brow. "I'm looking for an answer to a problem."

"I see," said the man. "What kind of problem?"

Doubtful folded up his handkerchief and placed it back in his pocket. "It seems someone came to our town and talked about a great debt that we owe to God and how there are terrible consequences for not paying it."

"Hmm, I understand why this is causing you some concern. My name is Witness, and I believe I can help you."

Finally, Doubtful thought. "Please sir, do you have any answers?"

Witness reached into his travel bag. "I have a Book that has all the answers. It's written by God himself."

Doubtful's eyes widened with excitement. "May I see it?"

"You may do more than just see it," said Witness, holding the Book out, "Here is your very own copy to read as much as you like."

"Thank you, sir," said Doubtful as he reached out and took it from him.

Witness smiled and nodded his head. "You're welcome."

Doubtful examined the Book. "Can you tell me a little bit about this debt that we owe?"

Witness told him the story of the first man and woman, Adam and Eve, how they were created perfect, and yet were deceived by Satan to commit sin. Witness explained to him that because Adam sinned, God counted it as if all human beings had sinned along with him, and this was why we all had this debt of sin.

Doubtful paused then shook his head. "It doesn't seem fair that I should share in the blame for a decision I didn't make. I wasn't there to eat the fruit."

Witness pressed his hands together as he nodded. "I understand that's how you may feel, but it's what God says, and if you think that's unfair, this Book also says that we get to share in something much greater that we also weren't there to participate in." He took off his glasses and wiped them off on his shirt. "And in addition to being counted sinful in Adam, we've also committed sin. 'For all have sinned, and fallen short of the glory of God.' Furthermore, because of Adam's sin, all of us are born with a sin nature. It says in this Book that we've been brought forth in iniquity and conceived in sin."

Doubtful put his hand to the side of his face. "So you're saying we were born with this debt?"

"That is correct."

Doubtful sighed. "So if I were to accept that I have this debt, what would I do about it?"

Witness took a deep breath as a serious look formed on his face. "You must be willing to go on a journey and leave everything of your old life behind."

Glancing over his shoulder, Doubtful said, "You mean I must leave the Town of Lost?"

"Yes," said Witness nodding, "The journey you need to begin is called The Quest. It is the most important journey anyone can take, for it is never-ending. It is full of adventure and excitement, but it is also full of challenges and hardships."

Doubtful scanned the area. "Where would I go to start this journey?"

Witness pointed out toward the distance. "To begin your Quest, you must go to a place just across that field, where you'll find a wooden structure called The Building of Reflection. But beware because what you'll find in that building will be disturbing. Most do not go far before they run back out, but if you are to pursue the answers you seek, you must go through this building and come out the other side."

Doubtful shook his head. "I don't know. This seems so sudden. I've lived my whole life in the Town of Lost, and now you're asking me to leave it all behind?"

Witness pointed at the Book. "I believe as you spend time reading you'll be convinced that you need to begin this journey."

Doubtful flipped through some of the pages. "Could you help me to know where to begin?"

"Sure," said Witness. "Hand me your Book, and I'll place some bookmarks in it for you."

After inserting the bookmarks, Witness handed it back to him. "I want you to know that this Book is the most important book you'll ever read. Study it, memorize as much as you can, meditate on what you've read, and talk about it frequently with others as you travel on your Quest."

"Thank you," said Doubtful as he threw his backpack over his shoulders, "but I'm not even sure I'm going on this journey you're talking about."

Witness pushed his hat a little further up on his head. "I believe you will."

Doubtful's eyes narrowed. "Why?"

"Because," said Witness as he smiled, "God would not have sent you to me if you weren't ready to begin The Quest."

2

THE JOURNEY BEGINS

Doubtful said goodbye to Witness and headed home. Along the way, he realized that while he'd solved one problem, another one had taken its place. Now that he understood what the stranger meant about a debt everyone owed, he must decide whether or not he believed it, and if so then what was he going to do about it.

Once he arrived back in his room, he sat down at the kitchen table and opened his Book to the first bookmark. 'All Scripture is God-breathed and is beneficial for teaching, for reproof, for correcting faults, and for instruction in righteousness.'

Immediately, he understood that the words of this Book claimed to be the very words of God. He then turned to the next bookmark, which was in the third chapter of Romans, and it had a note to start in verse 10. As Doubtful started reading, he was immediately confronted. 'There is no one who is righteous, not even one. There is no one who understands. There is no one who seeks after God. There is no one who does good.'

Doubtful set the Book down and stomped around the room. "What about me? I'm not a bad person. I do plenty of good things."

He suddenly stopped and shook his head. "Why am I letting this bother me so much? How do I even know these are God's words?" He thought back to his conversation with Mr. Brown. What if all this talk about a debt to God was just a scare tactic by some group to get him to run off and join them?

Thinking he just needed some rest after a long day, Doubtful flopped onto his couch and stared up at the ceiling. But even as he lay there, he couldn't help but think about his conversation with Witness. Why couldn't he dismiss all of this and get it out of his head? He glanced over at the table where his Book lay. ***No one is righteous. No one does good.*** The more he thought about those words, the more it felt as if something heavy was pressing down on him.

Doubtful jumped up and returned to the table. He started reading from where he left off, but the further he read the worse things seemed to get. He found himself being described as a viper and an open grave, even as someone who was able to do all manner of evil things. Could he really be that bad? Of course, he wasn't perfect and had committed some sins in his life, but wasn't there at least some good in him?

It was one thing to hear about this debt from others, but to read about it from a Book which claimed to be God's words was completely different. Suddenly, Mr. Brown's opinion seemed much less important as did the thoughts from the lady at the market.

Doubtful stared at the pages of his Book, feeling as if he had been dragged before a judge and declared: guilty, guilty, guilty. As he sat there reading the same verses over and over, he realized there was something much more powerful than his own skepticism. These words jumped off the pages, and they seemed to have life and energy, propelling him to take action whether his mind thought it was logical or not.

He closed his eyes and tried to clear his thoughts. After a few minutes, he stared back down at the page. What if he was as bad as these verses proclaimed? Was there any harm in taking a journey to seek answers? Maybe he should follow the advice of Witness and check out the building he had told him about. But was he ready to leave everything behind?

Doubtful closed his Book and meditated on what he had read. After a few minutes, he stood up, knowing what he had to do. He packed up everything he could carry and prepared for a long journey. He still wasn't sure what lay ahead, but he knew there wouldn't be any peace until he discovered some answers for himself.

He told Mr. Johnson, his landlord, that he was leaving and wasn't sure if he'd be back, then he headed over to the feed store.

Mr. Brown saw him approaching with a large backpack and knew Doubtful wasn't coming just to have another talk. "It looks like you're about to go on a trip."

Doubtful set his backpack down and held out his hand. "I came to tell you goodbye and to thank you for the opportunity to work here all these years."

Mr. Brown shook his hand. "I'm assuming this has something to do with what we talked about yesterday."

"Yes," said Doubtful, "I believe I need to go on a journey to truly figure things out."

Mr. Brown sighed. "You've been a good worker, but you must know that I'll have to immediately hire someone else, and I won't be able to give you your job back even if you did return."

Doubtful nodded. "I understand." He glanced around. There wasn't much to this little town, but it was the only life he had ever known. He turned toward Mr. Brown. "I don't know if I'm doing the right thing or not, but I feel like I have to try and find some answers."

"You know what I think about this whole thing," said Mr. Brown. "But I understand why you feel the need to go on this journey." He motioned for Doubtful to follow him inside. "Let me give you your wages for the week. You'll need a little bit of money if you're going to travel for any length of time."

"Thank you," said Doubtful as he followed him into the store.

After receiving the money from Mr. Brown, Doubtful shook his hand one more time and then walked out of the store. He thought about saying goodbye to his aunt and uncle, along with a few of his other friends, but he wasn't interested in hearing any lectures, so he just kept going.

Once outside the Town of Lost, he started toward the field Witness had pointed out to him. After traveling for an hour, he sat down under a maple tree to take a break. Seeing his Book protruding out of his backpack, he reached for it and opened it to Romans Chapter three. When he came to the part where it declared that no one was righteous, he once again felt the weight of the words pressing down on him. He tried to read further, but he couldn't.

As he closed his Book, Doubtful remembered the words of Witness, "For all have sinned and fallen short of the glory of God."

If these words were true, then this was an indictment against not only himself but the entire human race. He still wasn't sure if this Book was God's word, but the more he read, the more convinced he was that it was so.

He sat there for a few minutes, trying to wrap his head around the problem. So if everyone owed a debt of sin, but no one did what was good, then how could this debt ever get paid? If this Building of Reflection Witness had told him about was the first step in finding some answers, then he needed to get there as soon as possible. He placed his Book in his backpack and prepared to leave.

When Doubtful had traveled for another hour, he saw an old wooden structure about a hundred yards in the distance. He stopped and wiped the sweat from his brow. 'This must be the place Witness was talking about.' He started toward the building, and as he drew closer, he noticed two men talking to one another in an open field.

Doubtful recognized one of the men as the person everyone in town referred to as Mr. Enlightenment. He had long gray hair that was pulled back into a ponytail, and he wore a crystal around his neck. His clothes were clean, but they were all wrinkled as if they had been slept in. His head was tilted upward, and he clasped his hands behind his back.

Mr. Enlightenment eyed Doubtful approaching quickly. "I say, where are you going in such a hurry young man?"

Doubtful stopped and pointed toward the wooden structure. "I'm going to that building over there because I've been told it's the first step I must take on my Quest."

Mr. Enlightenment cocked his head to the side. "Uh hmm, what type of quest are you on, and who told you to go there?"

Doubtful took a moment to catch his breath. "Yesterday I learned that I owed a tremendous debt to God, and if I didn't pay it, I would spend all of eternity in terrible torment. I tried to find out why I owed this debt and how to pay it, but no one in town knew anything about it. So today I went to the countryside, and there I met a man named Witness. He gave me a Book and told me how I came to owe this debt in the first place. He then informed me that I needed to go through that building over there."

Mr. Enlightenment stepped toward him. "Why, that's terrible advice. The only debt that you or anyone else owes is to be the best person you can be. There is no such debt as you've been told."

Doubtful held out his Book. "But, it says so right in here."

Mr. Enlightenment angrily pointed toward the Book. "Well, those writings are thousands of years old and hardly relevant for today. You wouldn't exactly use two-thousand-year-old blueprints to build a house, would you? Of course not, and that book is just as useless. Besides, you don't need a book to tell you how to live your life. You have all you need right on the inside of you. You have your brain and an inner ability to attain all the knowledge you need if you'll pursue it. Why see here, I can point you to another path that goes around that building and is a much better way to achieve your quest." He shrugged his shoulders. "And besides, eventually, all paths lead to God anyway."

Doubtful shook his head. "But you don't understand. This Book was written by God Himself. It says that He worked within the men who wrote it in such a way that it was His words. If it's the words of God, then it would still be relevant for today, and even ten thousand years from now."

At this point, the other gentleman who most people in town called Mr. Good Works stepped forward. He was slightly overweight and mostly bald except for a little bit of hair above and around his ears. His clothes were neat and freshly pressed, and he wore a small brimmed hat that was just big enough to cover his head. He had a serious and austere look on his face, and his walk was rigid and stiff.

Mr. Good Works puffed out his chest and raised his hand. "Let me get a word in here young man. I've been listening to all your talk, and while it's possible that there is a certain debt that needs to be paid, there are better paths than the one you're heading for. Yes, you've done some bad things, and you'll likely do some more, but the key is to do more good works than bad, so when you die all of your good works outweigh the bad ones. Then your debts will be canceled, and you'll be accepted by God."

Doubtful shrugged. "But, my Book says there's nothing we can do to please God."

"Nonsense!" bellowed Mr. Good Works. "That book will be the end of you. Do you see that road over there that goes around the other side of that building? That's the path of Good Works, and you'll be much better off by following it." He turned and faced the

Building of Reflection. "And besides, you'll feel much better about yourself. Many of those who take your path are always talking bad about themselves. I hear one of the best of them once said, 'Oh wretched man that I am!' What kind of talk is that? Follow the path I will show you, and you can avoid such grief."

Off in the distance, they saw three men entering the Building of Reflection. Soon afterward, all three came running back out. One entered the path of Enlightenment, another fled toward the path of Good Works, and the other one just kept running.

Mr. Enlightenment chuckled. "If they don't listen to us before they go in, they certainly do when they come out."

"Ah yes," said Mr. Good Works, "A few moments in there, and they're much more ready to listen."

Doubtful looked back toward the building. "Why is that? What do they see in there?"

Mr. Enlightenment replied, "I hear that building is full of mirrors that show a person all kinds of awful things, very ugly things about themselves. They say it's quite a disturbing sight. I, myself, have never gone in there because I don't need such silly tricks. The mirrors that we have back in the Town of Lost are much better. They show us the very best of ourselves, and they help us to feel better about the things that we do. What good is it to dwell on the negative?"

Doubtful held out his Book again. "But, I've read that there is nothing good in us."

Mr. Good Works snorted. "There you go again with your book. Haven't you learned anything from what we've told you? Use your head young man. The answers you need are on the inside of you, and not in some old book."

Doubtful turned toward the Building of Reflection. "I'm going into that building, and I won't be running back out. I will go through to the other side, and I will start my Quest."

Mr. Enlightenment shook his head. "Very well then. We've seen a few make it to the other side. It's not a pretty sight though. They come out crying, weeping, and are all down on themselves. We see them again from time to time, and they insist that their path is the only true path. How narrow-minded of them to think they're the only ones who will end up with God."

Mr. Good Works nodded in agreement. "That's very true, and

then they have the nerve to tell me that good works don't earn you favor toward God. What kind of nonsense is that? Why, if everyone believed that good works didn't help to cancel your debt, then no one would do good works at all."

Doubtful was wearied from all the discussion. "I understand you don't agree with my decision, but I'm going to follow the advice I was given by Witness. And regarding my Book, I was skeptical too at first, but the more I've read it, the more I believe it's a letter written to me by God Himself. So I'm going into that building, and I will face whatever is in there."

Mr. Enlightenment and Mr. Good Works stepped aside, and Doubtful went on his way.

3

BUILDING OF REFLECTION

When Doubtful arrived at the building, he discovered that from the outside, the structure looked plain and simple. It was made of wood that had grayed with aging, and wasn't the kind of building one would think to enter without a good reason. Standing at the entrance, he heard the sounds of crying and deep distress and wondered if this was what he really wanted to do. Then the words from his Book flooded his thoughts, compelling him to go forward.

Taking a deep breath, Doubtful opened the door and entered the Building of Reflection. The inside of the building was also plain and unremarkable. There was just enough light to make out the unadorned walls and to see where he was going. The floors were solid, but they were obviously worn and old, making a creaking sound as he walked.

He took a deep breath and then crept down the hallway until he came to a door. Hesitating for just a moment, he turned the doorknob and entered the room. Immediately, he was confronted by a huge mirror that made him look like a giant. But it did more than just increase his size, for it showed him all his flaws as if they had been magnified a thousand times. It wasn't flaws of his physical appearance though, but it was flaws in his character and in his conduct. His face morphed into looks of pride, anger, and jealousy. He saw flashes of himself lying, cheating, stealing and committing other sins that seemed small and insignificant at the time, but in the mirror before him, all these things looked menacing and evil.

The sight was almost too much to bear, but Doubtful stood there, examining closely what the mirror revealed. After spending what felt like hours observing his reflection, he reached back to the door behind him and pulled it shut. The giant mirror sunk into the floor, revealing a path to another room. He walked down the narrow corridor wondering to himself, just what kind of place was this.

Doubtful opened the next door and walked into the room. Once inside, he saw a mirror on the ceiling. Looking up, he could see all his thoughts in large detail. There were thoughts of lust, blasphemy, murders, hatred, manipulation, pride, and other terrible imaginations. Feelings of guilt and shame overwhelmed him as he continued to stare into the mirror. He had always believed that only he knew about these thoughts and no one else, but this mirror showed that all of his thoughts were exposed and visible to God. Nothing was hidden from His sight.

Falling to his knees, he cried out, "God be merciful to me, sinful man that I am!"

A door opened at the back of the room revealing another hallway leading to another room. Doubtful plodded down the narrow hall, visibly shaken by what he had seen thus far. He entered the next room and noticed that the floor was one big mirror. He looked down expecting to see more terrible things, but this time the good things he had done in his life appeared in the mirror. A sense of relief came over him. Finally, it would be revealed that there was some good in him after all.

Doubtful bent down to get a closer look when suddenly, all of these good works began to transform into something different. Behind each good work, a dark shadow emerged and came into focus. Sometimes pride peeked out, or selfishness, or the desire to be approved by others. The shadows also revealed that there were times when he'd done these good works in order to feel better about the bad works he had done.

As terrible as the two previous rooms had been, Doubtful felt as if this room was even worse. He remembered reading in his Book about how sinful all men are. At that time, he comforted himself with thoughts that there was at least some good in him, but it was now clear that was not true. What he thought was good about his life was not so good after all.

Doubtful cried out, "All my works are completely rotten!"

Another door opened, leading to another room. Doubtful didn't want to go any further and see any more dreadful sights, but he couldn't go back. Feeling deflated and discouraged, he pushed on and proceeded to the next room. Upon entering, he saw an oval-shaped mirror located in the middle of the floor.

Slowly moving forward, Doubtful stopped in front of the mirror to see what it would expose. Suddenly, the room became dark, and glowing black sludge appeared in the mirror before him. After standing there for a few minutes, he realized that the purpose of this room was to show what was inside him. Doubtful understood that his problem was not just that he sinned, for his problem went far deeper than merely his actions.

Staring down at the floor, all he could say was, "I am completely sinful!"

Toward the end of the room, a small space opened at the bottom of the wall. After making his way to the opening, he got down on his hands and knees and crawled through to the other side. When he stood up, he saw a sign directly in front of him, which read, "Now You Must See What It Cost To Pay Your Debt."

After all he had seen, what could possibly be done to pay such a large debt?

As Doubtful walked forward, the narrow passageway opened up into a large room. There was no furniture, no mirrors, nothing. Written on the walls were verses from the third chapter of Romans, reminding him of his sinfulness. Toward the front of the room was an open door, and standing just inside it was a telescope pointing out toward a hill.

Suddenly, the awful sound of stone pounding on metal rang out from the direction of the hill. With each blow, someone was crying out in agony. It was the most horrible sound he had ever heard.

Doubtful looked up in anguish, placing his hands against his ears while pressing as hard as he could. "Please someone make this stop! I cannot bear to hear someone in such pain. Please help him!"

When the sounds didn't stop, Doubtful ambled toward the door and looked through the telescope. He saw a man laid out on a wooden beam, as his wrists were being nailed into the wood with large metal spikes. A hammer made of stone was being used to pound the spikes, and then the one who was holding the hammer turned and looked at him. What he saw brought terror to his eyes, for the person holding the hammer was himself.

Unable to take any more, Doubtful fell to the floor, sobbing and weeping. As he knelt crying, a hand touched his shoulder. He looked up but didn't see anyone. A gentle breeze swirled around him. Although he felt fearful and devastated on the inside, there was a feeling of peace all around him. "Who's there?"

A gust of wind swept through the room. "You cannot see me, but I am the Holy Spirit. I am also called The Comforter."

Doubtful looked around, holding his hands out in front of him. "How can I feel any comfort with what I've seen? I saw all my flaws and sinful deeds, and then I saw all my evil thoughts. Next, I saw that even the good that I thought I had done was actually bad. And yet what was worst of all, I saw that I was completely rotten and sinful in every part of my being. Now I see a man being tortured, and it is I that is doing this terrible thing!"

The Holy Spirit said, "As long as you stayed away from this building, only looking through the mirrors of this world, you saw yourself as you would like to be, but in here, you see yourself as you truly are."

Doubtful lowered his head. "If my debt is because of my sinfulness, then I have nothing with which to pay."

"That is why someone else had to pay this debt for you," said the Holy Spirit.

"Is that the point of the man being nailed to that cross?"

"Yes, the wages of sin is death. The Man you saw was the Lord Jesus Christ. He has existed as God the Son for all of Eternity where He, God the Father, and I lived in perfect unity together. The Father sent the Son to become a man by being born of a virgin. Jesus lived a perfect, sinless life before dying on that cross as a payment for your debt of sin. He then rose again on the third day and is in heaven now with the Father. They both sent me to be a Comfort and a Help for all who would come through this building and begin their Quest."

Doubtful pointed toward the direction of the cross. "I know I was born sinful, and I've done a lot of bad things, but would I have really swung that hammer and participated in the death of an innocent man?"

The Holy Spirit answered, "Think of all that you've seen in this building. Everyone has been born with the capability of doing the worst of things. It is God, because of His own goodness, who restrains people from being as bad as they could be."

Doubtful sat quietly for a few moments and then burst out, "What must I do to be saved?"

The Holy Spirit said, "Jesus did all of this so that you could receive the gift of Eternal Life. He lived the life you could not live and paid the price you could not pay. Through His shed blood, you can be completely forgiven of all the sin you saw in those mirrors. And because of his perfect obedience, you can be placed in right standing with God as if you have always done everything that was right."

Doubtful's eyes lit up. "That's great news! How does this happen?"

"When you leave this building, you will first go up a hill. The hill is called Calvary. There you will see the cross where Jesus was crucified. You will take all the sins you've seen in this building and lay them at the foot of that cross. You must look to the cross and receive what Jesus did for you, putting your trust in Him."

Doubtful stood to his feet. "I still feel the weight and shame of my sin, but I now have hope. This hope gives me strength to take my sins up that hill." He started toward the door but then stopped. "Before I leave may I ask one more question?"

"Yes go ahead."

"Mr. Enlightenment and Mr. Good Works said their paths led to the same place as the path I wished to take. Is that true?"

The Holy Spirit replied, "No, that is what they want to believe. There is only one path that leads to God, and it starts through this building and must go up the Hill of Calvary."

"Then where do those other paths lead?"

"They lead to a cliff, and at the bottom is a lake that burns with fire forever."

Doubtful held out his hands. "I'm so thankful that I heard about my debt and was led to this building. If not for such favor, I believe I would have gone on one of those paths myself."

"You have much to be thankful for. Keep that in mind as you proceed on your Quest."

Doubtful left the building and walked toward the hill called Calvary.

4

HILL OF CALVARY

Doubtful climbed up the hill to see the place where his debt had been paid. As he drew near to the top, an old wooden cross stood before him. He fell to his knees and bowed his head, pondering all the sin, all the awful sin, he had seen in the Building of Reflection. He then remembered the words of the Holy Spirit and gazed up at the cross, knowing that it was for his sins that Jesus died.

Lifting his eyes toward heaven, he cried out, "Lord Jesus, thank you for dying for me on this cross. I repent for all of my sins. I know that without your sacrifice my debt could never have been paid. I don't want to be the same person I was. I want to follow you. I want you to be my Lord and Savior."

Instantly, feelings of elation and euphoria swept over him, and he felt alive like never before.

A Voice thundered from heaven. "You are a new creation. Old things have passed away, behold all things have become new! No longer shall anyone call you Doubtful. From this point forward, you shall be known as Disciple."

"Disciple!" he said to himself, "What a wonderful name. I will try to live up to it for the rest of my Quest."

Disciple gazed toward heaven. "Thank you, Lord! Thank you for everything you've done for me!" He raised his hands and rejoiced, giving praise to God.

After a few minutes, Disciple stood up and climbed down the hill. When he reached the bottom, he saw another mirror. At first, he was hesitant to look into it because up to this point his experience with mirrors had not been positive. On top of the mirror was a sign that read, "How God Sees You." Disciple slowly stepped in front of it and saw himself clothed in a beautiful white robe. Words were stamped across the center of the robe which read, "The Righteousness of Christ."

Disciple realized he had been given a righteousness that he did not deserve, and now he understood what Witness had been trying to tell him. Although he might not feel it was fair to receive a debt of sin because of someone else's actions, it was the actions of someone else that canceled that debt for him. Even as he was counted as sinful because of Adam, he could now be counted as righteous because of Christ. Disciple thought this did not seem so unfair after all.

Staring into the mirror Disciple saw a light that seemed to be coming from inside him. He carefully opened his robe and saw that while there was still a lot of the black sludge in his body, in the center was a bright light.

He stepped away from the mirror and pondered all that had just happened to him. Hearing a sound behind him, he turned around and saw an elderly man approaching with a smile on his face and a bounce in his step.

As the man drew closer, he held out his hand. "Hello there, my name is Teacher."

"Nice to meet you, my name is Disciple." He shook Teacher's hand and realized he had just introduced himself for the first time with his new name. Joy swept over him as he was once again reminded of what had just taken place.

Teacher looked over Disciple's shoulder. "I see that you've gone through the Building of Reflection and have climbed the Hill of Calvary. I come by these parts from time to time to see those who have started their Quest, and to give them some instructions that will be helpful along the way."

Disciple stared back at the cross. "So much has happened today, and I'm so grateful for all that God has done for me."

Teacher lifted his hands and smiled. "Yes, Isn't God good?"

Disciple turned toward the mirror. "I do have a question for you. As I was looking in this mirror, I saw the black sludge of sin still running through my body, but in the center, I'm filled with light.

How do I get this light to spread out and remove all that darkness?"

Teacher walked up to the mirror. "I wish we could completely rid ourselves of the awful effects of sin, but the best we can do is to gradually diminish its influence in our lives. The light you see is the Light of Sanctification. As you spend more time on your Quest, you will grow in your relationship with God, and the light will start to spread. This light will affect how you think and what you do."

Disciple looked down at his hands, feet, and the rest of his body. "I feel a new powerful desire within me to do what is right, but I sense that my old ways have not completely gone. It's as if two people are living on the inside of me."

Teacher nodded and put his hand on Disciple's back. "Yes, it can certainly feel that way, but you are not two people. You are one person, a new person. The old nature is not who you are. It can still affect what you do, but it's powerless to stop you from obeying God whenever you wish."

Teacher motioned for Disciple to come and sit beside him on the grass, and then he opened up his Book to Romans chapter six. "You see here, it says that your old nature was crucified on the cross with Christ. It no longer has the power to dictate your thoughts or what you do. You are a new creation, and this new person is strengthened by the Holy Spirit, who now lives on the inside of you."

"I wish I could be perfect," said Disciple, "I wish I could be done with sin."

"We should all want to be holy even as the Father is holy, but we must understand that while this is our goal, it will happen a little at a time. We will never be perfect as long as we are in these bodies, but each day we can be transformed more into His likeness."

Disciple placed his elbows on his knees, thinking about his conversations just before entering the Building of Reflection. "Mr. Good Works seemed to make a good point to which I don't have an answer. He said that if good works have nothing to do with paying off our debt, then there would be no reason to do good works."

Teacher pointed toward the Building of Reflection. "As you saw in the room with the mirrored floor, what we humans think are good works, are not that good after all. None of them are perfect works, and only the works that Jesus did are perfectly pleasing to the Father. As you travel on this Quest, you will be motivated to do good works throughout your journey, but instead of doing these good works as payment on a debt, you will do them out of love to the One who paid your debt."

Disciple took a deep breath then slowly exhaled. "It would seem that I've got so much to learn. Is there anything else you can share with me before I start out on my Quest?"

Teacher stood up and pointed toward a meadow surrounded by small hills. "Look over there and tell me what you see."

Disciple rose to his feet. "I see a cave in the side of the hill with a large rock sitting beside the opening."

Teacher nodded. "That's the tomb where Jesus was laid. Of course, He didn't remain there, but He rose again early that Sunday morning. He showed himself to many of His followers, and then after forty days returned to heaven." Teacher gazed up at the sky and smiled. "And one day He's coming again."

Teacher turned to leave. "I must be going for now, but I believe we'll run into each other at another time. Keep that Book close by and read it daily."

"I will," said Disciple, grasping his Book, "I just wish I could take it in as one giant meal and understand all of it. I have a hunger and a thirst for every word."

"That's a great attitude to have. I wish all of those on this Quest felt the same way all the time. Many who started on this journey had the same hunger for the words in this Book, but over time they became neglectful and lost their zeal."

Disciple shrugged. "I don't understand. The way I feel right now is so much better than I've ever felt. Why would I give this up?"

Teacher shook his head. "That's a good question and one that is difficult to answer. I wish I could tell you that I've never strayed from my path, but that wouldn't be true. I learned from my mistakes, and I've been thankful for the grace that was always there for me when I acknowledged my faults and turned away from them."

Disciple stood up a little straighter. "I'm glad you got back on the right path, and I'm sorry you strayed at times, but I think I'll be different. I'm never going to leave my path to take another road, not even for a few feet."

Teacher looked at Disciple as if there were many things he wanted to say, but he just smiled. He held out his hand. "If you'll give me your Book I'll place a couple of bookmarks in it to help you get started with your reading."

Disciple gave it to him, and then Teacher placed the bookmarks and handed it back.

"I'd suggest you read where I placed the first bookmark now, and then read the second one after you've visited the empty tomb."

"Thanks," said Disciple. "I'll do that."

Teacher then prayed for him and went on his way.

Disciple plopped onto the grass and began reading from the first bookmark. He read about the life of Jesus from the time He started His earthly ministry until after His resurrection when he showed Himself to His followers. Disciple marveled at the sacrifice Jesus had made for him, and he felt even more love for his Savior.

He glanced down at his Book and remembered the struggle he'd had with reading Romans Chapter three. He turned over to this passage and read it again, but this time he saw these verses in a completely different light. Even as they pointed out his sin and guilt, he knew this wasn't the end of the story. He made his way to the end of the chapter and saw the blessed hope that was now his. Even though he was still sinful, God looked upon him as being righteous because he put his faith in Christ.

Disciple rose to his feet and strolled across the meadow toward the cave Teacher had pointed out to him. When he arrived at the tomb, he peeked in to see a slab of granite stretched out from end to end. He realized this was where they had laid Jesus' body. He stepped back out and leaned up against the large boulder, thinking about that glorious morning when this stone was rolled away, and Jesus came out of the tomb as the One who had conquered death and the grave.

Disciple took out his Book and turned to the second bookmark Teacher had placed. He then read about how one day his own body would be raised from a grave and would be a brand new body that would last forever.

Looking toward heaven, Disciple prayed. "Dear Lord, please never let me forget all that has happened to me on this day. May I live in a way that reflects my constant gratitude for all You've done for me."

Disciple gazed at the cross then at the tomb one more time, before leaving the meadow.

5

PASTOR SINCLAIR

Disciple peered up into the sky as the sun disappeared over the horizon and knew that soon he would need to find a place to stay for the night. He kept going in the same direction, and after a few minutes, he spotted a sign up ahead. "All who've just started their Quest are welcome to visit us at the House of Instruction."

Disciple trudged up a small hill until he arrived outside a large wooden building that was two stories tall. On top of the building was a steeple containing a bell. He thought this must be the House of Instruction the sign had pointed to, so he walked up to the door and knocked.

A kindly looking older gentleman came to the door. He was a tall, jovial person with salt and pepper hair, and appeared excited to have a visitor. As soon as he saw Disciple, he smiled and waved him inside. "Welcome, my name is Pastor Sinclair."

Disciple eased into the house. "Thank you. My name is Disciple." He ambled across the entryway, curious to see what kind of house this was.

Pastor Sinclair led him through a large room which had rows of benches on two sides separated by a walkway in the middle. Toward the front and in the center was a pulpit. After he had glanced around for a moment, Pastor Sinclair led him into a smaller room off to the side where there was a table and some chairs.

Pastor Sinclair held out his hand and motioned toward one of the chairs. "Have a seat. I'm so glad you stopped in to visit me."

Disciple set down his backpack and took a seat at the table.

Pastor Sinclair pulled out a chair across from him and sat down. "So tell me what brings you by this way today."

Disciple started from the beginning and shared all the events of the past two days. As he was speaking, Pastor Sinclair leaned forward, smiling and nodding as Disciple shared about each stage of his journey.

After listening to all of Disciple's testimony, Pastor Sinclair raised his hands. "This is wonderful. For even the angels in heaven rejoice each time someone goes through the Building of Reflection and climbs up the Hill of Calvary."

"It's been a great day," said Disciple. He looked around and noticed other rooms further down the hallway and an upstairs which appeared to be living quarters. "What is the purpose of this building?"

Pastor Sinclair pointed out toward the larger room. "It's a place where you can hear teaching from the Book, and you can meet and fellowship with others who are on the Quest. And since I perceive you are a weary traveler, it's also a place where you can rest before continuing your journey."

Disciple sat back in his chair, reflecting on all the circumstances which led him here. "So many wonderful things have happened today. I started off trying to find an answer to a problem, and along the way, I learned the best news anyone could possibly hear."

Pastor Sinclair smiled and put his hand on Disciple's shoulder. "The Gospel of Christ is such good news. It is the power of God to bring salvation to all those who believe."

Seeing that Disciple looked tired, Pastor Sinclair said, "You look as though you've had a long and eventful day, so let's get some rest, and we'll talk more tomorrow." He then stood up and showed Disciple to a room upstairs where he could spend the night.

Disciple settled in, then lay in his bed and read from his Book. After reading a few chapters, he set it on a nightstand and turned off his lamp. Once again he thanked God for His wonderful grace, before going to sleep.

The next morning Disciple woke up refreshed as the smell of eggs and bacon drifted up to his room. Anxious to begin a new day, he quickly got dressed and came downstairs.

Pastor Sinclair was singing as he placed the food on the table. "I hope you slept well. Sit down and have some breakfast with me."

While the aroma of the food was pleasant, even more noticeable was the peacefulness of the atmosphere. "Thank you. It looks and smells great. Yes, I did sleep well. In fact, I don't think I've ever had a more relaxing night of sleep."

Pastor Sinclair sat down at the table and took Disciple's hand as he closed his eyes. "Dear Lord I give thanks to you today that another one of your children has started their Quest. Thank you for this meal we're about to share and bless this time that we have together."

Pastor Sinclair tore off a bite of toast. "Last night you mentioned that you came from the Town of Lost. What did your family and friends think when you just up and left all of a sudden."

Disciple glanced down for a moment. "I don't have a lot of family. My parents died when I was younger."

Pastor Sinclair placed his hand on top of Disciple's. "I'm sorry to hear that. Were there others you were close to?"

Shaking his head, Disciple said, "Not really. I grew up with my Aunt Mildred and Uncle Bertrand, but we were never all that close. There were different people that I hung out with from time to time, but I never felt comfortable making close connections with anyone."

Pastor Sinclair took a drink of orange juice. "Another benefit of being on this Quest is that you are now a part of a very large family. God is your Father, and there are many brothers and sisters with which to build relationships with. As you progress on your journey be sure and take the time to form friendships with those you meet. Everyone needs encouragement and support as they travel along."

"I'll do that," said Disciple.

After they finished eating, Pastor Sinclair cleared the table. "I'll be right back. I have some important things I'd like to teach you."

Humming as he came back into the room, Pastor Sinclair sat down and eagerly began to turn the pages of his Book. "I would like to give you some instructions on two things. The first one is called Baptism. We see in the Book that after someone believed in Jesus, they were then baptized. This symbolized their new life in Christ by identifying with His death, burial, and resurrection."

After listening to Pastor Sinclair share some verses about baptism,

Disciple sat forward and placed his hands on the table. "I would like to be baptized."

Pastor Sinclair stood up and pointed toward the door at the end of the hallway. "There is a stream that runs behind this house, and I can baptize you there."

Pastor Sinclair and Disciple stepped outside and walked toward the stream. On each side of their path were fruit trees in full blossom, with songbirds nestled in the branches singing a harmonious tune. The sun had begun to rise above the forest in the distance, causing beams of light to bounce off the water. Wading into the stream, Pastor Sinclair led him to a spot where the water came up to their waists.

Looking up toward heaven, Pastor Sinclair said, "Dear Father, I thank you that Disciple has begun this Quest and that he has become a new creation. We come here today to honor Your command that we should baptize those who believe in Your Son."

Pastor Sinclair placed one hand underneath the upper part of Disciple's back and the other hand on his chest. "Disciple, as you have proclaimed your faith in Jesus Christ, and your desire to follow our Lord's command in baptism, I baptize you in the Name of the Father, in the Name of the Son, and in the Name of the Holy Spirit."

As Pastor Sinclair lowered him into the water, Disciple looked up to see the brilliance of the sun's rays coming through the trees, reminding him of the glory of God. Pastor Sinclair lifted him back up out of the water, and as he did, Disciple felt exhilarated. It was one thing to read that he had been buried with Christ and raised together with Him, but to experience something that represented it, made it all the more real. His old life was behind him, while laid out before him was his new life as a follower of Jesus Christ.

After they came out of the stream, they both went back inside to put on some dry clothes and then Disciple joined Pastor Sinclair again at the table.

Pastor Sinclair opened his Book. "The second thing I want to teach you is called Communion, or The Lord's Supper."

"I believe I read about this," said Disciple. "This happened on the last night before Jesus was crucified, correct?"

"Yes. On that night, Jesus took bread and gave some to each of His disciples. He told them the bread symbolized His body, which would be broken for them. Then He took a cup and instructed each of them to drink from it. Jesus taught them that the cup represented His blood which He would shed for them. He told them that as often as they did this, they would be doing it in remembrance of Him, and what He did for them in His death."

"So Communion is a reminder of the sacrifice of Jesus on the cross?"

Pastor Sinclair nodded. "Yes, it serves as a symbol. Communion is an opportunity to stop and think about what has been done for us, and it's an opportunity to reflect on how we are living our lives in light of what has been done for us."

Disciple was eager to experience Communion. "I hope we're going to do this as well."

"Yes, let me go get the items we need, and I'll be right back." Pastor Sinclair pushed his chair away from the table and headed off toward the kitchen. After a few minutes, he returned with two cups and a fresh loaf of bread. "I'm so glad you stopped by here yesterday. It's always nice to have someone to share Communion with."

Pastor Sinclair set the items on the table and sat down. He turned a few pages in his Book and then began to read. "For I received from the Lord that which I also delivered to you: that the Lord Jesus on the same night in which He was betrayed took bread; and when He had given thanks, He broke it and said, 'Take, eat; this is My body which is broken for you; do this in remembrance of me.' "

Pastor Sinclair tore off a piece of bread and gave it to Disciple, and then he tore off a piece for himself. "Let us eat."

They each ate the bread.

After handing Disciple one of the cups, Pastor Sinclair continued reading from his Book. "In the same manner, He also took the cup after supper, saying, 'This cup is the new covenant in My blood. This do, as often as you drink it, in remembrance of Me.' "

Pastor Sinclair said, "Let us drink."

They each drank from their cup.

Pastor Sinclair read once again. "For as often as you eat this bread and drink this cup, you proclaim the Lord's death till He comes."

Pastor Sinclair then bowed his head in prayer. "Dear Lord Jesus, thank You for giving Your body to be broken on the cross and thank

You for shedding Your blood for the forgiveness of our sins. May we never forget the great sacrifice that You made for us, and may we live in remembrance of what You've done every day of our lives. Amen."

Disciple said, "Thank you for teaching me these things. Experiencing Baptism and Communion gives me a deeper understanding of what they mean. I see that symbols are a way of teaching us things about God."

Closing his Book and holding it in both hands, Pastor Sinclair nodded. "Jesus and many of the writers of this Book used symbols as a way of teaching things. One symbol can represent pages of words to us. The next thing I'd like to show you also involves symbols. Let's go into that big room down the hall where I have many things I'd like to show you."

Disciple picked up his Book and followed Pastor Sinclair down a long hallway and into a large room where different pieces of armor lined the walls from top to bottom.

Disciple stared in amazement. "There's enough armor here to equip an army, but why would we need such protection? Will people try to hurt me along the way?"

"They may," said Pastor Sinclair, as he scanned the room, "but that's not its purpose. This armor is to protect you from the assaults of your enemy the Devil. He is a crafty foe that has been around for thousands of years. He and his army will try to keep you from being successful on your journey. He cannot change what's happened to you, but he will try to keep you from having success while on your Quest."

Disciple shifted his gaze from one piece of armor to the other. "Then please give me everything I'll need to stand against the attacks from my enemies."

Pastor Sinclair shuffled around the room like someone who was shopping in a store trying to find just the right item. He would hum and talk to himself as he studied the different pieces of armor, then glance back at Disciple. After a few minutes, he took down a large silver piece of metal and placed it over Disciple's head like someone would put on a shirt. It was strong and sturdy, and covered his entire front and back, from his neck down to his waist.

Pastor Sinclair stepped back. "This is called the Breastplate of Righteousness. It will protect your most important body parts. Do you remember seeing yourself in a robe when you looked into the mirror at the Hill of Calvary?"

"Yes," said Disciple, as he touched the metallic finish on the Breastplate.

"And what was written across the chest of this robe?"

Quickly looking up, Disciple answered, "The Righteousness of Christ."

Pastor Sinclair raised his index finger. "Correct. This Breastplate is to remind you that you must always put your trust in His Righteousness and Goodness and not your own."

After taking down a helmet from the wall, Pastor Sinclair turned it side to side, before placing it on Disciple. "Of course you must protect your head. This is the Helmet of Salvation. Your head is where your thoughts come from, and you must think on things that are pleasing to God. It is also called the Helmet of the Hope of Salvation. We place our hope in the salvation God has already given us, and we also hope in the salvation that is to come at the glorious appearance of our Lord."

Next Pastor Sinclair took down some shoes that had leather straps across the top and small spikes on the bottom. He handed them to Disciple who removed his sandals and placed these new Shoes on his feet.

"Those are Shoes of the Gospel," said Pastor Sinclair. "The Gospel Message is what you've learned so far. It teaches us that we must turn from our sin, while putting our faith in Christ and what He's done for us. We must walk daily in this Gospel Message and never forget what it means. As we do, our feet will always be firmly planted, and we'll not slip and fall when we're on unsteady ground."

While Disciple was admiring his armor, Pastor Sinclair set up a stepladder so he could retrieve the next item. Reaching up almost to the ceiling, he took down a large Shield and gave it to Disciple. It glistened with a bright metallic gray color and had a large red cross painted on it. The Shield was big enough so that Disciple could kneel down behind it and be completely sheltered from anything that came toward him.

Disciple held out the Shield. "I believe I understand what this is for, but please tell me more about it."

Tapping it with his finger, Pastor Sinclair said, "This is the Shield of Faith. It will block the attacks of your enemies, and if they shoot a fiery arrow at you, this Shield will quench the fire and cause the arrow to fall harmlessly at your feet."

Turning the Shield side to side, Disciple said, "Why is it called the Shield of Faith?"

"Because," answered Pastor Sinclair, "whenever we're attacked we must acknowledge that our trust is solely in God for our protection. It is through His strength and not our own that we can stand in the day of battle."

Pastor Sinclair showed Disciple that when the Shield was fastened to the back of his Breastplate, it would shrink to a very small size, and then once it was removed and held out in front of him, it would become full size again.

After marching toward the end of the room, Pastor Sinclair came back with a strong leather belt which he snapped as he handed it to Disciple. "Put this around your waist. It will anchor your Breastplate, and it will cause you to be ready for battle."

Disciple held out the belt. "What is it called?"

"It is the Belt of Truth. It goes around the very center of your body, and it symbolizes that you must always be centered in Truth. Meditate daily on the things you know to be true, and do not allow anything false to come out of your mouth."

Disciple examined each item he was given. "I noticed that all of these pieces of armor are for defense, but how can I participate in a battle with nothing to strike back at my enemy?"

Pastor Sinclair put his finger to his cheek. "That's a good point, but you already have an offensive weapon."

Disciple examined everything he was wearing. "I do? Where?"

Pastor Sinclair pointed toward the Book Disciple had placed on a table next to him. "Take your Book and hold it out in front of you."

Disciple held his Book out, and when he did, it became a Sword with a gold rounded handle and a silver blade. When he placed the Sword back down to his side, it became a Book again.

"Wow! I didn't know this Book was also a Sword."

"Yes," said Pastor Sinclair, "it is indeed a Sword. It was written by the Holy Spirit working through men, and it is called the Sword of the Spirit."

Disciple raised his Book again until it became a Sword, and then acted as if he was in battle, striking out into the air. At last, he put it back to his side.

"There is one more thing," said Pastor Sinclair, "but it is not a piece of armor, it is an attitude. You must always have an attitude of Prayer. When in battle, seek to stay in communication with God. He is the Supreme Commander who can see all things and knows all things."

Disciple looked in a nearby mirror, seeing himself with all of his armor. He was excited and felt ready to take on anything that would attack him.

Turning toward Pastor Sinclair, he said, "I'm grateful for all of this armor, but I'm concerned it's a lot to carry along with the other items I will need on my journey."

Pastor Sinclair looked down at his clothing. "Do you see me in my armor right now?"

"No. Where is it?" said Disciple as he inspected him from head to foot.

Pastor Sinclair tapped his chest two times, and immediately all of his armor appeared. He then tapped his chest again two times, and it disappeared. "When you're about to face an enemy, you can cause your armor to appear, but it will always be there whether it's visible or not. A person can take off their armor, but that wouldn't be wise."

Disciple looked back in the mirror while tapping his chest twice. Just like Pastor Sinclair's armor, his disappeared, and then when he tapped his chest twice again, it reappeared.

Pastor Sinclair put his hands on Disciple's shoulders. "Do be cautious, because when you leave here, you're likely to be in a battle very soon. Your enemy does not like the fact that you have started this Quest. He will do what he can to hinder you, and he watches to see when you're not on your guard."

"I will watch out and be alert," said Disciple.

Pastor Sinclair walked over to retrieve something from his workbench and held it out to him. "Let me also give you this satchel to carry your Book in."

After throwing the satchel around his shoulder, Disciple practiced putting his Book in his satchel, then pulling it out quickly, and raising it until it became a Sword.

Holding out his own Book, Pastor Sinclair said, "God's word is not just a weapon against your enemies, but it's also a weapon against your old nature—your flesh. When the words go inside you, it causes sin to leave you."

Disciple placed his Sword to his side. "So that's how I get the Light of Sanctification to spread out."

"Right. Study the words from your Book and meditate on them day and night. All Scripture is God-breathed and is profitable. It will teach you sound doctrine, correct you when you need it, and teach you how to conduct yourself while on your Quest."

"Thank you for this armor," said Disciple.

Pastor Sinclair patted him on the back. "You're welcome. You're equipped and ready to begin your journey."

As they left the room, Pastor Sinclair invited Disciple to have lunch with him before he left.

After they finished eating, Disciple pushed his chair back from the table. "Thank you again for everything. I will remember this time for as long as I travel on my Quest."

Pastor Sinclair stood up and hugged him. "I've enjoyed having you stay here with me. Let me walk you out."

As they made their way toward the door, Disciple stopped and turned around. "I do have another question for you. How do I know which direction I should go?"

Pastor Sinclair replied, "When you survey the land in front of you, your path will be raised a little higher than the rest of the ground around it. Also, as you continue to study your Book, you will notice that your path will be lighted as if a lamp were constantly at your feet."

"Does everyone travel the exact same path?"

"No, while everyone who starts on this Quest is heading for the same destination, we do not all experience the same journey."

Pastor Sinclair walked outside with Disciple. "I visit other Houses of Instruction from time to time, so maybe we'll see each other again."

Disciple held out his hand. "I hope so."

Pastor Sinclair shook his hand and then prayed for him before he left.

6

FIRST BATTLE

As Disciple left the House of Instruction, he noticed that his path stretched out before him. He traveled throughout the day, and when it wasn't as clear where he should be going, he stopped to read in his Book and pray. Afterward, he could see more clearly the direction his path was heading. Along the way, Disciple saw many others traveling their paths, and he made a point to stop and speak with them, even if it was for only a few moments to share some encouraging words.

After he had traveled for most of the day, he began searching for a place to set up his tent and camp for the night. The sun would be setting soon, and it would be getting dark in a couple of hours. As he moved forward, an intense quiet seemed to surround him, then suddenly, fiery arrows filled the sky, and he realized they were coming straight at him.

Disciple quickly knelt behind his Shield, and he could feel and hear the thumping of the arrows against the metal. One arrow zoomed just outside the perimeter of his Shield, grazing his exposed right arm, but the rest fell harmlessly in front of him.

Once the arrows had stopped, he relaxed for a moment, then suddenly an angry barking emanated from a thicket out to his right. He looked up to see a creature that resembled a large vicious dog coming toward him. It was as big as a small horse and had curved horns like that of a ram. He would later find out that this kind of beast was called a Karam. It was snarling and acting as if it was going to pounce any second.

Disciple was not sure how to fight such a creature, so he quickly prayed and asked God to give him wisdom. The Karam charged at him, and Disciple instinctively held out his Shield, while digging in with his Shoes. The Karam slammed into the Shield, knocking Disciple back a few steps.

Not knowing what the Karam would do next, Disciple dug in with his Shoes again and placed his Shield out in front of him. The creature retreated, and then a few moments later charged at him again. Bending his knees, while leaning forward into his Shield, he braced for impact. The Karam smashed into the Shield, but this time Disciple was only knocked back a few inches. The Karam retreated but looked as if it would pounce again at any moment,

Disciple remembered Pastor Sinclair describing the words of his Book as a weapon. He sensed that if he could remember a few verses it would help him to be more effective against this enemy. He was still very new to the study of God's word, but he prayed for the Holy Spirit to remind him of something he had read. At that moment, a verse came to his remembrance.

Looking the creature right in the eyes, Disciple shouted, "Thanks be to God, Who always gives us the victory in Christ."

The Karam stepped back a few feet, snarling and growling. Seeing that the fierce creature was about to charge again, Disciple braced for impact. The Karam pawed at the ground then lunged toward him, but this time the creature was stunned when it made contact with his Shield, and it tumbled backward.

Disciple knew this was his moment to go on the attack. Gathering his balance and reaching for his Book, Disciple shouted, "Blessed be the LORD my Rock, Who trains my hands for war, and my fingers for battle!"

He rushed the beast, striking it with his Sword on the side of the head. The Karam tried to charge, but Disciple thrust out his Shield and hit the creature on its horns, knocking it off balance. He then brought his Sword down on top of the Karam's head, and then followed up with a strike to the side of its jaw, driving it away.

Disciple tried to relax and catch his breath, but then all of a sudden a rattling sound echoed from above. He glanced up just in time to see a large cage dropping from the sky. He tried to get out of the way, but it landed on top of him, trapping him inside. Disciple took out his Sword, trying to cut himself free, but black sludge oozed out of the bars and kept his Sword from being effective.

Remembering that he had seen this same black sludge before, Disciple realized that the cage was fortified by sin. He once again searched his memory for a verse that would help him to be more effective. He then remembered his conversation with Teacher about his new life in Christ. Teacher had read the verse that said, "The one that has died, has been set free from sin."

Holding up his Sword, Disciple shouted, "I have died with Christ, my old nature was crucified with him, and I have been set free from sin's dominion in my life."

Disciple repeatedly struck the cage with his Sword until it was completely destroyed. He knelt down for a moment, leaning on his Sword to catch his breath. When Pastor Sinclair had said he was likely to face a battle soon on his journey, he didn't think it was going to be on his first day, and certainly not multiple battles from many different enemies.

Disciple stood up and surveyed the area. Out to his left, he heard sticks crackling on the ground as if multiple people were rapidly approaching. Just as he turned to see what it was, three creatures, covered in black from head to foot, darted toward him. They were the size and shape of men, but they had large hands with long, sharp fingernails. They each had a sword and shield of their own, and they all rushed at him simultaneously. Disciple struck at one with his Sword while blocking another one with his Shield. The third one swung at him with its sword, but he ducked just in time to get out of the way.

As all three enemies continued their attack, Disciple had to constantly alternate between blocking, striking, and dodging. Feeling worn down from the constant assault, Disciple cried out, "LORD, those who patiently look to you will regain their strength. They shall soar on the wings of eagles. They shall run and not grow weary. They shall walk and not be faint."

Disciple continued to fight them off for several more minutes, but he wasn't sure how much longer he could keep fighting. Just as he felt his strength was almost gone, another man appeared who was dressed in armor just like his.

Two of the creatures immediately broke off their attack on Disciple and charged this new warrior. He appeared to be experienced in battle, and he swung his Sword with extreme accuracy. He was steady on his feet, making it difficult for the creatures to catch him off balance or in a vulnerable position. He kicked out at one of the creatures with his Shoes, then whirled around and backhanded the other one with his Shield. Both creatures fell to the ground and then tried to scramble to their feet.

Disciple felt a renewed sense of energy, and he pressed the attack against the enemy he was facing. After blocking an assault, he lunged at the creature with his Sword and pierced it in its side. The creature tried to retaliate, but Disciple struck it on the side of the head and knocked it to the ground. The creature rolled over and saw that the other two were running away, so it quickly rose to its feet and ran after them.

Disciple glanced around, preparing for another enemy attack. When nothing appeared, he called out to the warrior who had aided him in the battle. "Thanks for the help. My name is Disciple."

"You're welcome. My name is Caleb. I've been fighting these battles for a long time. When I see a fellow soldier under attack, I join in the fight."

Caleb was a big man who was stout and muscular. He had curly hair with a full beard and mustache. He walked and fought with an air of confidence, but at the same time, his disposition was meek and humble.

Disciple noticed that Caleb's armor was a little thicker and fit better than his. "Your armor appears to be stronger than mine, and your Sword appears to be sharper."

Caleb held out his Shield. "As you travel on this Quest, you'll grow in your relationship with God, causing your armor to become more effective. And the more time you spend in your Book, the sharper your Sword will be."

"Why do we have to fight these battles?" asked Disciple.

Caleb reached over and tugged at Disciple's Breastplate. "How did your armor hold up during the battle?"

Surveying the battlefield, Disciple said, "I missed one of the arrows with my Shield, and then I noticed that my Breastplate left a small place on my left shoulder vulnerable. I was not as skilled with my Sword as I wanted to be, and I discovered I would need to know verses from this Book, to make my Sword more effective."

Caleb lowered his Sword to his side until it became a Book. "These conflicts expose your weaknesses. After every battle, ask God to show you where you need to be strengthened so you'll be ready for your next fight."

"Will all battles be like this one?" asked Disciple.

Caleb knelt down and tightened his Shoes. "They will not. Some battles will involve enemies that are very subtle and shrewd, and other battles will be with giants. Some battles you will fight by yourself, some with just a few people helping you, and other battles you may fight alongside many others."

Disciple shifted his weight from one foot to the other as he looked away. "I see."

Sensing that Disciple was concerned, Caleb said, "Don't be worried about what's ahead. God will not place you in a situation you aren't ready for."

Disciple lowered his Sword until it became a Book, and then put it in his satchel. "May I walk with you a little ways? I'd love to hear more about your experiences in combat."

Caleb glanced at the ground. "Sure, I see that our paths are heading in the same direction, so I'd be glad to talk along the way."

As they walked together, Caleb shared some insights into the enemy's strategies. He talked about how he had been attacked in different ways through the years, and Disciple carefully listened to each word. Their paths led them to the edge of the mountainside, overlooking a huge canyon which appeared to spread out for several miles. Large campsites filled the wide open space, and one of the camps was full of lights and had the faint sound of music.

Disciple peered over the side pointing to where the music was coming from. "What is that place?"

Caleb stared at the camp as dark smoke appeared to rise up from it. "That is the Camp of Sin. You never want to go down there. It will cost you dearly, and you will miss a lot of time that could have been spent making progress on your Quest."

Disciple noticed there was no way to get down to the Camp of Sin without falling off the side of the mountain. "How would someone even get down there?"

Caleb's eyes narrowed, as he folded his hands. "It's not an obvious path, for if it were, it would be more easily avoided. It's hard to know you are even going in the direction of the Camp of Sin in the beginning. The path to get there is through a series of winding trails that appear harmless at first, but the further you go, the more you have to compromise. By the time you arrive there, you've already compromised to the point that you are now ready to go in without thinking about the Quest you've left behind."

Disciple tightly grasped his Book. "I never want to go to the Camp of Sin, and I'll do whatever it takes to avoid ending up there."

Caleb paused, looking out over the canyon as if he was in deep thought. "The best way to avoid the Camp of Sin is not to leave your path to begin with."

Disciple pointed toward another section of tents further away. "What is that place?"

"That's the Camp of Religion. Each camp is designed to keep people off their Quests for as long as possible. Some will spend years going back and forth from one of those camps to the other. Stay on the path that God has revealed to you, and you will not end up in any of them."

Disciple and Caleb stopped for the night, camping near a big oak tree. When they awoke, they saw that their paths were going in different directions. After a quick breakfast, Caleb spent some time with Disciple, giving him advice on the things he would face on his journey. Caleb then read some of his favorite passages of Scripture to Disciple before saying goodbye and leaving.

As Caleb was walking off, he stopped and turned around. "I believe we'll see each other again. I'll pray for you as you continue on your Quest."

7

VALLEY OF DOUBT

Disciple continued on his Quest, making a lot of progress over the next three months. He faithfully read in his Book every day and enjoyed talking with others about what he had learned. When he would stop at a House of Instruction, it was always a joyous occasion of meeting many wonderful people. Disciple had not seen any enemies during this time, and following his path seemed easy. He wondered if his Quest would always be like this.

After traveling for three more weeks, Disciple noticed that his journey was becoming more difficult. His path took him up steep hills and across rocky terrain. The days were hotter, while the nights were colder. He did not see as many people along his path, and some of the ones he did see were not as friendly. After several days of hardships and challenges, he wasn't as cheerful and happy as he had been before.

Disciple wondered what was wrong. Had he done something that made things harder? Up until this time God always seemed close by, but now He seemed far away. Disciple found himself crying out, "God where are you?" But he didn't hear an answer.

On one particular day, he was going through a valley where every step seemed to be on uneven ground. There were rocks all over the trail, with thorn bushes lining both sides of his path. Then a violent storm erupted overhead. Torrential rain poured down so hard that he could barely see a few feet in front of him.

Disciple searched for shelter from the storm, but he couldn't find any place out of the heavy rain. He tried putting up a tent, but the wind beat ferociously against him, making it impossible. He thought the best thing to do would be to keep moving forward, and hope there would be something up ahead that could give him some relief from the awful pounding of the rain.

As Disciple continued to press on, he heard a peculiar swirling sound around his head, which turned into whispering voices.

"You don't belong on this Quest. You just think something happened at the Hill of Calvary, but it was a temporary emotional high. Nothing has changed. You are still on your way to the Lake that Burns with Fire."

Disciple wasn't sure where these voices were coming from, but doubts began to fill his thoughts. Maybe there hadn't been a real experience at the Hill of Calvary. Maybe he just wanted to believe his life had changed. The rain came down harder, and the wind blew even more fiercely. Disciple thought, if I really were a child of God and had become a new creation, would I be struggling like I am right now?

Miserable and drenched, Disciple crept forward. As each step became more challenging, he desperately wished the wind and the rain would stop. Then just as he felt he could go no further, a short break in the heavy rain revealed a small cave that was barely big enough for him to squeeze inside.

He ducked into the small opening and pressed inside as far as his body would fit. He crossed his arms and rubbed them with his hands, trying to massage some warmth into his body, but nothing brought relief as he stood there shivering from the cold. While the cave provided some shelter, the wind drove the rain toward him, making each drop feel as it was piercing through his clothes like a long needle. As Disciple waited out the storm, he thought about the voices and wondered if what they said was true.

Finally, the wind calmed, and the rain stopped. Disciple felt beaten down, but he gathered himself and left the cave. The ground was completely saturated with water, but he found one area that was a little dryer than the others. He set down his backpack, and then put up his tent.

After changing into a set of dry clothes, he built a fire and sat down to read in his Book. He came across the story when Jesus and

His disciples went on board a boat to go across the lake. While Jesus was sleeping, a storm arose that was so powerful His disciples feared for their lives. They woke Jesus up asking Him if He cared that they were about to perish. Jesus commanded the storm to stop, and it ceased immediately. Jesus seemed disappointed in His disciples' response to the storm, and He rebuked them for their lack of faith. Disciple thought, why does it seem like when the storms of life are all around us, God is asleep and doesn't care about us?

While he was reading, a bearded man in worn and faded clothing approached his campsite. His shoes looked tattered while his clothes were dripping wet.

The stranger's whole body shook and shivered. "May I warm myself by your fire?"

Disciple held out his hand. "Yes, come sit down."

The man knelt in front of the fire while holding his hands out toward the flames. "Thank you. That was a terrible storm."

"Yes I know," said Disciple. "My clothes have been drying for almost an hour, and they're still wet. If you'd like, you can go into my tent and change. If you don't have a set of dry clothes, you can take one of my blankets and wrap it around you while your clothes dry by the fire."

The man thanked him and went into the tent to change. He came back out wrapped in a blanket and put his wet clothes near the fire to dry. "Pardon my bad manners, I was so thankful to find you and your warm fire that I didn't introduce myself. My name is Joseph."

Disciple held out his hand. "Nice to meet you Joseph, my name is Disciple."

Joseph shook his hand and sat down. "When I walked up I saw that you were reading out of your Book. That's always a good thing to do, and especially after going through a storm like this. If you don't mind me asking, what were you studying?"

"I was reading about the time a storm arose while Jesus and His disciples were in a boat, crossing to the other side of a lake. Everything turned out fine, but the disciples were filled with fear and doubt during the storm. I know how they felt because I had doubts as I was going through this storm."

Joseph held his hands out toward the fire and then rubbed them together. "Doubts happen to everyone. I've had my share of doubts along the way."

Disciple sighed. "But, what bothers me is that the doubts made sense. I'm not making the same kind of progress that I used to, and the feelings of joy that I had don't seem to be as strong. In fact, I've had feelings of discouragement, and today I felt like I wanted to quit. If I had truly experienced something at the Hill of Calvary, how could I feel these things?"

Joseph sat up and pulled his blanket tighter. "I've gone through times like that in my life. You can't let your feelings dictate what you believe. What God says in His word is more certain than how we feel. The best way to know that you're truly on this Quest is to keep moving forward no matter what you're feeling. As you continue making progress, the Holy Spirit will bear witness with your spirit to give you the assurance you're looking for."

Disciple stared into the fire and nodded. "Thank you. That's what I needed to hear."

Disciple and Joseph continued to talk for a couple of hours. When Joseph saw that his clothes were dry, he went back into the tent and put them on.

After changing clothes, he returned and gathered up his things. "Thank you so much for your hospitality, but I must travel on. There is a place I want to be before it gets too dark."

Disciple stood up. "It was nice meeting you, and thanks again for your words of encouragement."

After Joseph left, Disciple noticed that his path was not moving away, so he prepared to stay for the night. He continued reading in his Book while thinking about the storm and what he could learn from it. When at last he lay down to go to sleep, he meditated on a verse he had just read: "We do not look at the things which we can see, but we look at the things which we cannot see. For the things which we can see are temporary, but the things which we cannot see are eternal."

During the previous few weeks, and especially during the storm, he had been focusing on the things which he could see around him. Discouragement had set in because all he saw were obstacles and hardships, but these were only temporary. Once he chose to focus on God's word, the doubts lost their power. Disciple told himself that the next time he felt doubts, he would remind himself of this storm and keep going forward.

Waking up the next morning, he felt refreshed and energized. The storm he went through the day before was challenging, but having gone through it, he felt even stronger. Disciple came out of the valley and made his way up a hill. Suddenly, three large vultures swooped down toward his head, trying to dislodge his Helmet of Salvation.

Disciple thought he heard voices again.

"You're not a new creation. You're the same person you always were," said the vultures.

Disciple ducked in behind his Shield of Faith and prayed. "Dear Lord I put my trust in You and what You've said in Your word."

The vultures regrouped and then flew at his head again. "You will end up in the Lake that Burns Forever."

Disciple once again ducked behind his Shield and prayed for wisdom. He thought of his struggles while traveling through the Valley of Doubt, and the Holy Spirit began to remind him of the things he had read the night before. He stood up and held out his Book until it became a Sword.

As the vultures swooped toward him, Disciple readied himself for battle. "I have repented of my sins, I have confessed with my mouth that Jesus is Lord, and I have believed in my heart that God raised Him from the dead."

Disciple struck one of the vultures with his Sword, knocking it back. "And I have called upon the name of the Lord! Therefore I am saved!"

Another vulture landed on his head and began pecking at his Helmet with its large beak.

Disciple stepped back and thrust his Shield upward toward the vulture.

At once he knocked the creature off his head, and then he pierced its wing with his Sword. "I have been given Eternal Life and promised that I shall never perish. I will spend eternity with my Lord, but it is you that will go to the Lake that Burns Forever."

Another larger vulture flew toward Disciple. "You are not saved. You're just trying to convince yourself that you are."

The large vulture smacked its beak together, making a loud, biting sound as it flew toward him.

Disciple reared back his Sword. "The Spirit Himself bears witness with my spirit, confirming that I am a child of God."

He swung at the large vulture and struck it in the chest. The vicious bird of prey flew up into the air and circled around before diving straight toward his head. Disciple lifted his Shield just in time as the vulture slammed into it and fell from the sky.

The other two had recovered and were flying toward him from opposite directions. As they came closer, he quickly struck out at one with his Sword, then ducked down just as the other was about to make contact. When he ducked, the second vulture flew into the first one, causing them both to fall to the ground. Disciple then struck them with his Sword, wounding them to the point that they were barely able to fly. They ran around, trying to avoid being hit again until they finally flew off.

The third larger vulture was not going to give up easily. It flew toward Disciple again, bearing its large claws as it came closer. As the bird of prey grabbed at his Shield, Disciple gripped it tighter and shook off the vulture. The angry bird tried to swing around and attack him from behind, but he turned just in time to strike its left wing. The vulture lunged for his Shield with its claws, but Disciple struck at its legs with his Sword until the bird had to let go.

The large vulture circled toward him again, but it was moving much more slowly. Disciple was able to time the swing of his Sword just as the bird came close and swatted it out of the air. The vulture tried to get away, but he hit it again as it hobbled on the ground. The vulture desperately flapped its wings and ran around until it was finally able to lift itself off the ground and fly away.

Disciple was wearied from the battle but pleased with the outcome. He had defeated the Vultures of Doubt. Now he understood that the storm of yesterday, prepared him for the battle today. Battling those doubts in the valley caused him to spend extra time in his Book, seeking answers about the assurance of his salvation. Rather than being upset about the storm, he thanked God for the storm.

8

FOREST OF FEAR

As Disciple continued his journey, a large forest appeared in the distance. Scanning the terrain ahead, he concluded there wasn't a suitable place nearby to set up camp. Since the sun would be setting in a few hours, he decided to try and make it through to the other side before it became too dark to see.

But after entering the forest, Disciple discovered that the further he went, the darker it became, as the thickness of the trees choked out the remaining sunlight. Loud screeching arose on both sides of his path, and sudden rustling sounds emanated from behind as if someone was always following him.

A howling wind swirled through the trees, while at the same time disturbing loud squawks and screams echoed through the forest. Disciple turned this way and that, not knowing when something might dart out to attack him. As he made his way forward, the coming of night produced a darkness that felt cold and smothering. He slowly crept forward, but only because he was concerned about what might be behind him.

Further ahead was a small open patch, where the beams of the moon filtered through the trees. As he drew closer to the small patch, the faint light revealed a large wolf stalking back and forth. The animal was bigger than anything Disciple had ever seen or heard about. Its fur was dark grey, and the look in its eyes was mean and angry.

The wolf growled and showed its teeth. "You have entered MY

Domain. This is The Forest of Fear. Do not challenge me, or you will be eaten alive. Go back the way you came, or be doomed to stay in this forest forever."

Disciple trembled with fear. He didn't want to retreat, and he didn't want to stay in this forest, but he definitely didn't want to be eaten. He stepped back and waited for what seemed like hours in the hopes that someone like Caleb would come along to help him, but no one arrived.

The wolf could sense Disciple becoming more terrified, so he taunted and mocked him. "Don't look so afraid. It's not as if you're about to be killed while experiencing extreme agony. Oh, wait a minute, that's *exactly* what's about to happen!"

The wolf acted as if it was going to take a step toward Disciple, causing him to jump back. This seemed to amuse the wolf who laughed even more. It held up one of its front paws, showing the sharpness of its claws. "Do not think that armor you wear will be of any use against me. I've eaten many of your kind who wore that same armor."

Disciple remembered reading something in his Book about fear, but the growling of the wolf, along with the noises from the forest, made it difficult to focus on anything other than being afraid. Disciple knelt down and prayed for help. While he was praying, the Holy Spirit brought to his remembrance verses he had read about fear. As the words from his Book rolled through his mind, he felt strengthened.

The wolf glared at him while stalking back and forth. "Don't be foolish. Think of the pain I will inflict on you as my teeth sink into your flesh and my claws rip you apart."

Disciple stood up and removed his Book from his satchel. He held it out until it became a Sword and steadily advanced toward the wolf. "Even though I walk through the valley of the shadow of death, I will fear no evil, for You are with me. Your rod and Your staff they comfort me."

The wolf growled loudly. "I will kill you slowly, and I'll enjoy every second of it." The wolf shot toward him.

Disciple managed to jump out of the way, but the wolf's claws skimmed the side of his arm.

Circling around, the wolf said, "You can't hold out much longer.

You're only delaying the inevitable. Soon I will rip into you with my teeth and the pain will be unbearable."

Suddenly the wolf pounced toward him, bearing its claws. Disciple lifted up his Shield just in time to block the assault, but the force of the attack knocked him off balance.

The wolf stepped back and started circling again. "That was close. I can feel you wearing down. It's only a matter of time now."

The wolf suddenly leaped at him again, and Disciple barely lifted his Shield in time, as the wolf's claws appeared over the top of it. The wolf brought all of its weight down on top of the Shield, trying to force it from his grip. Disciple strained to keep the wolf from getting through and was finally able to thrust it off his Shield.

Laughing as it continued to look for an opening, the wolf snarled, "I told you this was almost over. I can already taste your flesh in my mouth."

Stunned by the success of his enemy, Disciple realized he was allowing the words of the wolf to drown out the words from his Book. Leaning forward as he steadied himself, Disciple proclaimed, "The LORD is my light and my salvation; Whom shall I fear? The LORD is the strength of my life; Of whom shall I be afraid?"

The wolf stepped back a few paces and then took a running leap high into the air. Disciple raised his Shield above his head just as the wolf landed on top of it. The weight of the wolf knocked him backward and onto his back. The wolf tried to pounce on him as he lay on the ground, but Disciple rolled out of the way and jumped to his feet.

The wolf snarled. "Almost had you."

"No," said Disciple as his confidence began to rise, "It is the Lord that helps me, therefore I will not fear."

The wolf stepped to its left and then to its right to try and keep Disciple guessing. "Say what you will, this is about to be over."

Determined not to give into the wolf's threats, Disciple shouted, "Though an army encamp against me, my heart shall not fear. Though war may rise against me, even in this I will be confident."

The wolf ran toward him once again and leaped even higher into the air. This time though Disciple stepped to his right and swung his Sword down on top of its back. The wolf spun around and jumped toward him again, but Disciple slammed his Shield into the wolf's head, knocking it backward. The wolf was noticeably shaken and disoriented but still growling and snarling.

Disciple took a step closer to the wolf. "Through my God I shall do valiantly, for it is He who will tread down my enemies."

Disciple lunged at the wolf with his Sword. The wolf tried to move away, but it was too late. Disciple's Sword had pierced it through the heart. The wolf yelped in pain and then collapsed to the ground.

Disciple knelt down and leaned against his Sword. He was both relieved and exhausted. Bowing his head, he thanked God for the victory. As he knelt while trying to recover from the battle, the sun began shining through the forest. Disciple did not realize it, but he had been there through the entire night.

Suddenly the sound of rustling leaves resonated to his left. He grasped his Sword and readied for another battle. But as the sun's rays broke through, they revealed a group of people who were crouched down behind some trees.

Disciple lowered his Sword and strode over to them. "Why are you hiding?"

A slender young man named Mark stepped out from behind a tree. "I, my three brothers, and my three sisters have been traveling on this Quest together, but when we came through this forest, the wolf blocked our way. We didn't want to go back, but we were afraid to go forward. So we've been here all this time, paralyzed by our fears."

All of those who had been hiding held their arms tightly across their chest.

Disciple glanced at the wolf lying on the ground. "Well, now that the wolf is dead, we can all leave this forest together and continue with our Quest."

Nobody moved. Disciple was puzzled at this. The wolf was dead, so why were they still hesitant to go forward?

One of Mark's sisters named Helen stepped out into the sunlight. "Sir, we are grateful that you killed the wolf, but perhaps there will be another enemy up ahead. We see that you were able to kill this wolf, but will you always be with us? We aren't so sure that we'll be able to do what you did."

Disciple realized that the biggest enemy they all faced was not the fear of the wolf, but the fear that was on the inside of them. He could not conquer that for them. They would have to fight that battle for themselves. Disciple took out his Book, motioning for the others to do the same.

He read to them where it said, "For God has not given us a spirit of fear, but of power and of love and of a sound mind." He also read, "I sought the LORD, and He heard me, And delivered me from all my fears." Together they read through all of Psalms 91.

As they read and discussed portions of God's word, Disciple saw the same confidence appearing in their eyes that he had felt while battling the wolf. They had been reading and meditating on God's truth, and this truth was setting them free.

Disciple stood up. "Let's leave this forest and continue on our journey."

Everyone rose to their feet, some quicker than others, but they all stood up and left the forest together. As they were walking, Disciple thought to himself that the real power of fear was not what it could do to you, but what it would try to make you *think* it could do to you.

Disciple saw that his path was the same as Mark's and the others, so they all continued on their journey together. After traveling for an hour, Helen spotted a house in the distance, and as they drew closer, they could hear singing. Everyone thought it must be a House of Instruction, so they hurried toward the entrance and knocked. They were welcomed inside and started singing with all those who were there.

The owner of the House, whose name they learned was Pastor Bill, stood up and read from the Book. He covered many of the same portions of Scripture that Disciple had read while in the forest, and he taught about overcoming fears.

When the service was over, Pastor Bill invited them to stay and have some lunch. Mark and his siblings had not eaten in days, so they were very grateful. After getting cleaned up, they all sat down at the table. Pastor Bill's wife, whose name was Judy, brought out dishes of roast beef and mashed potatoes with gravy.

Pastor Bill noticed that many were gobbling down their food as if they were starved. "Tell me about where you all have been, and what your journey has been like the last few days."

Mark took another bite of his roast beef and then gulped down some of his lemonade. "It's been terrible. We've been stuck in a forest for days, trapped by a mean and angry wolf."

Everyone took turns talking about their experiences in the Forest of Fear, and then they told how Disciple arrived and defeated the wolf. Disciple shared that he had been paralyzed by his own fears when he first entered the forest.

After finishing his last bite of mashed potatoes, Disciple said, "We enjoyed your message today. Could you teach us some more about overcoming fear?"

Opening his Book, Pastor Bill said, "Why of course. Fear is a dreadful thing. It keeps you all knotted up on the inside, so you aren't able to move forward."

Pastor Bill read from the Book where the Israelites had come out of Egypt and were about to go into the Promised Land. Moses sent twelve spies to search out the land, but when they came back, all but two had a negative report. These spies convinced the rest of the children of Israel that they would not be able to defeat the giants and the other enemies in the land. As a result, God did not let them enter the Promised Land.

Pastor Bill turned several pages. "Another writer in this Book says that they were not able to enter in because of their unbelief and their refusal to trust in God."

Mark quickly swallowed a bite of mashed potatoes. "It wasn't God that I didn't trust, but it was that wolf."

The others chuckled.

Pastor Bill smiled. "Ah yes, it does seem that way at times. We all have fears, but we must not allow these fears to stop us from doing what God has called us to do."

Pastor Bill saw that they were all tired so he invited them to stay the night. Everyone, including Disciple, was thankful for the opportunity to get a good night's rest. While Mark and his brothers and sisters had been in the forest, the wolf kept them awake and fearful with its constant growling and taunting. After settling into their beds, they each meditated on the verses they had learned from the Book and thanked God for delivering them from their fears. One by one they drifted off to a peaceful sleep.

In the morning they all came downstairs to eat some breakfast, and when they were done, Pastor Bill opened up his Book. "I wanted to start this morning off with some more teaching about fear. I shared last night about how the children of Israel did not go into the Promised Land when they first had the opportunity. But forty years later the next generation did get to go in. As they were about to enter the Promised Land, Moses said to them, 'It is the LORD who will go before you. He will be with you, and He will not leave your side nor abandon you. Do not fear or be discouraged.' "

"Were the people still afraid of the giants and other enemies?" Mark asked.

Pastor Bill nodded. "I'm sure they were, but they didn't let the fear stop them. Just before they were to enter into the land, God told Joshua to be strong and of good courage. In another place in the Psalms, it says, 'do not fear bad news or live in dread of what might happen.' You cannot travel on this Quest while being in constant fear of what may be around the next corner. The reason we aren't to be afraid of what lies ahead is because God goes before us, and He already knows what's ahead and will be with us every step of the way."

Pastor Bill prayed and asked God to help all of them overcome their fears. After he finished, he looked around at those who had come out of the Forest of Fear. "I would like to invite all of you to stay with me for a few weeks to recover and become stronger."

Mark looked at his brothers and sisters who were all nodding. "We would love to stay with you, but we insist on working and helping out while we're here."

Pastor Bill then turned toward Disciple. "Will you join us as well?"

"I'll stay for as long as my path remains here."

Two days passed, and then Disciple saw that his path was moving on. He said goodbye to Mark, Helen and the others, and then reached out to shake Pastor Bill's hand. "Thank you for all your kindness and hospitality. I know that Mark and his brothers and sisters will grow stronger while they're here."

9

ORCHARD OF VANITY

Disciple forged ahead on his Quest for the next several months. He continued to make progress, and he won many more battles along the way. But over time he began to lose sight of who it was that was empowering him to win the battles he faced, and who it was that was enabling him to move further ahead. Disciple started to become over-confident in his own strengths and abilities, and he began to spend less time reading in his Book and in prayer.

As time passed by, Disciple realized it had been a year since he went through the Building of Reflection and up the Hill of Calvary. He considered how far he had come and how much he had accomplished. After walking a little further, he heard sounds of distress as if someone was under attack. He ran toward the voices and saw a family, consisting of a father, mother, and two children fighting off a group of bats.

They were all battling bravely, and even the children were using their Sword and Shield as best as they could, but the bats continued to harass them. Disciple held out his Book until it became a Sword and charged forward to join the family in their battle.

The bats were swarming like bees, and Disciple took aim at several of the larger ones and knocked them out of the air. With Disciple's help, they were able to drive all the bats away.

The father walked up to him and extended his hand. "Thanks for the help. My name is Sam. This is my wife Jill, and these are our two children, Susan and Sean."

Disciple shook his hand and nodded toward the rest of the family. "It's a good thing I was nearby."

Jill knelt next to her backpack. "Would you like to stay with us for lunch."

"Sure," said Disciple.

Jill set out the food, then they all sat down to eat.

Disciple took a bite of his chicken. "So what brings you all out this way?"

Sam smiled. "We've just recently started our Quest, and not long after attending a House of Instruction the leader invited us to sing at their services."

"And soon after that," said Jill, "we started getting invitations from other Houses of Instruction to share our testimony and sing."

Sam reached out and grasped his wife's hand. "We're honored that God has been able to use us this soon on our Quest."

Disciple smiled. "That's great. God used me to help many others in the early days of my Quest, and as you can see he's still using me to help those in need."

As Disciple continued to talk with the family, he couldn't help but think they didn't seem to know as much about the Book as he did, and he had noticed during the battle, they were not as experienced and effective in using their Swords.

The family was sharing all the things which led them to start their Quest, but Disciple wasn't paying attention. He noticed off in the distance what looked to be a beautiful orchard. When they were finished eating, the family picked up their belongings and prepared to start back on their path.

Sam threw his backpack over his shoulders and motioned toward Disciple. "Will you be joining us as we travel?"

Disciple pointed toward the orchard. "I want to go over there and get a closer look at those beautiful fruit trees."

"But isn't that off your path?"

Disciple looked down at his feet. "It's not that far off my path. I'll get some fruit and be right back. Go on ahead, and I'll catch up with you later."

The family thanked him again for his help and went on their way.

Disciple was feeling good about all he had accomplished on his journey so far, and he thought it was no big deal to get off his path for a little while. Besides, if there were any threats he had all his armor and his Sword, and he could quickly jump back to his path and be on his way.

As Disciple entered the orchard, he glanced around at all the different kinds of fruit trees. The fruits themselves appeared exotic and vibrant, teeming with a myriad of colors. Beautiful flowers sprung up from the ground all around him, giving off a pleasant fragrance. All of the smells from the orchard seemed to combine into a calming and relaxing aroma.

Disciple closed his eyes and breathed in deeply. Suddenly, he heard scurrying in the tops of the trees.

"Look who has visited us. Is this not Disciple, that great warrior on the Quest?"

Disciple scanned the trees trying to see where the voices were coming from. "Who's there?"

"No one has come so far on their journey in so little time as you. You are truly a special man."

At first, Disciple was cautious, keeping his hand on his Book ready to raise it at the first sign of danger. But the more the voices spoke, the more he relaxed and let down his guard.

"Who was the one that killed the wolf in the Forest of Fear, and who rescued all those people from that forest? Was it not you?"

Disciple put his Book back in his satchel and lowered his Shield to his side. "Yes, that was me. I killed the wolf in the Forest of Fear, and I did help many escape from there so they could continue their Quest."

"Yessss, yessss, and we've heard that you've accomplished a lot more too. What other things have you done?"

Disciple continued to look up into the trees, but he couldn't locate where the voices were coming from. "The first battle I was in, I won easily. I had a little help from another person, but the battle was mostly over by that point."

"We're quite sure you could have won that battle with no help at all. What else have you done?"

Disciple walked up to a tree where he thought he heard the sound of scurrying and stared into the branches. "I fought off a vicious army of vultures."

"That is quite impressive."

Disciple still couldn't see who was speaking to him, but he was no longer concerned. "I've helped many travelers on this Quest, and before coming here, I rescued a family that was under attack."

"Yes that is true, you've done so much to help others, and we're sure you will do even greater things."

Disciple sat down under one of the trees and thought of all the victories he had achieved. He rehearsed them over and over in his head and thought about how far he had come.

The voices spoke again. "Why do you think others have not made as much progress as you?"

That was a question that Disciple had asked himself many times lately, but he didn't have an answer. Now that someone else was asking the same question he thought about it some more.

Disciple heard more scurrying in the trees.

"Is it possible that they are not as dedicated as you are, Disciple, or maybe they aren't working as hard as you?"

That did seem like a logical explanation, he thought.

"And don't you think that family probably did something to attract that attack from those bats? If they had been more like you, perhaps they would not have been attacked at all."

Again Disciple thought that was a good point.

"Stay a little while and have some fruit. You have accomplished much on your journey, and you deserve some rest."

Disciple picked a piece of fruit off the tree and brought it to his mouth. It was the size of a small apple, with a deep bluish color, and it tasted like watermelon and grapes were mixed together. As soon as he swallowed the first bite, he felt as if he was in a daze. He closed his eyes and pictured all of his achievements, concluding he must be more gifted than all others on this Quest. Continuing to think about his many victories, he drifted off to sleep, unaware that he been seduced by the Orchard of Vanity.

Several hours later, he suddenly awoke to the sound of laughter. At first, he was alarmed because of how dark it was. He rubbed his eyes, realizing he must have slept long past sunset. He glanced around and noticed the glimmer of flames coming from the direction where he heard the laughter.

Disciple stood up and shouldered his backpack, then made his way toward the flames, not realizing he was drifting even further from his path. As he came closer, he saw several young people close to his age singing and laughing around a campfire. At first, he stayed behind a group of trees and observed all those who were there. After a few minutes, he concluded that they didn't appear to be a threat, and they seemed to be having a good time.

Disciple stepped out and approached the group. As he did, those on the near side turned and faced him.

One of the young men strode over to him. "Hello, my name is Michael."

"Nice to meet you, my name is Disciple."

"That's an interesting name. What brings you around these parts?"

Disciple looked back. "I've been on a Quest, and I —"

Michael put his hand on Disciple's back to quickly turn him around toward the campfire. "That's great. Do you have time to join us for a little while?"

"Sure," said Disciple. "I can't travel very far at night anyway."

Michael was a clean cut and handsome young man who seemed cheerful and carefree. He appeared to be the center of attention, and it was apparent that everyone liked being around him and wanted his approval.

Michael pointed toward a table. "Go on over and get you something to eat. We have plenty."

Disciple sat down with his food, still observing everything that was going on. Everyone was having a good time, and he thought it was nice to be able to just sit and relax. These people didn't appear to be concerned about anything other than just enjoying themselves. After finishing his last bite of food, Disciple stood up and joined the others around the campfire. Everyone stayed up late laughing, singing, and talking, and then just before the sun rose, they all lay down to get some rest.

When Disciple awoke, he noticed from the position of the sun that it was already late afternoon.

Michael walked over to him. "Well good morning, or afternoon, or whatever it is. How did you sleep?"

Still groggy, Disciple sat up and wiped his eyes. "I slept well, but I really should be on my way."

Michael put his hand on Disciple's shoulder, gently pushing him down. "Sit back and relax. You have to get something to eat first, so at least stay with us for a little longer."

Disciple lay back down and closed his eyes, while he waited for someone to let him know it was time to eat. By the time the food had been prepared, and he had finished eating, the sun was already beginning to set.

Michael sat down next to him. "Well, you can't travel in the dark, so stay with us another night and enjoy yourself some more."

Disciple knew he couldn't make much progress while it was dark, so he stayed for another night. Once again, everyone stood around talking and enjoying themselves until it was almost morning, and then after sleeping most of the day, they awoke just in time for the sun to set. This went on for several days, and Disciple thought there wasn't anything wrong with taking some time off. After all, he wasn't doing anything that was bad or harmful.

As the days and nights passed, Disciple became less concerned about his Quest. When he first arrived, he spent a few minutes in his Book, but after three days he wasn't reading it at all.

One night Disciple noticed that two new girls arrived. From time to time, one of them would quickly glance in his direction and smile. He liked the attention, and he would sheepishly smile back.

Michael strolled over to him and glanced over his shoulder. "Hey, do you see those two girls?"

Disciple shot a quick look in their direction while trying not to be too obvious. "Yes. What about them?"

"I think one of them likes me, and the other one seems to be interested in you. They want to go for a walk, but they insist on going together, so I need someone else to go with me. Would you like to come?"

Disciple looked around. "Where will we go?"

"Do you see that path over there just off to the side? We're going to go a short distance in that direction. We'll be back before time to get some sleep."

Disciple wanted to spend some time with the young woman, so he agreed to go.

Michael had noticed that when Disciple first arrived he would tap his chest, causing his armor to appear. "Why don't you take off that armor until we get back. When it's visible, it causes you stand out, and it might make the girls a little nervous."

Michael looked back at the girls. "We don't want them to be nervous now do we?"

Disciple tapped his chest until his armor appeared. "But, I haven't taken it off since I received it."

Michael tugged at the back of the Breastplate. "It's only for a little while, and then we'll be right back."

Disciple took off his armor and set it next to a tree where he had laid his satchel with his Book. He then followed Michael toward the two girls. Both girls were slender with long blonde hair, and Disciple was captivated by how beautiful they were. As Michael and Disciple approached, both girls stared at the ground and smiled as if they were bashful and shy.

Michael stopped and gave the girls a slight grin. "This is my friend Disciple."

The girls introduced themselves as Innocence and Purity. They talked for a little while, and then Michael asked if they would like to go for a walk. The girls smiled and nodded. Michael led everyone to a path that was heading away from the campsite. Disciple felt uneasy, but at the same time, he felt a rush of excitement. It was a different kind of feeling, but he liked it.

As they strolled along, the girls came up with the idea to play hide and seek. They wanted to hide first, so they took off further down the trail to hide while Michael and Disciple counted to one hundred. When they were finished counting, they headed off to find the girls. About fifty feet ahead, the trails forked. Michael thought he heard sounds coming from the path to the right, so they went that way.

Not too far down the trail, they found the girls hiding behind a clump of bushes. Now it was the guys turn to hide.

Michael took Disciple to the side and whispered, "I know a place not too far up ahead with a thick group of pine trees. It will be hard for them to spot us in there." He turned toward the girls. "See you soon, but not too soon." He tugged on Disciple's arm, and they hurried off.

Michael and Disciple sprinted down the trail, and when they came to a fork, he motioned for them to go to the left. They briskly walked for another five minutes, and then they arrived at the group of pine trees Michael had described. They waited and waited for the girls to come by, and after thirty minutes they finally heard the girls talking as they drew near.

Michael appeared to slip, and when he crashed into the pine branches, it gave their position away. The girls strode up to them, and Michael and Disciple came out from behind the trees.

"That was a great hiding place," said Purity.

"Yes it was," said Innocence. "Now it's our turn to find one even better."

Once again, the girls headed off.

The guys and the girls continued to alternate hiding and then seeking for several hours, all the while traveling on several different winding paths which led them further away from where they had started.

The last time the girls found the guys, both Innocence and Purity slipped up close to them.

Innocence leaned over and whispered in Disciple's ear. "If you find me this time, I'll have a special surprise for you."

Disciple observed how excited Michael was and concluded he must have received the same message. They closed their eyes and began to count, and then immediately they heard the girls take off running.

Michael quickly finished counting and then looked over at Disciple. "Come on! We've got to find them."

The guys headed off and traveled further and further taking different trails, but they couldn't find the girls. It was getting close to the time for the sun to come up, and they were both exhausted.

Michael ambled over to a small clearing next to some trees and sat down. "Let's stop here and take a short nap. After we get some rest, we'll set off to find them again. They couldn't have gone far, and they may even come back to find us once they realize we weren't able to find them."

Disciple was exhausted and desperately wanted to get some rest, so he agreed. When they awoke, they discovered that they had slept so long that the sun had already set, and the last bit of light was fading over the horizon.

Michael sat up. "I think I know where the girls may have gone. Follow me. We can also get something to eat and drink there as well."

Disciple followed Michael to the entrance of what looked to be a large camp. They could hear music and singing, and there appeared to be all kinds of entertainment going on. Two men were stationed out front who seemed to be in charge of letting people in.

Disciple strolled up to the men. "We were walking with two young women last night, but we seemed to have lost them. Did they come this way?"

One of the men adjusted his hat and squinted his eyes. "I don't know. We get a lot of travelers through here. What did they look like?"

Disciple described the two girls and told the men that their names were Innocence and Purity.

The men laughed and nudged one another. "Oh, we know who they are, and yes they did come here, but we don't call them Innocence and Purity. Their names are Lust and Seduction, and they bring us quite a lot of business!"

Disciple noticed a banner above the entrance. It read, "The Camp of Sin."

10

CAMP OF SIN

Disciple was not sure what to think or feel. Before him stood the entrance of what he knew to be wrong. His path was far away, and he had taken so many different and winding trails to get here, that he wasn't sure how he could get back even if he wanted to. He had been off of his path for weeks, and the desire to continue it was no longer as strong as it once was. In front of him were all kinds of exhilarating sights and sounds. Everything seemed to be electric and pulsating with energy.

Disciple had made his decision; he was going into the Camp of Sin.

Michael patted him on the back. "Hey, don't worry about those girls. I'm sure we'll run into them, and if not, there's probably plenty more who are even better."

Disciple turned to the men who stood at the entrance. "Is there a cost for all of this?"

The men slapped their hands down on the counter. "Why of course there's a cost. Nothing's free. But, our costs are very reasonable. You just place your hand on this small table, and it will take a little bit of your energy. Every place you go, you'll see these tables, and after you place your hand on them, you can have whatever is there."

Disciple examined his hand. "How will that affect me?"

"Don't worry," the men said, "a young man such as yourself, so full of energy, will have plenty to spare."

Disciple placed his hand on the table. It felt like a small shock, but at the same time, it felt kind of pleasant. Michael did the same, and then they both went in.

Michael started toward a tent that was serving beverages. "Come over here first. We have to get you something to drink to loosen you up a bit. A few cups of this fine liquid, and you'll be ready for everything here."

Michael led Disciple over to where they were serving drinks. "Give my friend here something fruity but strong."

Disciple reached out to get it, but the attendant pulled it back.

Pointing to the small table, he said, "You must first pay."

Disciple put his hand on the table like he did at the entrance, and then the man gave him the cup.

Michael ordered something and then held up his drink. "Let me propose a toast. To good times and a never-ending party!"

Michael and Disciple both turned up their cup and drank. Disciple thought at first that it seemed like any other drink made of fruit he had tasted, but as it went down, it had a bite to it. He glanced around, realizing he was in the midst of everything he knew to be wrong, but yet he felt drawn to it.

When they finished their drinks, Michael tapped on the counter. "Give me and my friend another round."

Michael and Disciple drank another cup and then a few more. By now Disciple started to feel detached from himself, as if he was in a dream but still awake. He felt a sense of bravado, as he strolled along with Michael observing the sights. The next tent they entered was raucous and lively with activity. The first booth they walked up to featured a man named Lucky shuffling a deck of cards. Lucky wore a visor on his head and a leather vest on top of his shirt.

"Do you feel lucky?" he said as he pulled his visor a little further down.

Disciple wiped his eyes. "What are the rules?"

Lucky shuffled the cards some more. "Place your hand on the table to pay for your chance to win a free ticket to any attraction in the camp. I draw a card, and then you draw a card. If my card is higher, you get nothing, but if your card is higher, you get the free ticket."

Disciple looked over at Michael.

Michael shrugged his shoulders and smiled. "Why not? Give it a try."

Lucky drew a card and then gave him a card. After they both revealed their cards, Disciple saw that he won.

"Hey I like this game," said Disciple. "Let's do it again."

"Sure," said Lucky, "just place your hand on the table and pay for another turn."

They each drew another card, but this time Disciple lost. He quickly placed his hand on the table to pay for another turn, and just as quickly he lost again. He paid for another one, and again he lost.

As Disciple reached out to pay for another turn, Michael grabbed his hand. "Hey, slow down a little bit. There are a lot of games in here. Let's not spend all our time on the same one."

They walked around to different tables where the games varied, but the idea was the same. Disciple won a couple more times, but he lost much more than he won.

As they were walking out of the games tent, Michael pointed to another attraction. "Come with me. You've got to see this."

Michael led Disciple over to a tent that was completely closed off so you couldn't see what was inside. They could hear yelling and cheering, and it sounded like everyone was having a great time. They each put their hand on the table and went in. It was mostly dark inside, and toward the front, there was a stage where women who were wearing very little clothing were dancing. Disciple knew he shouldn't be there, but at the same time, he couldn't look away. When the show was over, the announcer said that as they went out, they could purchase pictures of the women that were on the stage.

Several men lined up, and although he knew it was wrong, Disciple got in line behind Michael. After getting the pictures, Michael handed him a satchel to put them in. As Disciple swung the satchel over his shoulder, he remembered how he once carried his Book in another satchel on the same shoulder. He quickly suppressed the memory because it was too much for him. He couldn't enjoy his sin if he thought about the Quest he'd left behind.

Michael then led him over to a group of guys that were singing, but the songs were far different from what they had been singing back at the campfire. These songs were about women and contained the worst words he had ever heard. Each word felt as if it was stinging his conscience. The guys then started to tell jokes that were crude and vulgar. As much as Disciple knew it was wrong, he couldn't help but laugh because he thought some of them were funny.

Eventually, he and Michael left. As they were walking around, Disciple hit his foot on a large tent spike, and immediately curse words flew off his tongue. Realizing what had just happened, he put his hand over his mouth in shock.

Michael laughed. "Hey, it's ok. It's just words."

They continued going throughout the camp and seeing all the sights. A few hours later, just before it was time for the sun to come up, several men started closing everything down.

Michael slapped Disciple on the shoulder. "Come on. I know a great place to get some sleep."

Michael led Disciple to a nice tent with soft beds. They paid the man at the entrance and went in and slept. When they awoke, the sun was going down again, and they could hear lots of activity outside. Disciple felt like his head was going to explode, and all the sounds were making it worse.

Michael walked over and grabbed him by the shoulder. "Come on. The party is about to start all over again. We'll get you a few drinks to patch up those headaches of yours."

Disciple rose up slowly from his bed and put his hands on his head. "Is it like this all the time?"

Michael held open the tent door, waiting for Disciple to follow. "Why yes. It's non-stop fun for as long as you're here."

Michael and Disciple once again strolled through the camp, and that night was much like the first. Night after night went by, and instead of having to be led to different sites and attractions, Disciple began telling Michael to come on or to go to certain tents. His language became worse to the point that he didn't even think about what was coming out of his mouth. He knew what he was doing was wrong, but instead of turning from it, he plunged even deeper into sin to try and make the guilt go away.

What Disciple didn't realize was that slowly, night after night, his energy was being drained.

After months of following the same routine, nothing seemed as fun anymore, and he could barely get up and get started for the next night. The last time he went to pay for something, the men frowned at him because he was barely able to make the payment. The next night Disciple stopped into the tent to go to bed much earlier than previous nights, and once again was barely able to make the payment. He collapsed on his cot and started to feel sick, very sick in fact.

Michael came into the tent, laughing and joking with some guys that Disciple recognized as having been around the campfire when he first met Michael.

Disciple placed his hand on his stomach and tried to sit up. "I feel awful, and I don't think I've got enough energy to pay for anything else."

Disciple was expecting Michael to have sympathy for him and to offer him some help, but he and the other guys just started laughing.

Michael pointed at him. "You fool! You have nothing left because you're all spent out."

Disciple was startled and sat up as far as he could. "What do you mean, Michael?"

"Stop calling me Michael! That's not my name." A hideous look formed on his face. "My name is Rebellion."

Disciple shook his head. "What are you talking about?"

Rebellion shrugged his shoulders and held out his hands. "You don't get it do you. Do you think it was an accident that you happened to find me and my friends that night you came out of the orchard? We were waiting for you. We heard about your exploits and adventures, and we set up that orchard just for you. It was the Orchard of Vanity, and you fell for it completely."

Rebellion began speaking in a mocking tone of voice. "Oh, Disciple, how great you are. Oh, Disciple, tell us about all the battles you've won."

Rebellion and his friends laughed. "You were bursting with pride and arrogance."

Disciple lowered his head into his hands. "I can't believe I fell for that."

Rebellion smiled an evil smile as he nodded. "It works with a lot of people on the Quest. We lure them off their path for a while and then watch to see how they respond. Once we see they're no longer interested in their Books and haven't looked back toward their path, then we take the next steps."

"So it was a trap?"

Rebellion smirked. "I wouldn't call it a trap. We put the temptation out there, but you're the one that took the bait. It was obvious you were intrigued by Lust and Seduction, so it was easy to get you to come along. You practically jumped out of your armor once you thought you had a chance with those girls."

Disciple turned over on his side and groaned. "I'm so weak I can barely walk, and I won't have any energy to pay for anything else. I don't even know where I'll sleep tomorrow."

Rebellion kicked at his leg. "We have the perfect destination for people like you. It's where we dump all the garbage from this place. It's about a mile away. You can sift through the trash during the day and sleep on the filthy ground at night. Sometimes people from the Camp of Religion come near there, so maybe you can beg for a few things from them."

Disciple tried to sit up. "That's terrible. There has to be something better."

Rebellion leaned forward and shook his fist at him. "There's not! And didn't you notice that as you got weaker and weaker, I had more energy?"

Disciple looked down at his hand. "But how?"

Rebellion wagged his finger at him. "Because, I get all of my strength from people like you. When you deposit energy into those tables to pay for sin, I make a withdrawal and become stronger. Once someone like you runs out of energy, we dump you with the rest of the garbage. After that, we go back up and find someone else to lead down here, and then we drain them too. You see, we work for your enemy, and we take as many people off their path as we can."

Disciple thought of all he had left behind to come here. "I wish I had never gone into that orchard or followed you in the first place. I desperately want to go back to my path."

Rebellion glared at him. "Never! You could never find your way back up those trails. The only other way out of here is straight up the side of the mountain, and that's impossible. You're stuck here, and besides, do you realize what people would think about you if you could go back? Do you know what they're already saying about you? They're ashamed of you. They've heard so many good things about your successes and now look at you. Think of the shame you would feel if you saw them again."

Everything Rebellion was saying made sense. Disciple felt so much shame. Suddenly he started to cough and couldn't stop.

Rebellion grabbed up a dirty sock and threw it at him. "Get out of here if you're going to be sick! Stay outside in the dirt until we wake up, and then we'll carry you to the garbage dump where you belong."

Disciple crawled out of the tent on his hands and knees, feeling devastated that it had come to this. Once looked upon as a mighty warrior, now he was weak and about to become a beggar. He didn't want to spend his life begging and surrounded by a heap of garbage, but wasn't that what he deserved? Why did he take those first steps off his path? Why didn't he recognize the evil in those voices in the Orchard of Vanity? How could he have fallen for all the things that led him here to this awful place?

As the sun was coming up over the horizon, Disciple surveyed the top of the canyon. The light of the sun was illuminating a place that looked familiar. It was the spot where he and Caleb stood and talked after his first battle. It was there that Caleb had shown him the Camp of Sin. Disciple remembered thinking that he would never go down to that place, and yet here he was.

Disciple remembered back to the day he entered the Building of Reflection and climbed up the Hill of Calvary. How could he have done this to the One who gave His life for him? Jesus had suffered and died so that he would never have to be in bondage to sin ever again. Disciple realized he had sinned against his Savior and his God. He was sorry for all his sin and would do anything for another chance.

He cried out, "Lord Jesus, I have sinned against you! I am so sorry that I walked off my path. I want to serve you again. I'll wash dishes at any House of Instruction. I'll be a slave to all those on the Quest, and I'll carry their belongings for as far as You command. I'll do anything for You if I can just walk my path and serve you again."

At that moment a heavenly figure appeared in shining white clothing. "Disciple, your prayers have been heard. You have repented of your sins, and your Lord wishes to restore you to your path."

Disciple gazed up at the heavenly figure. "I'll do anything my Lord wishes of me. I'll walk ten miles up a mountain carrying a bag of rocks that represent my sin. I'll suffer as many lashes as a man can strike me with. I'll do anything to get rid of all these awful feelings of guilt that I have."

The heavenly figure held out its hand. "My Lord does not require any of that, for He is the One who paid the price for sin. I have come to offer you grace from my Lord and your Lord."

Disciple lowered his head. "I don't deserve grace. I feel as if I must do something to earn back the favor of my Lord."

"If you feel you've earned it, then you will have reason to boast in yourself, but it is of grace so that no one can boast except in God."

Disciple held out his hands. "Then what must I do?"

The heavenly figure turned around and knelt on the ground. "Get on my back and hold on."

11

PRODIGAL SON

Feeling a surge of strength Disciple climbed onto the back of the heavenly being. They rose into the air and ascended up the side of the mountain. After they reached the top, the heavenly being took him to the place where he had first veered off his path and headed toward the Orchard of Vanity.

Disciple looked around. "This is where I helped that family defeat a group of bats." He reflected back to that time, remembering how he felt superior to the family. "What happened to them?"

The heavenly being pointed in the direction the family traveled that day. "They have made much progress on their journey. They had a lot to learn, but they were humble and grew quickly. Our Lord led them to many different Houses of Instruction, and through this experience, they gained much knowledge and understanding. They now have their own House of Instruction and are doing well."

Disciple glanced around. "I thought I'd have to go back to the beginning of my Quest and start over."

"No, this is where you left off, and this is where you will begin again."

Disciple turned toward the area where the Orchard of Vanity used to be. "But, it seems as if there should be a punishment. Shouldn't there be a higher cost for going off my path?"

"There is a cost," said the heavenly being. "Sin is like seed sown into the ground. When you plant a crop of sin, you will reap a harvest from it."

"What do you mean?" asked Disciple.

"You will read in your Book about David. He was a faithful servant of our Lord who became a great king, but who also gave into sin. Many on the Quest will speak of him as an example of God's forgiveness even when the sin is severe. And it is true that God does forgive when His servants turn to Him in repentance, but many don't often speak of what happened to David after that. He lost his newborn child, there was awful violence among his children, and one of David's own sons tried to kill him and take his kingdom. David was forced to leave his palace and wander around like a nomad until he was finally restored. So as you see, sin has consequences."

Disciple appeared concerned. "What will my consequences be?"

"I don't know," said the heavenly figure, "but it is good that you stopped putting more bad seed into the ground when you did. Now that you are back on your path, you will not have to go through those consequences alone. Our Lord will be there with you. He will not remove the consequences from you, but He will be there with you as you go through them."

"So these consequences serve to teach me and others the results of sin so that we learn not to do them again?"

"Yes, and just as you sowed bad seed, you have the opportunity to sow good seed. And our Lord promises that you will reap a harvest from this good seed in due season if you don't grow weary and leave your path."

The heavenly figure took him to a small clearing where his armor and the satchel with his Book were lying on the ground.

Disciple threw his satchel over his shoulder and picked up his armor. "I'm so glad to have these back again." After he wrapped the Belt of Truth around his waist, he noticed that his armor wasn't as strong as it once was, and when he held out his Book, his Sword was not as sharp as it used to be.

The heavenly figure said, "As you continue on your journey, you will restore more strength to your armor, and your Sword will become sharper."

Disciple realized that this too was another consequence of going off his path, and he wished he could make up for it all in one day.

The heavenly figure said goodbye then disappeared into the clouds. Disciple finished putting on his armor and then traveled forward. After he had gone about a mile, he heard singing, but it was vastly different from the singing at the Camp of Sin. It was songs of joy magnifying his Lord. He concluded that the music must be coming from a House of Instruction.

How long had it been since he had been to one? What would people think if he went in? Would they know who he was? Would they have heard about his time at the Camp of Sin? Would they look at him with shame and disappointment?

Disciple entered the building and took a seat on the back row. The singing was uplifting and inspiring, but he just sat and listened, not feeling worthy to join in. He remembered a time when he was one of those singing the songs of joy.

After singing one more hymn, an elderly man approached the front and prayed for the service. Then a familiar figure walked up on the stage and stood behind the pulpit. Disciple recognized him immediately. It was Pastor Sinclair, the man who had explained so much to him the day he had gone through the Building of Reflection and up the Hill of Calvary.

Pastor Sinclair opened his Book and taught about The Prodigal Son. Disciple listened closely to every word. He could identify with the son in the story who had walked off with such an arrogant and prideful attitude to follow rebellion. Just like the rebellious son, he too had enjoyed the fruits of his sin, and he too knew what it was like to end up with nothing.

Listening to how the prodigal son came to himself and repented, Disciple thought back to when he knelt down in the dirt at the Camp of Sin, as he cried out in sorrow for what he had done. He listened intently to what would happen to the son next, still wondering what he could expect in his own life.

Pastor Sinclair taught that the father saw his son from a distance and then ran out to welcome him back. Disciple thought, why was the father running toward him? Shouldn't he have let the son walk into the village by himself and at least suffer some of the shame of walking in alone? But Pastor Sinclair made the point that the father wanted to let everyone know, "This is my son. I accept him."

Tears began to flow down Disciple's face as he thought about how he didn't deserve such love from his Father. Pastor Sinclair asked everyone to bow their heads for prayer. Disciple buried his face in his hands and once again told God how sorry he was for his sin.

After Pastor Sinclair said goodbye to the others, he joined Disciple and sat down beside him. Pastor Sinclair put his arm around him, and Disciple began to cry even more. He felt such love and acceptance from him. For several minutes Pastor Sinclair just sat there and held him as he cried.

Disciple kept his head bowed to the floor. "I've sinned against God. I left my path, and I went to the Camp of Sin. I've been there for many months. It was terrible. I thought I would end up begging in a garbage heap, but our Lord sent a messenger with words of grace. I don't deserve such grace!"

Pastor Sinclair held him some more and then softly spoke. "I know where you've been. Many of us have been praying for you. I knew you would return."

Disciple was still crying. "How could I have done such a thing?"

"Sin is deceptive," said Pastor Sinclair. "All it takes is one moment where we look the wrong way and make the wrong decision."

Disciple shook his head. "But how do I make sure it never happens again? I don't ever want to end up there again. Please tell me what I can do."

Pastor Sinclair put his hand on Disciple's shoulder. "The best way to avoid sin is to know that you're always capable of it. No matter how far you go on your journey, you are still capable of going off your path and following rebellion."

They continued to talk for many hours, then Pastor Sinclair invited him to stay the night. Disciple didn't recognize how tired he was until he lay down. As his body sunk into the bed, he realized that it was the first time in a long time that he was lying down in peace.

He slept well that night and woke up refreshed the next morning. Pastor Sinclair prepared a nice breakfast for them both, and they talked some more.

Disciple asked, "May I stay here for a little while with you? I feel I need to spend some extra time in my Book, and I want to learn more from you before I go back out and continue my Quest."

Pastor Sinclair smiled and nodded. "Of course, stay here until you feel you're ready. I've been invited to fill in at this House of Instruction for a few weeks so there will be plenty of time."

Disciple finished his last bite of breakfast and pushed his plate to the side. "I've been meaning to ask you some questions about a couple of people I met at the Camp of Sin."

"Go ahead."

"While I was there, I ran into some young men who said they too had been on this Quest. One said that he tried it, but it didn't do him any good, and the other said he would come back, but he wasn't ready yet."

Pastor Sinclair drank some orange juice and wiped his mouth with his napkin. "Well the one who said he just tried it, probably never came through the Building of Reflection and the Hill of Calvary in the first place. And if the other one was truly on this Quest, then at some point he will come back."

"But what if he doesn't come back?" asked Disciple.

Pastor Sinclair paused and took a deep breath. "If he doesn't come back, then it means he was never on the Quest to begin with."

Disciple leaned forward. "So what will happen to him?"

Pastor Sinclair stared straight ahead. "He will end up in the Lake that Burns Forever."

Disciple looked concerned. "Is that where I would have gone?"

Pastor Sinclair shook his head. "No, a person that comes through the Building of Reflection and takes his sin up the Hill of Calvary cannot end up in the Lake that Burns Forever because he is kept in the hands of both the Father and the Son. He can never perish."

Disciple thought about this for a moment. "I know that verse, and I know what you're saying is true, but it makes you wonder if some would try to take advantage of that and stay in the Camp of Sin."

Pastor Sinclair leaned forward and put his hands on the table. "A person that has truly been on this Quest would not think in such a way. A person that has become a new creation wants to do what is right even though there is still sin within him. But let me ask you this, now that you've been reminded that you cannot perish, does that make you want to go back to the Camp of Sin?"

Disciple sat straight up. "No! I don't ever want to go back there."

Pastor Sinclair held up his hand. "Why not?"

"Because, I do not want to rebel against God. Although sin seems fun at first, over time, it just makes you miserable. There were many times I thought of coming back, but I didn't know how."

"That's correct," said Pastor Sinclair. "Someone who is truly on this Quest can only enjoy sin for so long until it makes them miserable. Sin grieves you because it grieves the Holy Spirit who lives inside you. If someone does not have the Holy Spirit, then they are not God's child."

Disciple put his finger to the side of his forehead. "How long can someone stay in the Camp of Sin and still be truly on this Quest?"

Pastor Sinclair sat back in his chair and folded his arms across his chest. "That's a good question. The only answer I can give you is that only God knows for sure those who are His. He has promised that for those which He has begun a good work in, He will surely complete it. A person who truly belongs to God will not go on continuously practicing sin."

Disciple thanked Pastor Sinclair for teaching him this important lesson, and he went into a small room to pray and read. Later that evening he joined Pastor Sinclair for dinner.

After praying over the food, Pastor Sinclair passed Disciple a pot of stew. "I want to ask you a question."

"Sure," said Disciple as he placed some fresh steamed vegetables on his plate.

"When we first talked together over a year ago you mentioned that you grew up without a mother and father."

"That's right," said Disciple as he reached for his fork.

Pastor Sinclair poured some gravy over his rice. "From listening to your experiences as you grew up, it seemed that you had a hard time getting close to people and letting them get close to you."

Disciple stopped eating for a moment. "I never thought about it like that. I guess I just got used to doing things on my own."

"It's a good thing," said Pastor Sinclair, "to know how to take care of yourself, but at some point you need others. I feel this may be something that's been missing in your life, and it might have played a part in what led you off your path."

"How so?" asked Disciple as he took a drink of tea.

Pastor Sinclair sat back in his chair. "Developing relationships with others causes us to see things in ourselves that we ordinarily wouldn't see. It's like a mirror to our souls."

"That makes sense. I guess it's something I'm going to have to work on."

Pastor Sinclair nodded. "I'll be praying that God gives you that opportunity. Relationships cost you something though. They cost your time and your attention. They require you to take your eyes off of yourself and to see life through the lens of someone else's perspective. Relationships teach you that life is about giving and not always receiving."

Disciple took another drink of tea and stared out across the room. "You know, that helps me to understand something. When I met Lust and Seduction, I was immediately drawn to them, although in the past I wasn't that interested when a young lady showed me attention. Now I think I understand why. Lust and Seduction offered me a way to interact with them without having to develop a relationship. I didn't have to see them as real people but only as objects of my desire."

"That's great insight," said Pastor Sinclair. "Many young men need to understand that."

Disciple pushed his chair back and set his napkin down on the table. "Before I entered the Orchard of Vanity, I thought I had everything figured out, but now I realize how much more there is to learn and how far I still need to progress."

Pastor Sinclair placed his hand on Disciple's shoulder. "That's the attitude we must always have while we are on this Quest."

Disciple stayed with Pastor Sinclair for another week, and he grew in his understanding of the Book. They continued to have many conversations, and Disciple soaked up everything he could learn. One day they both saw that Disciple's path was leading away, and they knew it was time for him to start on his journey once again.

Disciple gathered his things, and as he was about to leave, he turned and gave Pastor Sinclair a hug. "Thank you so much for all that you've done. You're just the person I needed to see after I came out of the Camp of Sin. The love and acceptance you showed me reminded me of just how much God cares about me."

Pastor Sinclair patted him on the back and grasped his arm. "You're welcome. I'll continue to pray for you as you travel on your Quest."

Disciple and Pastor Sinclair prayed together, and then Disciple left.

12

MR. REGRETFUL & MR. FEARFUL

As Disciple continued his journey, he took notice of how good it felt to be making progress. Instead of feeling as if life was passing him by, he felt like a full participant once again. After traveling for hours, he took some time to stop and read. Ever since he had been delivered from the Camp of Sin, he couldn't get enough of God's word. The Holy Spirit was teaching him things as he read, and he could feel strength returning to his armor.

Disciple understood how great a privilege it was to be able to read the very words of God. It occurred to him that he had taken this for granted earlier in his Quest, and he was now realizing just how special it was to have this experience.

After starting back on his path and traveling for a little while, Disciple noticed two men up ahead who were both mumbling and pointing into the air with their index fingers as if they were trying to solve a problem. They were spaced about fifty yards apart, with one facing forward and the other backward.

As Disciple drew closer, he saw that each of them would start to take a step, and then pull their foot back, so that they never actually moved. After watching this for some time, he decided to talk to the men.

First, he called out to the one who was facing backward. "Excuse me, sir, what are you doing?"

"Hello, my name is Fred, but people have taken to calling me Mr. Regretful. I want to move forward, but each time I think about turning around, I remember something negative about my past. Then as I dwell on this event, I feel as if I must go back and do something to change it. However, after thinking about it for a few minutes, I realize there's nothing I can do, so I just stand here. Then after a few minutes, I think of something else negative from my past and end up doing the same thing again."

Disciple asked, "If you know it's in the past, and you can't change it, then why can't you turn around and go forward."

Mr. Regretful threw up his hands. "Because, I feel as if I must find a way to make up for the things I've done. I've made so many mistakes, and I feel as if each and every one of them haunts me. I'm determined to go over them in my mind, again and again until I find a way to make up for them."

Disciple pointed in the other direction. "But, I've learned that you can't do anything about the past except repent and move forward."

Mr. Regretful waved his hands at Disciple. "I've already heard all that. Let me be. There has to be a way to fix this."

Disciple tried to talk to him some more, but Mr. Regretful wouldn't listen. He just kept acting as if he would take a step, only to stop and then start all over again.

Disciple approached the other man and asked him who he was and why he was there.

"Hello, my name is Jeb, but people have taken to calling me Mr. Fearful. I feel as though people misunderstand me, because I do want to go forward, but I'm concerned about what might be ahead. I think of all the things that could go wrong, and I feel as if I must solve all of them in my mind before I can advance onward."

"How many of the things that you're fearful of, have actually happened before?"

Mr. Fearful looked agitated. "Well, none to me, but I've heard of them happening to others, and besides, how can I go forward when I'm not ready to deal with every possible thing that could happen?"

Disciple shrugged his shoulders. "But, if you stand here all day, you will never go forward anyway."

Mr. Fearful shook his finger at Disciple. "Let me be. I don't need any lectures from you. I can't move forward without first knowing that I have everything under control."

Disciple shook his head and started forward. Along the way, he reflected on his conversations with Mr. Regretful and Mr. Fearful, realizing that at times he struggled with the same anxieties they did. He still felt regret because of his time in the Camp of Sin, and he wished there was a way to go back and undo all the things that happened there. He remembered reading in his Book that we are to forget those things which are behind and press forward to those things which are ahead. He knew he could not change the mistakes of his past, but he could move forward and put more distance between himself and those mistakes.

Disciple then thought of Mr. Fearful. While being with Pastor Sinclair over the last few days, he was concerned about what would happen when he returned to his Quest. So many negative things could occur, but he finally concluded that it was better to take a risk than never having the opportunity to move forward again.

Disciple wondered how much time he'd spent either in regret about what happened yesterday or in fear of what might happen tomorrow. How much better it would be, if he concentrated on the things of today, while it was still today, and let tomorrow take care of itself.

After traveling for another hour, Disciple came to a wide rushing river. There was no way he could wade or swim to the other side because the water was too deep, and the current was too strong. He searched for a way across, but couldn't find one. He started walking downstream and came upon what looked to be a bridge with ropes extending from one side to the other. However, after surveying the bridge he noticed there was nothing to walk on, and there was no way he could hang onto those ropes all the way across. As he drew closer, he saw a sign: "We Walk by Faith and Not by Sight."

Trying to decide what to do next, Disciple sat down to read in his Book and pray. He remembered the story of how Jesus walked on the water while his disciples were in a boat, so he turned in his Book until he came to the passage. Peter asked if he could come out on the water with Jesus. When Jesus told him to come, Peter stepped out of the boat and walked toward Him. Understanding what the Holy Spirit was showing him, Disciple stood up and approached the bridge.

The ropes hung twenty feet above the river and were four feet apart. Using the ropes as handrails, Disciple stepped out with his right foot. As he did, a board appeared under his foot, and he stepped firmly on the board then brought his other foot onto the board. He extended his foot to take another step, and another board appeared. He placed one foot on that board and then the other foot as well. Each time he would step out, a wooden board would appear.

When he was halfway across the bridge, the wind began to blow. It gusted harder and harder until the bridge rocked back and forth. Disciple became afraid, but he remembered what happened to Peter. When Peter was walking on the water, a fierce wind began to blow, and he became afraid and started to sink. But it wasn't the wind that caused Peter to sink, but his fear of the wind.

Calling out to God, Disciple shouted, "Whenever I am afraid, I will trust in you."

As Disciple continued to step out, the boards continued to appear. Despite the wind, he did this until he reached the other side of the bridge and was safely across the river. Turning back and seeing the sign, he realized this was a Bridge of Faith.

Disciple had heard the phrase, "taking a leap of faith," but he thought taking a careful step was better than a full leap. He could have stayed on the other side and never crossed the river, or he could have taken a running leap and ended up in the river. Instead, he walked by faith and was able to safely cross the bridge.

Disciple thought of the words he had read in his Book: "Trust in the LORD with all your heart, And lean not on your own understanding; In all your ways acknowledge Him, And He shall direct your paths." Disciple thanked God for all He showed him that day, and he continued to meditate on what he had learned while traveling forward.

13

GIANT OF SHAME

After three days of a quiet and pleasant journey, Disciple noticed that a crowd was gathered up ahead. He hurried forward to check out what was happening, but before he was close enough to see, he spotted a large sign: "All those on this Quest must defeat the Giant of Shame and enter the River of Healing. Once you bring the Giant to his knees, he must let you come back and forth as you wish."

Disciple drew closer taking notice of his surroundings. A massive rock wall appeared to rise up out of the ground a thousand feet into the air. The wall stretched for miles on either side, with a small opening carved out in the middle. The Giant of Shame stood in front of the opening, blocking the entrance to a beautiful river which flowed with crystal-clear water. The ground leading up to the Giant was packed down from all the battles that had taken place there. Those waiting to face the Giant would set up camp on either side of the narrow path leading to the battle area.

As Disciple looked around, he saw many sitting on the side looking defeated, so he strolled up to them. "Why are you all still here? Why haven't you brought the Giant of Shame to his knees?"

One replied, "Because, it's too difficult. It seems the harder we fight, the stronger he gets."

Disciple felt confident that he could easily defeat this enemy. His armor was strengthened, and his Sword had become much sharper. He stepped marched toward the Giant, but as he came near, he observed how much bigger the Giant looked the closer he got to him.

The Giant of Shame was about nine and a half feet tall. He had large, broad shoulders; strong, muscular arms; legs that were the size of a tree trunk; and a thick, scruffy beard that looked as if it hadn't been cleaned in months. His armor was made out of thick black leather, and he carried a large club which he could swing so fast that it created a gust of wind when it went by.

The Giant of Shame spoke in a loud and obnoxious voice. "Ah, I've heard of you. You are Disciple, or should I call you Doubtful? How was your time in the Camp of Sin? Got any pictures of those women you'd like to show me? Perhaps you could tell me a few of the jokes you learned, or sing me a few of the songs." The Giant then let out a roaring laugh.

Disciple was enraged that he would bring these things up. He glared at the Giant, then lunged at him with his Sword. But the Giant seemed to anticipate his every action and easily blocked everything he tried to do. When Disciple did make contact with him, it was as if the Giant's armor became even thicker.

The Giant of Shame appeared to be amused with how hard Disciple was trying, and then after a few minutes the Giant took his club and swatted him away. "Next!"

Disciple limped off to the side, wondering how he was going to defeat this enemy. The Giant of Shame brought up all the awful things of his past and then laughed at him. The harder he fought, the stronger the Giant of Shame seemed to become. Disciple read in his Book and prayed, and then rose up to fight the Giant again.

The Giant of Shame waved his hand toward Disciple. "Back again so soon? I ran into an old friend of yours the other day, Michael was his name. He and I did lunch, and he had a lot to say about you."

The Giant then transformed his voice to sound like Michael's. "Oh, Disciple, how brilliant you are. Oh, Disciple, you're so much better than everyone else."

Disciple was still upset with himself for falling into that trap in the first place.

The Giant of Shame pointed his club at him. "Michael tells me you may have been the most enthusiastic sinner he ever saw. He could barely keep up with you."

Once again the Giant roared with laughter.

Disciple felt the shame of what he had done and desired to be rid of those feelings more than anything. He took out his Sword and ran up to the Giant attempting to pierce him in his gut. But before his Sword even got close, the Giant once again swatted him away with one blow of his club.

The Giant of Shame smirked and shook his head. "Poor Disciple, if only you could fight as well as you can sin."

Disciple retreated and sat down next to the others who were waiting to face the Giant. He now understood what they had been talking about. Defeating this enemy was not going to be easy. Throughout the rest of the day, he watched others battle the Giant of Shame with the same failed results. They too became angry when the Giant hurled accusations at them. Spurred by their feelings of shame and guilt they rushed toward him only to be easily defeated.

Disciple set up camp preparing to stay there a few days. He realized it wouldn't do any good to keep fighting with the same strategy, only to be defeated again and again. Over the next two days, he continued to read in his Book and to pray. On the third day, he thought back to his time in the Building of Reflection, remembering the shame he felt after seeing all of his sinfulness. There was nothing he could say that would explain away or excuse anything he saw that day. All of that sin had to be carried up the Hill of Calvary. He had to face his sin in all of its ugliness, bringing it to the foot of the cross.

Disciple stood up with confidence and marched toward the Giant.

The Giant of Shame held out his club, motioning for Disciple to come forward. "Ah, you're back for more. That's great because I have more to give. You were so easy to lead into the Orchard of Vanity, in fact, you may have set a record for how fast you fell for that."

This time though, Disciple did not become angry. He looked up at the Giant of Shame and nodded. "You're right. I did all those terrible things, and there's no excuse. I went to the Camp of Sin, I told those jokes, I used those words, and I looked at those pictures. It was my own pride that caused me to be seduced by the voices in the Orchard of Vanity. All that you say is true and more."

The Giant of Shame frowned, but he quickly started speaking again. "Everyone thinks you are a failure since you went to the Camp of Sin. No one will be able to count on you ever again. They will always know you as the person who abandoned his Quest."

As Disciple thought about his reputation, he lowered his gaze to the ground. "I cannot control how others see me. They have a right to measure my life by the fruit I produce, but I do not have to earn my way back into God's favor. God does not deal with me according to my sins, nor does he punish me according to what my iniquities deserve."

The Giant smirked. "Why am I even bothering with someone such as you? You were a nobody before you started this Quest, and you will always be a nobody. You will never accomplish anything for God!"

At these words Disciple paused. This struck at the heart of his insecurity. He had such big dreams of what he'd like to do while on this Quest, but he wasn't sure any of his dreams or aspirations would come to pass. Then the Holy Spirit brought a verse to his remembrance.

Disciple took a step forward. "There once was a great man who said, 'For a day in Your courts is better than a thousand anywhere else. I would rather be a doorkeeper in the house of my God than live in the tents of the wicked.' It does not matter what my Lord gives me to do while on this Quest. It only matters that I serve him faithfully each day that I'm on it."

Starting to become concerned, the Giant pointed his club at Disciple as he smirked. "You tell everyone that you keep to yourself because you like to be alone." The Giant then waved his hand toward all those watching from the sidelines. "But why don't we go ahead and tell everyone the truth. After your parents died, no one wanted you. You were a burden, and that's all you are now. You're a burden to Pastor Sinclair and everyone else on this Quest. Why don't you just quit and save everyone else the trouble."

Disciple lowered his Sword and Shield then stared at the ground. There was some truth in what the Giant said. He never felt wanted by any of his family, and he always felt like a burden to his friends. He was relieved when he could finally afford to live on his own, so he didn't have to depend on anyone else anymore. But deep down inside there was always that fear of rejection that drove him to remain alone.

As he stood there, verses that Pastor Sinclair had taught him began to rise up in his thoughts. Even though he did not feel like he had an earthly family, God had adopted him into His family and made him an heir with Christ. He didn't need to fear rejection by God because it was God that had chosen him. He didn't have to earn his way into this family, for it was God Himself who made him qualified to share in the inheritance of all His saints.

Disciple stood up straight. "God sees all my weaknesses and failures, yet He still loves me and accepts me into His family. This is not because of anything I ever did or ever could do for Him. I am a frail human who withers like the grass and whose life is only but a vapor. It's true I've been a burden to others, and in fact, it was the burden of my sinfulness that was laid on Christ on the cross. But Jesus willingly took on all my burdens and through His death and shed blood, He wiped them all away so that He could present me completely without blame before the Father."

The Giant of Shame let out a yell. "Come fight me now!"

Disciple reached out with his Book until it became a Sword, then darted toward the Giant. But just as he came into range of the Giant's club, Disciple swerved out to the right, then sprang back in and struck the Giant on the leg with his Sword. "There is no one that does anything good, and that includes me."

The Giant temporarily lost his balance, but quickly recovered and tried to kick him.

Disciple jumped out of the way. "There is none that seeks after God, and left to my own decisions, I never would have either. Everything I am or ever will be is because of His grace."

The Giant of Shame swung his club at him, but he ducked just in time and then brought his Sword down on top of the Giant's arm. Rocked by the blow, the Giant dropped his club to the ground.

Disciple struck him in the leg again. "There is no one who is righteous, and I know that the only righteousness I have is of Christ. It is no longer I that live, but Christ that lives in me. I don't care what people think of me. I only care to show people Christ in me!"

When the Giant of Shame reached down to pick up his club, Disciple clobbered his skull with his Sword. The Giant shook his head trying to recover from the blow, but Disciple quickly followed up with a strike to each of the giant's knees. The Giant was now wobbling. Barely able to stand, he desperately swiped at Disciple with his fist but missed wildly.

Disciple struck the Giant in the stomach, causing him to double over. "If the LORD kept a record of our sins and held them against us, who could stand before Him? But with Him, there is forgiveness that we might fear His Name."

Disciple brought his Sword down on the back of the Giant. "For as far as the east is from the west, so far has He removed our sins away from us."

The Giant rocked back and forth then collapsed to his knees, shaking the ground all around him.

Disciple knelt and thanked God for his victory. He then stood up and waded into the River of Healing. He felt the waters washing away his guilt, as it brought healing to his soul. As he stood in the river, he could overhear some of the people talking about his battle with the Giant of Shame.

One of them said, "Did you see that? How could you admit such awful things about yourself? That has to be worse than any blow that Giant could inflict on you. I could never do such a thing. People have said some awful things about me, and it would just make them think they were right all along."

Disciple knew what it took to defeat the Giant of Shame, and he wondered if he should go back and try to teach them. But as the waters continued to wash over him, he felt the Holy Spirit leading him to stay in the river and pray.

He remained in the river for over an hour and watched to see who else would challenge the Giant. As he looked on, a young woman bursting with energy strolled up to the battlefield. She had dark brown hair that came down to her shoulders, and she wore a determined look on her face. Although she appeared to be small in stature, she carried herself as a fierce warrior. Her armor looked strong, and her Sword appeared sharp. Later he would learn that her name was Overcomer. Disciple believed this young woman had a good chance of defeating the Giant, so he was anxious to see what would happen.

Overcomer stood up to fight, and the Giant of Shame, who had recovered to full strength, began to hurl accusations against her just as he had against Disciple.

Overcomer yelled at the Giant. "You are wrong! You will not steal my joy, and you will not steal my victory! I am none of those things that you say that I am!"

Some of the other young women stood up and cheered. Overcomer then rushed toward the Giant, striking at him with her Sword, but the Giant of Shame easily blocked everything she tried to do. The Giant yawned, leisurely covering his mouth with one hand, then he swatted her away with the other. Overcomer tumbled backward and landed next to where the others were sitting on the sidelines. Some of the other young women felt inspired by Overcomer's speech, so they rose up to charge the Giant, but he swatted them away in the same manner.

The Giant of Shame laughed at them all. "Sit Down! And while you're over there why don't you make me a sandwich."

After watching all of this take place, Disciple again wondered if he should go back to teach them what he had learned. But as he stood in the river, he continued to feel his assignment was to watch and pray. He knew though that just yelling at the Giant of Shame while proclaiming your victory, was not going to win the battle.

Overcomer set up her tent then sat down for an extended time of reading and prayer. As nighttime approached, Disciple set up camp on the other side of the river.

The next day, Disciple waded back into the River of Healing. Again, he watched what those on the other side would do and continued to pray for them. A few people tried to fight that day, but none were successful. As the day was ending, Overcomer slowly rose to her feet. She walked toward the Giant with an appearance of humility and confidence. Once again, the Giant of Shame started hurling demeaning accusations at her. This time though, Overcomer didn't try to defend herself.

The Giant of Shame became angry and shouted every negative and hurtful thing that men in her past had said about her. Then the Giant transformed his voice and facial expressions to look and sound like the men who had abused her. Overcomer winced at every abusive word the Giant repeated.

The Giant of Shame yelled at her, "Those men gave you exactly what you deserved. You're nothing but a pathetic little slut."

Overcomer fell to her knees and buried her face in her hands.

Those words cut through her like a knife because they were almost exactly what one man had said to her after he used her for several days then kicked her out of his house. Before she started her Quest, she looked for shelter and refuge wherever she could find it, and this meant she couldn't always be picky about the people she accepted help from.

Overcomer knew she had made some bad choices in her life, but did she deserve to be treated with such cruelty? Did she still deserve to be treated that way? All of the positive affirmations she had memorized weren't of any help in this moment.

She meditated on the Scriptures she had been reading and suddenly realized it didn't matter what she did or didn't deserve because that wasn't where her worth came from. She was in Christ, and when He took her sinfulness, she received His worth and His value.

Overcomer stood to her feet then held out her Book until it became a Sword. She stared defiantly at the Giant of Shame then shouted with a strong and confident voice, "There is no condemnation for those who are in Christ Jesus, and that includes me!"

Overcomer rushed the Giant so fast that before he had time to swing his club, she lunged at him with her Sword and plunged it into his right foot.

Groaning in pain, he hopped around and glared at Overcomer. "I'm going to tear you apart, you sinful little girl!"

Holding out her Sword toward the Giant of Shame, Overcomer shouted, "My sinfulness is always before me, but the answer to my sinfulness, the Lord Jesus Christ, is always before the Father on behalf of me."

The Giant gave Overcomer a fierce look, then tried to bring his club down on top of her head.

After stepping back and blocking the Giant's attack with her Shield, Overcomer said, "I have become the righteousness of God in Christ! It does not matter how others see me, or how you see me, or even how I see myself. It only matters how God sees me."

Overcomer raised her Sword with both hands and then brought it straight down piercing the Giant's left foot. Once again, the Giant groaned and hopped around in pain. The Giant was so angry that he tried to stomp down on top of Overcomer's head, but she dashed out of the way.

Darting from side to side to keep the Giant guessing as to where she would attack next, Overcomer held up her Sword and proclaimed, "It is the Lord My God that helps me, therefore I will not be disgraced. I have set my face like flint, determined to do his will, therefore I will not be put to shame."

After dodging another blow of the Giant's club, Overcomer struck him with her Sword on both his legs. "I will set my focus on Jesus, Who is the author and the perfecter of my faith, Who endured the cross and despised the shame that went with it, because of the joy that was set before Him."

The Giant of Shame lunged wildly at Overcomer, swinging his club back and forth toward her head, but she was so fast that he wasn't able to get close to her. Each time the Giant missed, Overcomer struck him with her Sword. She pummeled the Giant, beating him down so he could barely swing his club anymore.

Just as the Giant gave one last desperate swing with his club, Overcomer stepped out of the way. "I have boldness to enter into the Most Holy Place because of the blood of my Lord Jesus. Because of His sacrifice, I am able to draw near to the Throne of God, with full assurance of faith, and receive cleansing from all the guilt and shame that assaults my thoughts."

Overcomer beat the Giant down to his knees, and then just for good measure, she hit him on his head a few more times until the Giant of Shame collapsed face down in the dirt.

Overcomer raised her hands toward heaven, then strode past the Giant of Shame and into the River of Healing. She closed her eyes as the water flowed all around her. Then she leaned back, submerging her entire body in the river. After several minutes, she stood and waded over to Disciple.

Reaching out her hand, she said, "Hello, my name is Overcomer."

"My name is Disciple," he said, shaking her hand. He glanced over at the Giant of Shame, who was now getting up and recovering to full strength. "I was here when you first arrived, and I saw how you struggled on that first day. I also struggled when I first tried to fight the Giant."

Overcomer nodded. "I was confused at first. I thought I was

saying all the right things, and they certainly felt empowering, but they had no effect on that Giant. Later, as I was reading in my Book, I saw where it said that there is no one that can bring a charge against God's chosen ones, but I wanted to understand why."

"What did you discover?"

Overcomer glanced down at her Breastplate. "So many times I've quoted, I'm the righteousness of God in Christ, but as I read and prayed, I realized that the most important part of that truth was the *In Christ* part." Overcomer shook her head as she held out her hands. "I knew the words, but I didn't understand the meaning. In myself, I was not the righteousness of God, but it was IN CHRIST where my righteousness resided. The reason no accusation can be brought against us is because we are in Christ, and no accusation can be brought against Him!"

Disciple clasped his hands. "That's a great point. That's why there is no condemnation for us because we are in Christ and He cannot be condemned."

"Exactly," replied Overcomer.

Disciple reflected on his battle. "I found that the more I tried to defend myself against the Giant's accusations, the stronger he became."

"Yes," said Overcomer. "We desperately want to prove there's something good about us. We're afraid that if we admit to our sins and shortcomings, we'll feel more shame, but I learned that freely admitting these things is the only way to be free of shame."

Disciple pointed toward the Giant. "I heard him repeat some awful things that men have said about you in the past. I saw how much that hurt. How did you not let those words defeat you?"

Overcomer lowered her head. "You're right, those words hurt. At that time in my life, I thought I deserved everything those men said and did to me."

"How did you get past that?"

Overcomer put her hands on her hips and glanced around. "Throughout much of my Quest, I tried to convince myself that every negative and hurtful word which was ever said to me wasn't true. In fact, I came to believe that I couldn't admit anything negative about myself, or I would be agreeing that it was my fault those men had abused me."

Disciple put his finger to his chin. "So the Giant of Shame thought he had you trapped. The only way you could battle his accusations was to deny them."

"At first he did have me trapped," said Overcomer as she looked back at the Giant, "but I realized that we do not overcome the Accuser of the Brethren by denying his accusations, but by the blood of the Lamb and the word of our testimony in Christ."

"That's great insight. There are a lot of people who need to hear that," said Disciple.

Overcomer sat down in the River of Healing until it came up to her neck. "For the first time, I was able to approach God in complete honesty, allowing Him to show me anything of my sinfulness that He wished. I was no longer going to fight for my own reputation. My identity is in Christ, and I don't have to defend myself any longer. Even if some of the things those men said about me were true, the Holy Spirit showed me that I still didn't deserve to be abused."

Disciple and Overcomer overheard some of the women sitting on the sidelines talking about her battle.

"Did you hear what that Giant said to her? Why didn't she defend herself? She just gave in as if she agreed with them."

Overcomer shook her head. "They still don't understand. I want to go back and teach them and others what I've learned because I want to see more defeat that Giant."

Disciple nodded. "As I've been watching and observing over the last two days, I felt my place was to pray. Now I know that it's you that God wants to minister to these people. I'll continue on, but I'll remember to pray for you as you minister to others."

"Thank you," said Overcomer as she turned to go back across the river.

Disciple waded from the River of Healing and continued on his journey. Along the way, he thought of all that had happened with the Giant of Shame. This would not be the last time he battled shame, but defeating the Giant gave him the tools he needed to face it again in the future. Each day he would need to die to his own reputation and identify with the cross of Christ.

14

MOUNTAIN OF UNFORGIVENESS

As Disciple was traveling, he saw two men up ahead laughing and talking. When he got closer, one of them headed off in the other direction, and the other one picked up his backpack and threw it over his shoulder. When the man turned around, Disciple immediately recognized him.

"Caleb!" shouted Disciple. He hurried toward him and extended his hand. "It's good to see you again."

Caleb shook Disciple's hand and clasped his shoulder. "It's good to see you again too. How has your Quest been going since I last saw you?"

Disciple told him all that had happened since the day they first met. He talked about his victories as well as his failures. As he was telling Caleb how God had bestowed grace on him and restored him to his path, he saw a few tears on Caleb's face.

"There have been times when I needed His wonderful grace as well," said Caleb as he wiped his eyes.

Disciple and Caleb walked for a few miles, enjoying their conversation with one another and discussing things they had read in their Book. After a while, they came upon a group of people who looked very distraught. Some were even crying.

Disciple strode up to them. "What's wrong? What happened?"

An older gentleman with a kind smile stepped forward and introduced himself as Edward. "We've been traveling together as a group for over a year, but recently two of our members have been struggling because they didn't feel they've been treated fairly by some of the people on this Quest."

"What happened?" asked Caleb.

Edward put his arm around one of the young ladies who was crying. "Those two men let their anger build to the point that they became more difficult to get along with, and they seemed to get offended over even minor things. Today they became furious because we asked them to look at how they've been treating us. They took off their armor, threw down their Books, and stormed off their path. As they were walking away, two winged creatures flew by and snatched them up. They flew in the direction of that mountain, and we don't know what to do."

Caleb peered toward the mountain. "I know what's happened. I've seen it before. When someone doesn't walk in forgiveness toward others, this builds up into bitterness and resentment. It starts out as a small root and then grows to the point that it consumes their thoughts. They feel justified in keeping this bitterness and resentment because they believe they've been wronged and deserve justice. They determine that they will not let it go until everything has been made right. This leads them to have an increasingly negative attitude about everything. They even become hostile toward those who love and care about them."

Edward nodded. "Yes, that sounds exactly what happened to these men. Please continue."

Caleb could see the desperation on the faces of those gathered around. "Some will allow these feelings of bitterness and resentment to drive them off their path, causing them to become prey for the enemy. The winged creatures you described are called the Pikron, and they've taken your two companions to the Mountain of Unforgiveness. That's a tough place to escape from. I've heard of people being held captive there for years."

A young woman named Charlotte stepped forward. "Please tell us what we can do. These are not bad men. They were helpful to many of us until they gave into these feelings of bitterness and resentment. As they were being carried off, we heard them call out for help. We don't want to see them trapped on that mountain."

Caleb glanced over at Disciple. "We'll camp here for the night and pray. We'll know by tomorrow morning if we should pursue them or not. If they're not ready to fight for themselves, then it will be useless for us to go after them, but if they're ready to repent, we can help them."

Charlotte looked relieved. "Thank you for staying and praying about this."

When the others filed off toward their tents, Disciple leaned closer to Caleb. "How will we know if we should go or not?"

Caleb spread out his tent, preparing to set it up. "We'll see where our paths are leading tomorrow. If they're heading toward the mountain, then that means we're to go and help rescue these men."

When Disciple and Caleb awoke the next morning, they spent time reading in their Books and praying. After coming out of their tents, they immediately saw that their paths were leading toward the mountain.

Caleb asked everyone to gather around. "We're going to help rescue these men. Those of you who also see that your path is heading toward the Mountain of Unforgiveness can join us."

Three men and two women, including Charlotte stepped forward. They all joined hands and prayed for God's guidance and protection.

Caleb glanced around at those who would be going with them. "This will not be an easy task. I haven't climbed this mountain before, but I've talked to some who have. They say that the trail leading up to the top is treacherous and dangerous, and we'll face different enemies and obstacles as we get closer to the place where your friends are being held. Those of you who will remain here should pray for us, and please continue praying until we return."

Those staying behind, including Edward, agreed to be in constant prayer while the rescue party was gone.

Caleb, Disciple, Charlotte, and the others gathered up supplies, and then set off toward the mountain.

As they were walking, Disciple had some questions for Caleb. "I want to learn more about how bitterness and resentment can become such a problem that it causes someone to leave their path."

Caleb replied, "It happens much the same as the two men who were carried off. It starts out with us feeling wronged by someone. How we handle that determines whether bitterness is able to take root in us. We are taught in our Book that we are to forgive others just as we have been forgiven."

Disciple thought for a moment. "I can understand forgiving someone when they may have unintentionally offended us. I'm sure I've done things that have offended others when I didn't realize it, but what about when someone intentionally tries to harm you in some way? How do we handle that? Do we forgive them and treat them as if nothing happened?"

Shifting his backpack, Caleb answered, "Forgiveness is between you and God and does not depend on the other person. When we forgive, we give up our rights to hold a grudge and seek revenge. But there is a difference between forgiving them in our hearts before God and how we relate to them afterward. We can totally forgive them in our heart, but still hold them accountable for what they've done. If they have intentionally harmed us, then the relationship cannot be restored until they've taken responsibility for what they've done and have asked for our forgiveness."

Caleb signaled for everyone to stop and take a break. They all set down their backpacks and took out their canteens. While they had been walking along, Charlotte and the others were paying close attention as Caleb and Disciple discussed bitterness and resentment.

After taking a drink of water, Charlotte turned toward Caleb. "I was listening to your answer to Disciple about forgiveness, but what if someone has done something to offend us, but they don't know it?"

Caleb nodded as he knelt down to put his canteen in his backpack. "That's a good point. It may just be a misunderstanding. There will be times when we feel it's best to forgive and not say anything, but if we can't get past something, then we may need to talk to someone else about it, even if we don't confront the person who did it."

Others in the group began discussing their experiences with bitterness and resentment, and they all realized that at times, they had held resentment toward someone.

After a few more minutes of discussion, Caleb said, "We're almost at the Mountain of Unforgiveness, and before we get there let's pray together and repent for the times that we've held grudges toward others."

After they all prayed and confessed their shortcomings, Caleb led them to the base of the mountain.

Heavy gray clouds surrounded the Mountain of Unforgiveness,

shielding it from most of the sunlight. The vegetation and trees appeared to be brown and dying. Instead of hearing the usual singing of birds, only the gawking of vultures could be heard as they circled overhead. The air smelled like ashes that were left over from a fire that had been burning all night. The trail was extremely steep and wound around the mountain so that it was difficult to see too far ahead.

Caleb told everyone to check their armor and especially their Shoes of the Gospel to make sure they were on securely. Since the ground was slippery and loose, they each would need to maintain firm footing as they climbed.

Caleb stepped forward to lead them up the trail. "As we climb this mountain, meditate on parts of the Book that speak about the grace and forgiveness of God."

Disciple thought about the forgiveness he had experienced at the Hill of Calvary, and also after coming out of the Camp of Sin. He desired to show this same love and forgiveness to others. He then thought of the story of the wicked servant who had been forgiven of a very large debt by his master. This same servant then went out and showed no mercy to a fellow servant who owed him a much smaller debt. Jesus told this story to illustrate that even as we have been forgiven much, we should also extend this forgiveness to others. These men they were about to rescue would need to learn this same lesson.

One by one they climbed the winding trail. At one point Disciple thought he heard something moving in the trees, then all of a sudden, the branches turned into tentacles and began creeping toward them. The tentacles reached out as if they were trying to wrap around their bodies.

Caleb shouted, "These trees are searching for areas of unforgiveness in your heart. If they find such a place, they can latch on and capture you. If anything is revealed to you, repent quickly, and then take out your Sword and cut off the branch."

Disciple felt one of the tentacles digging into his shoulder, and he realized that he was holding resentment toward Michael and his buddies. They had used him until all his energy was gone, and then they were going to throw him away like garbage when he was no longer of any benefit to them.

Disciple held out his Sword. "God, give me the ability to love my enemies, to do good to those who hate me, and to pray for those who spitefully use me." He then cut off the tentacle and beat back the other branches that were coming toward him.

The rest of the group battled back the tentacles while confessing any lack of forgiveness toward others that was revealed to them. Finally, after another thirty minutes of relentless combat, they fought off the last branches. Anxious to get out of this area, everyone picked up their pace.

As they hiked up the trail, Disciple said, "It's a good thing we talked and prayed about areas of unforgiveness before we reached the mountain, or that would have been a lot harder."

Caleb nodded. "Yes, even after we've prayed about an area, there's usually still more that needs to be revealed."

After walking a little further, the ground began to vibrate. Stopping for just a moment, everyone looked up to see large rocks tumbling downhill toward them.

Caleb shouted, "These are rocks of offense. They represent the things that others do, which can cause you to be offended. If you do not avoid them, they will cause you to stumble and lose your balance. And if the larger ones land on you, they can crush you, so be ready to use your Shields."

Boulders of different sizes came bounding down the hill. Three boulders rolled straight toward Disciple. He was able to dodge the first by jumping over it and then darted to the side to miss the second, but there was no time to get out of the way of the third. As the boulder bounced toward him, Disciple quickly ducked down and thrust out his Shield, knocking the boulder up into the air and safely out of the way.

Suddenly, a large boulder that was big enough to mow down three of them at one time came rolling down the hill. Caleb was in the lead, and he knew that if this boulder was allowed to keep going, it could take any one of them out.

Bracing for impact, Caleb knelt down behind his Shield as the massive boulder approached. "Hatred stirs up strife, but love covers up all offenses."

The large boulder crashed into Caleb's Shield and instantly broke into small pieces.

Several small boulders rumbled toward Charlotte. She thrust out her Shield to the left and to the right, knocking the rocks away while shouting, "Love is not easily offended, and it does not keep a record of suffered wrongs."

More rocks tumbled toward the group, but by now they were all adept at dodging and knocking the boulders out of the way.

When the boulders finally stopped, Charlotte took a deep breath. "That was a lot of work."

Caleb reached for his canteen. "There are many things that happen around us every day that we could get offended about if we wanted to. It takes hard work and persistence to walk in love toward others sometimes."

The group moved cautiously forward again, not knowing what they might encounter next. As they came to an open area, several lions appeared. The lions roared loudly and steadily crept toward them.

Caleb motioned for everyone to stop as he studied the lions. After a few moments in prayer, he said, "These lions can sense fear."

"What does fear have to do with bitterness or resentment?" asked Disciple.

Caleb kept an eye on the lions as they drew closer. "When people do things that cause us offense, we can experience anger. And if we stuff our anger instead of dealing with it properly then it turns into fear. It's our fears that will give these lions the ability to overpower us."

Disciple quickly read out loud from his Book. "Be angry and sin not, do not let the sun go down on your rage, and do not give such place to the devil."

Caleb held up his hand. "If you have suppressed any anger in your heart, then release it to God now. Tell Him what you're angry about and lay it at His feet."

Each member of the group searched their heart, and as they released their anger to God, the lions backed off and retreated into the woods.

Caleb motioned for everyone to stop and take a break. As the others gathered around, he said, "Those lions represent an important lesson. Walking in love does not mean walking in denial. If something causes us to be angry, then we must deal with it appropriately. Taking our anger out on someone is wrong and harmful, but it's also destructive to deny anger and suppress it. Stuffing our anger causes fear and depression, and it can also cause us to act in passive-aggressive ways."

Charlotte said, "I perceive that the command to be angry, means to express anger in a way that does not do damage to others. We can be angry without sinning."

Caleb nodded in agreement. "Great point." After taking another drink of water, he pointed ahead, "Let's keep going."

The group hiked up the steep trail for another thirty minutes, then Caleb motioned for everyone to stop. "I believe we're getting close to the place where the Pikron have taken your friends."

The group crept closer until they reached the next corner, then Caleb motioned for everyone to duck in behind a large rock. Peeking out from behind it, they could see the two winged creatures standing beside a cave with prison bars in front of it. The two men, who had been carried off, were imprisoned inside.

Caleb tapped Charlotte on the arm. "Did you bring the armor and the Books these men left behind?"

"Yes," said Charlotte. "We're each carrying some of it in our backpacks."

Caleb said, "Good, we can only do so much. These men will have to fight the decisive battle against these winged creatures if they want to be free. Some of us will need to fight with the Pikron and keep them busy while the others help to free the men."

It was decided that Caleb would lead four of the group to fight the Pikron while Disciple and Charlotte rushed toward the prison bars to help free the men. Caleb and those with him held out their Books until they became Swords, then they inched slowly toward the winged creatures. They were able to stay hidden as they crept forward for about twenty feet, but when the Pikron spotted them, they angrily flapped their wings and rose up a few feet into the air. They seemed agitated that someone had come to rescue their prey. The Pikron were not used to losing what they snatched up.

These winged creatures were seven foot tall with dark grey faces that looked like that of a bat. Black slime covered their entire body, and large claws jutted out from their feet. Acid dripped from their long spiked teeth, and they emitted a high-pitched hissing sound.

Caleb and the others attempted to encircle the Pikron, but the winged creatures flew into the air and then dove toward them with their claws extended as if they intended to force them off the mountain.

Caleb shouted, "Duck down and hold up your Shields!"

Their Shields momentarily held the creatures back, but the Pikron thrust out their claws and knocked them on their back.

Caleb quickly regained his footing and pointed toward his feet with his Sword. "Dig in with your Shoes, and do not let these creatures push you around."

The Pikron flew toward them again. This time though they crouched as low as they could while holding their Shields above them. When they felt the creature's claws pressing down on them, they sprang up and thrust their Shields into the Pikron, knocking them out of the air. As soon as the Pikron hit the ground, Caleb motioned for the rest to attack with their Swords.

Disciple whispered to Charlotte. "Now that they have those creatures occupied, let's get over to those prison bars. Hand me the armor and Book for one of your friends, and you take the other."

Hoping the Pikron would be too busy to notice them, Disciple and Charlotte quickly made their way to the cave where the two men were being held. They then took out the armor and the Books and handed them to the men through the bars.

Caleb saw Disciple and Charlotte moving toward the cave, so he tried to keep the pressure on the Pikron in order to keep them from noticing what was happening. But, the creatures managed to get away from the battle and flew into the air. When they did, they saw Disciple and Charlotte trying to free their prey. The Pikron realized what was going on, and dove toward them.

Caleb motioned for the others to move between the cave and the creatures to give Disciple and Charlotte more time. The Pikron tried to bite them so they could inject them with their poison of bitterness, but Caleb and the others held them off. One of the Pikron was able to grasp the youngest member of the group with its claws and was trying to lift him off the ground. Caleb quickly struck at the feet of the creature, until it dropped the youth.

Caleb glanced back at Disciple and Charlotte. "Get those prisoners free as soon as you can. We can't hold these creatures off much longer."

Disciple shouted at the men being held captive. "We'll help cut through these bars to free you, but you must take out your Swords and help as well. As we strike these bars, we're going to quote verses from the Book about forgiveness. You must do the same, for if you do not fight from the inside, we will not be able to free you from the outside."

Disciple struck the prison bars with his Sword. "Help us to be kind to one another, tenderhearted, forgiving one another, even as God in Christ forgave us."

Charlotte struck the prison bars with her Sword as well. "Help us to bear with each other, and forgive one another. If any of us has a complaint against someone; even as Christ forgave us, so let us do also."

Disciple noticed that the men on the inside were not fighting as hard as he and Charlotte were. Disciple gave the men a stern look. "If you want to be free then you must let go of all your bitterness and resentment and forgive those who have wronged you. If you don't, you'll stay trapped on this mountain for the rest of your lives."

Charlotte grasped the prison bars. "Let go of your stubbornness and pride, and realize you are in need of forgiveness as well."

The men on the inside forcefully swung their Swords, and the iron bars began to fall apart. Disciple and Charlotte struck the bars a few more times until they were completely destroyed. Finally freed, the men climbed over the rubble and out of the cave.

Disciple and Charlotte turned to help Caleb and the others with the Pikron. The creatures became more ferocious, flying higher and diving toward them more swiftly in an attempt to knock them out of the way.

Caleb whirled around toward the two men who had just been liberated. "Now that you're free, only you can drive these creatures away so we can get off this mountain."

The two men struck out at the creatures with their Swords. "Lord, forgive us of our sins as we also forgive those who have sinned against us."

The men successfully struck the Pikron with their Swords, but the creatures were determined to keep their prey. The Pikron dug their sharp claws into the men's shoulders, but they fought back, slamming their Shields into the creature's heads, and knocking them back into the air. The Pikron flew upward several feet and then rushed toward them again.

The men reared back with their Swords. "Even though Jesus suffered tremendous injustice, He cried out, 'Father forgive them.' Lord Jesus, give us the courage and the faith to forgive as You did."

The men struck the creatures even harder this time, rocking them back to the point that they almost fell to the ground. The Pikron flew out of reach trying to recover. As they descended toward the two men again, the faces of the creatures began to change into the faces of those who had offended them. Recalling all the times they had felt wronged, the two men lowered their Swords and stared at the ground.

Disciple shouted toward them. "You must strike these creatures while giving up the right to get revenge."

Just as the Pikron were about to make contact, the men lifted their Swords and lunged at the creatures while yelling, "Vengeance belongs to the Lord. It is His place to repay and not ours!"

The first man struck one of the Pikron and gashed its head, then followed up with slashing its wing. The second man struck out at the other Pikron catching it just under the chin with his Sword and then pierced its wing. Both of the Pikron fell to the ground and then wobbled away. As the creatures came to the edge of the mountain, they jumped off, flapping their wings. Descending down the side, they fell a hundred feet before finally taking flight again. They circled overhead a few times, then disappeared into the dark grey clouds above. The battle was finally over. All those involved with the rescue hugged the men and congratulated them.

Caleb looked around and smiled. "It's time to get off this mountain."

The group traveled down the trail and back toward their camp. When they arrived, everyone was full of joy as they reunited with their two companions.

Edward stepped forward. "Thanks to all of you who helped bring back our friends. We haven't stopped praying since you left."

"We could feel your prayers, and we needed them many times while on that mountain," said Caleb.

Edward embraced the men who were rescued. "Josiah, Malcolm,

it's so good to see you again."

Josiah and Malcolm were both younger men in their early twenties. Their clothes were filthy and torn from having been grasped by the Pikron's claws, and their hair and face were grimy and dirty. But although their appearance was rough, they looked humbled and relieved.

Josiah stepped back. "Thanks for not giving up on us. We learned a valuable lesson."

"Yes," said Malcolm. "I just wished we could have learned that lesson without getting ourselves into so much trouble."

Edward smiled toward them. "What's important is that you're back."

All the others embraced the two men with tears, and Josiah and Malcolm cried as well.

Josiah took out a handkerchief and wiped his face. "I'm so sorry for how I treated all of you. Please forgive me."

Malcolm gazed into the sky. "God has forgiven me for so much, and from now on I'm going to walk in forgiveness toward others as well."

One by one the members of the group approached them and let them know that they were forgiven. Some even confessed their own areas of bitterness and resentment that they'd been holding onto regarding other situations.

After a meal was prepared and everyone sat down to eat, Caleb, Disciple, and the others took turns sharing what happened on the Mountain of Unforgiveness. Those that stayed behind were thankful that God had guided and protected them through every part of the mission to rescue their friends. Edward asked Caleb and Disciple to stay longer, but they saw that their path was continuing on. Everyone thanked them once again and wished them well as they departed.

15

PERSONAL RESPONSIBILITY

Disciple and Caleb continued to travel together over the next week. One day, just as they were cresting a hill, they saw that their paths were splitting up, but a hundred yards in the distance, they came together again. On Disciple's path was a thicket made up of small trees, bushes, and Thorn Plants. There was no way to go around it, so he would have to go through it.

Disciple turned to Caleb. "Any idea why our paths are splitting up like this, and why there's all these obstacles on mine?"

Caleb took a deep breath and nodded. "Yes, I came across those same Thorn Plants earlier in my Quest. They represent the seeds of rebellion and the sin that you sowed earlier in your journey. Not I or anyone else can help you cut through it, but I can be here to support you as you go through it."

Disciple followed his path, and soon he reached the dense foliage that he would have to pass through. He took out his Sword and began to cut through the thicket. It was hard work, and as he swung his Sword, the Thorn Plants dug into his arms. He knew this was part of the consequences the heavenly figure had told him about right after being delivered from the Camp of Sin. All those seeds he had planted there had grown up and created this thicket.

Each time Disciple felt a thorn pressing into his flesh, he remembered the sins he had committed in rebellion. He prayed and asked God if there were still things he needed to repent for. He also asked if there were things he still needed to forgive himself for.

Disciple remembered the promise that if we confess our sins, thus taking full responsibility for them, then God would be faithful and just to forgive us and cleanse us.

Disciple saw others in the distance traveling on their paths, and he felt a sense of shame. But the Holy Spirit quickly reminded him that Jesus had carried his shame, as well as all the sins he had committed that produced that shame. This adversity was not happening because God was angry at him or punishing him for his sin. Jesus had suffered to take care of all of that, but this thicket was God's discipline to train him regarding the consequences of sin.

At some places, the shrubbery was thicker, and the thorns were sharper. Disciple remembered the times when he had plunged deeper into his sin even though he had felt the Holy Spirit convicting him. He realized that when we press further into rebellion, there is a heavier cost later.

His journey through the thicket took most of the day, but Disciple worked his way through to the other side where his path joined Caleb's again. Upon stopping at a stream a little further ahead, Disciple waded into the water and let it flow over his wounds. When he came out of the stream, Caleb gave him some salve to put on his cuts and scrapes, which also provided great relief.

Disciple and Caleb set up camp and stayed there for the rest of the day and through the night. The wounds from the thorn plants made it difficult for Disciple to sleep, and another three days would pass before he could rest well without the pain and itching from the wounds.

As they were sitting around a fire one evening, Disciple said, "Thanks for being here as I've gone through this ordeal. I never had a family, but you're the closest thing I've ever had to a brother."

Caleb smiled as he threw a chunk of wood on the fire. "You're welcome. We all need someone to be there for us during our times of struggle. There were many who supported me during these times, and I know you'll be there for someone else one day."

Disciple tightened his blanket around him. "I hope I can be there for others. Learning to trust has not been easy for me. Things seem much simpler just being on my own."

Caleb nodded. "They're simpler, but they aren't as rewarding. I see God doing a work in you, and I know He has a call on your life. Stay in the process and surrender to whatever needs to be done to complete this process."

Disciple held his hands out over the fire and then rubbed them together. "I'll try to remember that, but I've got a feeling it's not going to be easy."

Caleb stood up to fix the fire for the night. "Nothing that produces lasting results ever is."

After retiring to their tents, they both got some sleep and then began traveling on their path again the next day. As they were walking, Caleb and Disciple spotted a man who was hunched over and dragging a large bag of garbage behind him. His hair was uncombed, and his face appeared wearied. The man looked exhausted as he trudged up his path dragging the extra weight behind him.

As the man struggled along, little pieces of trash spilled out. Small but fierce creatures that looked like large rats with sharp claws and jagged teeth were following the man as if drawn by the garbage. The creatures tried to bite him on the leg, and he swatted at them with his Sword, rebuking them in the name of Jesus. The rat-like varmints scurried away for a moment, but then they came right back to the garbage.

Disciple stopped and shook his head. "Doesn't that man understand that he's never going to get rid of those creatures until he gets rid of the garbage he's dragging around?"

"That's a good point," said Caleb. "Let's ask him."

Disciple and Caleb marched up to the man, though they stayed just out of range of the garbage around him.

Raising his voice, Disciple called out, "Hello there. I'm Disciple, and this is my good friend Caleb."

The man shook one of the creatures off his leg. "Hello, my name is Simon."

Disciple pointed toward the creatures. "How long have you been having this problem?"

Simon swiped at another one that hissed at him. "I don't know really. It wasn't that bad at the beginning, but lately, it's been much worse. These varmints are constantly bothering me, and I can't seem to ever get a good night's rest."

Disciple pointed to the bag. "Why are you dragging all that

garbage around?"

"This isn't garbage. Sure, it's not the best looking stuff in the world, but I've been carrying it with me for some time now on my journey."

"Do you not see that these creatures are attracted to all that trash?"

Simon shook his head. "Oh no, I don't believe that at all. These creatures were sent by the Devil to steal my peace and my joy. It's my duty to battle them until they leave."

"But," said Disciple as he held out his hand, "can't you see they're not leaving? They're attracted to the garbage, and as long as you're dragging that around, then they won't leave. You've given them permission to stay."

Simon was upset when he heard this. "Why are you bringing such an accusation against me? You talk like this is my fault, as if I brought it on myself."

At this point, Caleb stepped forward. "We're not here to condemn you, but you need to understand that you're carrying around things that give these creatures a right to hang around you. You won't be free of them until you get rid of that garbage."

Simon was angry, but he examined the garbage as if he was taking note of it for the first time. After a few minutes his countenance changed, and instead of appearing angry, he looked sad.

Simon pulled on the bag. "I've always thought each of these pieces of trash was something that others had thrown at me. It was much easier to blame someone else than take responsibility for it myself. If anyone asked me what I was dragging around, I could always tell them about all the wrongs I had endured. I could get people to feel sorry for me, and then they didn't look down on me for dragging this trash around."

Disciple said, "Why didn't you try to do that with us when we asked you about it?"

"You two didn't look like people that would listen to that kind of talk. You seemed like the kind of people who would try to get me to take responsibility. When I've encountered people like you, I've tried to deny there was any garbage at all."

"So why are you being honest with us now?"

Simon took a deep breath and then breathed out slowly. "To tell you the truth, I'm tired of playing the victim to get sympathy from others. I'm tired of telling stories to get people to feel sorry for me, so they won't hold me accountable for the problems in my life. I know that if I get rid of this garbage, I will no longer be able to blame others, and I will have to take responsibility. It's going to be tough, but I'm ready to get rid of this. Will you help me?"

Caleb nodded toward Disciple to let him know that he had confidence in his ability to handle this.

Disciple opened his Book. "We will be glad to help you. Let me start by sharing something from God's word. 'Stop being deceived; God is not mocked, for whatever a man sows, this will he also reap. For he that sows to his flesh shall of the flesh reap destruction, but he that sows to the Spirit shall by the Spirit reap eternal life.' "

Disciple closed his Book. "God tells us that we reap what we sow. We reap according to what we've planted in our lives, and not according to what others have planted for us. The garbage that has come up in your life is not the result of other's sins, but your own. Others can do a lot of things to us, but they cannot make us sin. We can't be free until we're ready to admit that."

Simon paused for a moment and stared at the garbage. He wondered if he was ready to give up blaming others for his problems.

"I guess I've always known the truth you just read," said Simon as he kicked the bag of trash, "but admitting it out loud is a different thing entirely." Simon lifted his eyes toward heaven. "I want to be free from all of this."

Disciple pointed to his Book. "Take out your Sword and pierce the garbage with it. As you do, confess the things you've done that have brought these problems into your life."

Simon struck the garbage with his Sword, and Disciple and Caleb took out their Swords to help him. Simon confessed his responsibility for his sins and gave up the right to blame others. As they all hacked at the bag, it disappeared, and the creatures started to leave.

When all of the garbage was gone, only one of the creatures was left. Simon swung at it with his Sword, rebuking it in the name of Jesus, and the rat-like varmint ran off immediately.

Simon stood upright as a look of contentment and peace filled his face. "I feel so light. It's like someone took a hundred pounds off my back. Thank you so much for helping me."

Disciple put his hand on Simon's shoulder. "I believe the Holy Spirit sent us to talk to you because you were ready to do something about your problems. From this point forward immediately take responsibility for your sins and shortcomings and never go back to blaming others or making excuses."

Simon thanked them again and went away rejoicing.

Disciple turned to Caleb. "I'm so glad we were able to play a part in helping that man."

Caleb returned his Sword to his side and placed his Book back in his satchel. "Yes, it's a great thing when the Holy Spirit leads us to someone in their time of need. I've had other experiences that didn't go as well as this one."

"What happened?" asked Disciple.

"You should know that everyone will not respond as Simon did. Some people aren't ready to give up their garbage. They'll continue to make excuses and want you to feel sorry for them, but that's not going to help them get free from their problems."

Disciple said, "I can see how our first reaction would be to feel sorry for them and try to fix them."

Caleb nodded. "Too often we think the first thing we should do for such a person is to get into their past and try to work through all the negative things that have happened to them. This seems like the caring thing to do, but if they're actively giving into sin, then they first have to take responsibility for what they're doing now."

"So what do we do when we encounter someone who wants to stay a victim and not repent for their sin?"

Caleb shook his head. "We can't do anything."

Disciple knew what Caleb was saying was correct, but he felt very uneasy about the results of such an encounter. "But, if we just point them toward personal responsibility, we're going to be accused of being uncaring and harsh."

Caleb threw on his backpack preparing to move forward. "Correct. If you don't go along with trying to fix them, you can be accused of not caring about them. But if we're not careful, we can spend most of our time trying to help people who really don't want to be helped."

Disciple shrugged. "So what do we do?"

Caleb brought his index finger to the side of his face. "We have to let people know that when they're ready to start taking steps, even small ones, toward accepting responsibility, we'll be more than willing to get in the middle of their garbage with them and help them get rid of it. But until they do that, we'll keep pointing them toward the truths they need to hear."

Disciple continued to think about this as they walked along. He hoped that he would be wise enough to discern when he needed to jump into the middle of someone's problems, and when he needed to keep a healthy distance until they were ready to take responsibility.

After traveling for the rest of the afternoon, they arrived at a stately looking inn surrounded by a vast and beautiful piece of property.

16

INN OF EXPERIENCE

Disciple and Caleb went up to the inn and knocked on the door. A kind elderly gentleman wearing a dapper-looking suit greeted them. After introducing themselves, they asked him if there were any vacancies.

The gentleman smiled and opened the door wider. "Yes, yes of course. Come on in, and I'll have someone show you to your room. My name is Giles, and if you need anything while you're here just let me know."

Giles summoned a young lady who took them upstairs and showed them to a nice room with two beds. They'd both been camping for the past several weeks, so they welcomed the opportunity to sleep in a nice warm bed. They settled in for the night and went to sleep. When they came downstairs for breakfast the next morning, there were already several people sitting at a long dining table.

The room was strikingly elegant, with beautiful paintings along the walls, depicting different kinds of nature scenes. In the center of the room was a gigantic table, which looked as if it came out of a king's palace. A large antique china cabinet stood against the wall at the head of the table, and old mahogany end tables, each standing three feet tall and holding a custom piece of porcelain, occupied each corner of the room.

The floors looked like they could be a hundred years old, but they were freshly stained with a deep rich maple color. The ceiling towered twenty feet above them, and a large candle chandelier hung above the center of the table. All of the food was laid out, and each of the guests was helping themselves to a buffet of biscuits, ham, eggs, bacon, and different kinds of fruit.

Disciple and Caleb sat down and began to fill up their plates with food. Everyone seated around the table was lively and full of energy. Most of the guests were older and had been on their Quest for a long time. The main topics of conversation centered on the different experiences they had while on their Quest and the lessons they had learned. Disciple and Caleb quietly listened as they ate, taking in all the knowledge that was being dispersed by the guests.

After most were done with their breakfast, an elderly gentleman sitting at the head of the table called down to Disciple and Caleb. "Hello, young men. My name is Elder Jenkins. I see that you're new here. Would you tell us a little bit about yourselves and some of your experiences on your journeys?"

Disciple and Caleb both introduced themselves and shared various adventures they'd had together and individually. The other guests listened intently to all their exploits, enjoying the stories of the different battles they fought. They always liked to hear accounts of how different ones defeated the Giant of Shame, and they all laughed a little when Disciple told how Overcomer decided that she would not only bring the giant to his knees but put him face down in the dirt. They thought that was only fitting and a well-deserved outcome for that giant.

Both Caleb and Disciple told them about the Mountain of Unforgiveness, and all the guests were fascinated by what had happened. Disciple then told them about his experiences with the Bridge of Faith and the Forest of Fear, but there was one thing that he was hesitant to bring up.

When Disciple had finished speaking, they asked if there was anything else he would like to share. Disciple sat quietly and glanced around the table. All of these guests were great warriors who had accomplished much on their Quest. He could see that while he was speaking of his triumphs, they looked at him with approval, but what would they think of him if they knew he went off his path for almost a year?

Elder Jenkins sensed that Disciple was hesitant. "Those are some great things that both of you have accomplished while on your

Quest, but all of us have experienced victories and defeats."

Disciple glanced around the room. "Yes, I know what you mean. I wish I could tell you that my entire Quest has been one victorious battle after another, but that wouldn't be the truth. I became prideful at one point, and this led me to the Orchard of Vanity, and then to the Camp of Sin. I spent almost a year there before turning back to God in repentance and experiencing His grace. I wish I could have learned what I needed to without having gone there, but I did learn a valuable lesson. I discovered that the moment I think I'm standing, I should take heed lest I fall."

Elder Jenkins replied, "As much as I enjoyed hearing of all your battles and triumphs, that last part you shared may be the most important thing of all. I too am sorry that you had to experience those awful things, but you learned some important lessons. And the truths that you share from that experience may be what keeps someone else from having to go there and experience it for themselves."

Disciple was greatly encouraged. He thought this experienced group of warriors would look down on him because of his past failures, but he found they were accepting and loving.

Disciple and Caleb finished breakfast and then walked outside onto the porch. They gazed out over the countryside, which was teeming with acres of beautiful grass and towering trees.

While they were enjoying the scenery, Elder Jenkins came outside to join them. Although it was clear that he didn't move as quickly as younger men, his face had a determined look as if he could spring into battle at a moment's notice if necessary.

Elder Jenkins sat down in one of the rocking chairs, and after rocking back and forth for a minute, he smiled and said, "It was so nice having you two join us this morning. We love hearing about other's adventures. Most of us have been on this Quest for a long time, and we gather here for several months of the year. This inn has come to be known as the Inn of Experience. We enjoy hearing the stories of others, and we also enjoy sharing the things we've learned along the way."

Disciple looked out over the countryside and then back toward Elder Jenkins. "Don't you all still go on adventures yourselves?"

"Sure," said Elder Jenkins as he continued to rock in his chair.

"As long as we still have life in these bodies we'll still go forward on the path God has for us. But as we've gotten older we've come to understand that part of our path is to share our experiences with those who are still in the earlier days of their journey. So we gather together at this Inn and welcome those like yourselves to stay a few days with us before continuing on."

Caleb leaned against the railing on the porch. "Too many of the younger generation don't understand how valuable the experiences are of those who have gone before them. They think that just because someone is no longer as fast or as strong as they once were, they don't have the same value they used to."

Elder Jenkins sat up. "That's true. Although my body is not as strong as it once was, my mind is as sharp as ever, and with time I've been able to soak in more and more of God's word."

Disciple told Elder Jenkins about Simon who had been dragging around a bag of garbage and their encounter with him.

Elder Jenkins said, "I'm glad that man took responsibility for his sin. It's much easier to blame someone else rather than accepting responsibility. Why look at the first sins that were committed in the Garden of Eden. When God confronted Adam, he blamed Eve, and then Eve blamed the serpent. As soon as we sin we want to find something or someone to blame."

Disciple crossed his arms. "I guess it's easier to blame than change."

"Yes it is," said Elder Jenkins, nodding his head. "When David took full responsibility for his sin with Bathsheba, he gave us some good insight into our sin. He wrote, 'For I acknowledge my transgressions, and my sin remains continually before me. Against You, You only, have I sinned, and done this evil in Your sight, so that You may be justified when You give your sentence and be blameless when You judge.' Our sin does affect others, but ultimately all sin is against God Himself. When we recognize that our sin is against God, this gives us no one else to blame but ourselves, leaving us without excuse."

Disciple walked over and sat down in a rocking chair next to Elder Jenkins. "Did you have experiences with those who wouldn't take responsibility?"

Elder Jenkins leaned forward. "Oh yes. There was a time when I had my own House of Instruction, and I saw many who didn't want to give up their garbage. They wanted to sit down and talk for hours about the problems their garbage was causing them, but then they'd go out the next week and do the very things that caused the problems in their life to begin with."

"How did you respond?" asked Disciple.

Elder Jenkins put his hand to his chin. "I began to handle counseling differently. When people came to me for help, I would first give them basic instructions on what to do to start making changes. If they came back and only wanted to cry or complain, but had not made any effort to change, I'd tell them that our time was over. I would then tell them they could come back for more of my counsel when they had acted on the counsel I had already given them."

Disciple said, "That's very bold, but weren't you accused of being harsh?"

Elder Jenkins nodded as he rocked back in his chair. "Yes, many times. Some said they were never coming back to my House of Instruction again. They would tell others that I didn't care about them and that I wouldn't take the time to listen to them. What I tried to help people understand is that there's a difference between worldly sorrow and godly sorrow. Worldly sorrow will make you sorry about your problems, but godly sorrow will cause you to do something about your problems."

Caleb nodded. "That's a great point. I wish I had learned that earlier in my own journey."

"Me too," said Elder Jenkins. "We all learn by experience. No one enjoys seeing their faults, but going back to what David said in the Psalms, he emphasized that his sin was continuously before him. Some don't want to hear talk like that today because they think it interrupts their joy. But if we are constantly aware of our sinfulness, then we will constantly approach God for His grace. And it's in the presence of God where there is fullness of joy."

Disciple sighed. "There's so much I need to learn. Being around you, and all the other guests at this inn challenges me to press ahead in my Christian life. But sometimes it seems I have so far to go that I wonder if I'll ever make it."

Elder Jenkins put his hand on top of Disciple's and stood up.

"The further you go in your journey, the further you realize you still have to go. That is a tension that will exist until you die. It's meant to be like that. We're always to be content and at rest with our standing in Christ, but we're never to be satisfied in our progress with Christ. The Apostle Paul said that he pressed toward his goal and calling as if he was continuously straining forward. Always be content but never satisfied."

They continued to talk for a little while longer, and then later that afternoon Elder Jenkins led Disciple and Caleb on a tour of the grounds. After dinner, they gathered out on the porch again, and others came outside and joined the conversation as well. Disciple and Caleb listened carefully as Elder Jenkins and the other guests shared with them numerous things they learned while on their Quest.

Over the next few days, it became customary for everyone to gather around the porch after meals and talk about their experiences. During these occasions, Disciple learned many things listening to those who had traveled on this Quest for decades.

When it came time to leave, both Disciple and Caleb recognized their paths were going in different directions. Disciple looked disappointed that they were about to part ways.

Caleb put his hand on Disciple's shoulder. "God is going to do great things with you."

Disciple nodded. "Thank you. I'm glad we were able to spend this time together over the last couple of weeks."

Caleb threw his backpack over his shoulders. "You've made much progress since I fought by your side at the beginning of your Quest, and I don't believe it's the last time we will be in a battle together."

Before Caleb and Disciple went their separate ways, they prayed together and wished each other continued success.

BLACK KNIGHTS OF LUST

After traveling for most of the morning, Disciple stopped at a big oak tree and decided this would be a good place to eat some lunch. Some of the women at the inn had packed him a nice meal, which he was looking forward to enjoying. When he finished eating, he took out his Book and read in the Psalms. "Search me, Oh God, and know my heart. Examine me, and know my thoughts. See if there is any wicked way in me, and lead me in the way everlasting."

This was a bold prayer, Disciple thought. David was asking God to go deep into his thoughts and show him anything that wasn't right. David didn't want anything standing between him and God.

Disciple reflected on this while thinking about the things in his own heart. Most of the time his thoughts were on good things, but there were times when he would allow his mind to drift into lust. He always repented afterward, but he knew this was not the best way to handle sin. A battle needed to take place in his mind before thoughts of lust had the opportunity to get a foothold.

Disciple determined that the next time these thoughts tried to dominate his mind, he was going to put up a fight. He traveled on, finding a nice place to camp. He realized that if he was going to battle the lust of the flesh, he would need to know certain parts of his Book by heart. He searched for verses with which to do battle and began to memorize them. After a few hours, he realized it was getting late, so he settled down to go to sleep while continuing to meditate on words from his Book.

The next morning Disciple ate a quick breakfast and studied some more. Three verses stood out as being the best weapons against lust. The first was, "I call on you brothers, by the mercies of God, that you present your bodies as a living sacrifice, holy, acceptable unto God, which is an act of your spiritual worship." Disciple wanted his mind and his body to be a continuous living sacrifice that was pleasing and acceptable to God at all times. No longer did he want lust to be able to dominate his mind at any time.

The next verse was, "But put on the Lord Jesus Christ, and stop making provision for the flesh, in order to fulfill its lusts." Disciple saw that while thoughts of lust could introduce themselves to his mind, he had to provide space for them to operate. If he didn't make provision for lust, then it could not be fulfilled.

The third verse he would use was, "Beloved, I plead with you as foreigners and pilgrims, to refuse to give into fleshly lusts, which wage war against your soul." He was a foreigner and a pilgrim while on this present journey. His citizenship was in heaven, and while on this temporary portion of his Quest, he wanted to do all he could to not give in to fleshly lusts. These lusts were waging war against his soul, attempting to bring him into sin.

Disciple prayed, "Dear Lord, I know I cannot do this on my own. I have tried so many times. I surrender myself to you, and I acknowledge that I will need your strength to win this battle."

Feeling he was now ready, Disciple stepped out of his tent. All of a sudden a small army of Black Knights came rushing over a hill, heading straight toward him. These knights carried long spears and wore metal suits of armor that clanked as they ran. On the front of their armor were flashing pictures intended to induce thoughts of lust. Some were pictures he had seen at the Camp of Sin. He also saw pictures he had created in his mind. By giving place to these sinful thoughts, he had given ammunition to his enemy.

Once the Black Knights were upon him, Disciple vigorously swung his Sword while holding out his Shield. When his Sword made contact with the enemy's armor, it made a screeching sound as metal struck metal. When he knocked the first knight to the ground, he discovered that once they were knocked out, they would disappear.

As several more Black Knights rushed at him from all directions, Disciple held up his Sword. "I present my mind and my body as a continuous sacrifice to God."

Disciple ducked as one of the knights swung his spear toward his head. "I will not make any provision in my thoughts for the lust of the flesh."

Crouching down and swinging his Sword at the legs of three knights running toward him, Disciple sent them flying in the air. "I will not surrender to the lusts of my flesh which wage war against my soul."

While the knights were in mid-air, Disciple brought his Sword down on their backs causing them to disappear before they even hit the ground.

More waves of knights charged him, and some were able to burst through his defense and slip in behind him. Disciple turned to strike them with his Sword, and as he did, a few of the knights coming from the front hit him on his arms. Disciple kept fighting, but it seemed like after he took care of one wave of knights, another wave followed right behind them. After destroying four waves of fighters, he fell to his knees.

Exhausted and out of breath, Disciple cried out, "Dear God, I need your grace, and I need the power of the Holy Spirit. I know I can't fight this battle on my own. I can only win with your strength."

Disciple stood up again and readied himself for more combat. After persevering through the battle for a little longer, the waves of Black Knights finally stopped. With the last bit of his energy, he finished off the few knights that remained. Too tired to travel, he went back into his tent and collapsed.

After resting for hours, Disciple awoke and began reflecting on the battle with the Black Knights. It hadn't gone as well as he hoped, and the scrapes and bruises on his body revealed the times when his enemies were successful. All that time he had spent in preparation didn't seem to manifest itself on the battlefield.

He repented for the thoughts that had momentarily gotten through and asked God to cleanse him from these thoughts of lust. As he read from his Book and prayed, the Holy Spirit helped him to see that while it was not a flawless battle, the Black Knights never completely dominated him. He had gone to his knees a few times but was never knocked out. And while not perfect, it was still his best effort against lust so far. Feeling encouraged, Disciple spent the rest of the evening reading and then lay down to get some sleep.

When the next morning arrived, Disciple once again spent time meditating on his verses and praying for strength. As soon as he was out of his tent, waves of Black Knights rushed toward him. The sounds of clanging metal echoed all around while pictures arousing lust flashed on their armor.

As the first knights approached, Disciple recited his verses and readied himself for battle. One knight flashed a picture of the girl named Seduction who had flirted with him at Michael's camp. The knight began to whirl its spear in front of him, and then quickly jabbed at his stomach. Disciple jumped to the side as the spear sliced past him. The knight then twirled its spear above its head before trying to bring it down on top of his head. Disciple quickly raised his Shield, and the spear glanced off. The knight then thrust its spear toward his legs, but Disciple pinned it to the ground with his Shield and stomped on it.

He then pulled back his Sword and glared at the knight. "The Lord is my portion, so therefore I will put my hope in him. I will not place my hope in what seduction promises, for I know that only God can supply what truly satisfies."

Disciple plunged his Sword into the knight. As soon as the Sword made contact, the picture vanished, and the knight disappeared. Another knight attacked from the left, and Disciple kicked out toward its shins with his Shoes. As the knight tumbled forward, he stepped back and swung upward with his Sword, knocking it out.

As more knights approached, Disciple shouted, "I will not live according to my flesh by setting my mind on things of the flesh, but I will live by the Spirit and set my mind on things of the Spirit."

He then fought off the remaining knights, until they were all gone. Once back in his tent, he examined his body to find some more scrapes and bruises, but not as many as the day before.

Disciple felt better about today's battle, but he still wished the struggle wasn't so difficult. It was dawning on him that every thought of lust he allowed to take hold in his mind could be used against him at another time. He realized the best plan was not to let these thoughts get a foothold to begin with. He spent more time reading and praying, before laying down for another night's sleep.

The next morning Disciple started out the same way as the two other days before. When he came out of his tent, he braced himself for battle, as a wave of Black Knights charged toward him. He was determined not to be distracted by the flashing pictures so he could focus more succinctly on the battle.

As the first group of knights reached him, he shouted, "I have been raised with Christ and seated with Him in heavenly places. Therefore I will seek those things which are above where Christ is sitting at the right hand of God."

Disciple jumped as one of the knights swung its spear at his legs. "I will set my mind on things that are above and not the sinful desires of this world."

Disciple swung his Sword at the feet of five knights and sent them tumbling backward. Another knight thrust his spear toward his chest, and he blocked it with his Shield. The knight tried to pierce his feet, but Disciple jumped out of the way. When the spear plunged into the ground, Disciple sliced it in two with his Sword. He then backhanded the knight with his Shield and knocked it out.

Disciple shouted, "Those who belong to Christ have crucified the flesh along with its cravings and lusts."

Two fierce looking knights raced toward him and immediately jabbed at his head.

Disciple slipped to the left to avoid one of the spears and then quickly raised his Shield to block the other one. He stepped back and shouted, "I will walk by the Spirit so that I will not fulfill the lusts of my flesh."

Disciple lunged at the two knights with his Sword and struck one under the chin. He then jumped into the air and brought his Sword down on top of the other's head. Both fell and instantly disappeared.

A larger knight marched up to him as it snorted out black smoke. Disciple felt weary from the battle, but he had come too far to give in now. The knight grasped its spear and plunged it toward Disciple's shoulder. Deflecting it with his Shield, Disciple moved to his right.

The knight flashed several pictures in rapid succession to distract him, as it thrust out its spear. Disciple was caught off guard for a moment, but then quickly ducked as the tip of the spear was about to reach his forehead. He realized that if he allowed his thoughts to drift for even a moment, he would be vulnerable to attack.

Backing up a step Disciple declared, "I will keep a constant watch over my heart, for out of it flows the wellsprings of life."

The knight lunged toward him, but Disciple moved to the side and slammed his Shield into its head. As the knight tried to recover, Disciple jumped into the air and drop-kicked it. The knight staggered backward. After regaining its balance, the knight let out a large snort of smoke and charged toward him. Disciple stormed forward as well, and as soon as they met, he thrust out his Shield and sent the knight reeling backward to the ground. Disciple then stood over the knight and plunged his Sword into its chest. The knight let out another snort of black smoke and then disappeared.

When Disciple defeated the last remaining Black Knights, he thrust his Sword into the air. "The LORD is my strength and my song, And He has become my salvation; He is my God, and I will praise Him; My father's God, and I will exalt Him."

Disciple walked back to his tent reflecting on the battles of the last three days. On the first day he declared war on the lust of the flesh, and in return, the lust of the flesh declared war on him. By taking the fight to lust, he was slowly reclaiming the ground that had been given to his enemy. When he relied on the grace of God, the strength of the Holy Spirit, and the power of God's words, the Black Knights were no match.

After staying over for one more night, Disciple came out of his tent the following morning to see that there were no Black Knights. He packed up his belongings and started out on his path. Disciple realized this would not be the last time he would see these enemies, but he knew how to deal with them now. As soon as a thought of lust tried to seduce him, he was going to shut it down by quoting from his Book and asking God for grace and strength.

18

TEACHER'S HOUSE OF WONDERS

As Disciple strode down his path, he spotted a group of people gathered around someone. When he came closer, he saw that it was Teacher, the person he met at the Hill of Calvary. Teacher was sharing some truths from the Book, while those surrounding him paid close attention. Always interested in learning more, Disciple set down his backpack and listened too.

After Teacher finished with his lesson, he spotted Disciple and walked over to him. "Hello, it's good to see you again. Let me say goodbye to these who came, and then I'd love to hear about how things have been going on your Quest."

Teacher spent a few more minutes with those who had gathered and then told them goodbye. He returned and gave Disciple a hug. "How has everything been going?"

Disciple told Teacher about all the things that had happened since he last saw him. When he finished, Disciple added, "The day we met, you said that there were times when you strayed from your path, and I remember saying that I believed I would be different. I was so full of zeal that I was over-confident. I also recall that when I was speaking with such zeal, you looked as if you were going to say something, but you didn't."

Teacher put his finger to his cheek and nodded. "Ah yes, I do remember that. There's not much you can say to someone at that point. Each person has to walk their own path and learn through experience. We've all had to do that. Some learn quicker than others, but I also knew that the One who began a good work in you would continue to perform that good work until the day of Christ. I didn't know what all you'd go through, but I knew you'd get through it."

Disciple sighed. "I've learned a lot of things since that day."

Teacher smiled. "If you have some time, I'd like for you to come stay with me for a few days. There are many things I can show you that will help on your journey."

"I'd love to," said Disciple.

Teacher's house was a few miles away, so they had more time to talk and get caught up as they traveled. Disciple told him about his latest battle with the Black Knights of Lust.

Teacher folded his hands behind his back as he walked. "You learned a lot during that battle. When we get to my house, I'll show you some things that will add to what you've already learned about dealing with sin."

When they arrived, Teacher welcomed him into his spacious home and gave him a tour. There were several rooms downstairs, and there was an upstairs with several more rooms. All along the walls were paintings of different scenes from the Book. The floor was covered with a beautiful carpet that was embroidered with the picture of Jesus coming up out of the water when He was baptized by John the Baptist.

A grand mural overlay the ceiling. The painting depicted a scene in heaven with a multitude of people kneeling before two thrones occupied by God the Father and God the Son, Jesus Christ, as the Holy Spirit swirled around like a mighty wind.

Disciple roamed around, noticing large bookshelves filled with hundreds of books. He glanced through some of them, and then Teacher invited him to sit down and have some tea.

When they finished, Teacher stood up from the table. "Let's go out on the porch. There's something I want to show you. Keep in mind though that what you will be seeing is not actually happening but will be a three-dimensional moving picture."

When they reached the porch, they saw a large number of sheep grazing on the grass. Off to the side, a shepherd sat under a tree.

Teacher leaned over and whispered to Disciple. "That shepherd represents some who are on this Quest."

After a few minutes, a lion crept slowly toward the sheep, staying low to the ground, as it quietly stalked its prey. Finally, it pounced, snatched one of the sheep by its neck, and carried it off.

Disciple abruptly turned toward Teacher. "Why didn't the shepherd do anything about that?"

Teacher pointed toward the sheep. "Continue watching."

Time seemed to pass by quickly because the sun set and then rose again within a matter of minutes. The sheep were once again grazing, and the lion came out and snatched another one of the sheep. Disciple noticed that while the shepherd was not doing anything about the lion, the lion was not bothering the shepherd either.

This happened three more times, but then the next time the lion came, the shepherd rose up and marched toward it. The lion roared and showed him his teeth. The shepherd held out his rod, as the lion leaped toward him. After an intense battle, he defeated the lion and drove it away.

Teacher motioned for them to go back inside and sit down. "What did you see?"

Disciple slid into a straight-backed chair at the kitchen table and pointed outside. "The lion was stealing the sheep, and at first the shepherd didn't seem to care. As long as he stayed under that tree, the lion didn't bother him, but once he stood up to fight, then the lion attacked."

Teacher said, "That's correct. The lion represents sin. Sin is content to kill you slowly, but if you decide that you're going to battle back, it becomes fiercer in its attacks."

Disciple leaned forward, placing his hands on the table. "That's exactly what happened to me when I determined to battle lust."

Teacher nodded. "Yes, and it's that way with any sin. The moment you decide you're no longer going to tolerate it, then it becomes threatened. Sin will rise up to protect the ground it has gained, but as you saw in your own battle with lust, once you begin to take a stand, sin is not able to dominate you. You'll have to fight to retake the ground you've surrendered, but once you've taken it, you can hold it."

"It seems like there's always going to be a battle," said Disciple.

"That's true. You must always be killing sin, or sin will be killing you." Teacher stood up. "There's something else I'd like to show you. Follow me to the roof."

He led Disciple upstairs and then out on a balcony where there was a set of steps. When they reached the roof, Disciple saw three soldiers who were stationed at different sides of the house. Each had a cannon with several cannonballs and a bow with many arrows. Both the cannon balls and the arrows had verses from the Book written on them.

Teacher led him to the soldier on the north side who was shooting cannonballs onto the lawn below. As soon as they landed on the ground, a small barrier appeared. These barriers lasted for several minutes and then they would disappear.

The soldier constantly shot cannonballs covering as much of the ground below as possible. He also kept a constant watch on all the area to the north side. All of a sudden, he spotted an enemy. But the assailant wasn't able to get far into the lawn because of all the barriers that slowed him down. The soldier picked up his bow and shot an arrow toward his enemy. Because the barriers held up the attacker, the soldier easily picked him off with an arrow.

Teacher then led Disciple over to the soldier who was supposed to watch the west side. This soldier sat daydreaming, not shooting any cannonballs or keeping watch over his side of the lawn. When he heard an enemy approaching, he stood up quickly and started shooting arrows. But, without any barriers, the enemy was able to move more quickly, making it harder to hit. Disciple watched this go on for some time. Some of the enemies were able to get to the wall and damage it before the soldier was finally able to hit it with an arrow.

Teacher then led him over to the east side where the soldier was asleep. Enemies were able to run toward the wall, put up ladders and climb toward him. Once the enemy was almost to the top, the soldier woke up and desperately tried to fight off his attacker. He was eventually able to shoot the enemy down, but not before much damage had been done to both the wall and to himself. Once the battle was over, this soldier went back to sleep, and another enemy would attack. Once again he suffered damage before forcing the enemy back down.

Teacher then led Disciple over to the south side where there was only a black flag. Disciple walked around the wall for a little while longer, carefully observing each soldier, and then Teacher led them off the roof and back downstairs.

When they were seated at the table again, Disciple said, "I believe I understand some of what was happening, but please tell me what it all means."

Teacher placed his elbows on the table and clasped his hands. "The different areas that the soldiers were defending represent your mind and thoughts. The enemies that were trying to attack represent sin. The further that sin penetrates your mind, the more damage it can do. The first soldier was constantly keeping his mind saturated with God's word, forming barriers that made it harder for the enemy to break through. This soldier was keeping a constant watch for things trying to enter his mind. When an enemy attacked, he easily picked it off by shooting more of God's word at it."

"I noticed that the first soldier was constantly alert."

Teacher sat back in his chair. "Yes, but as you saw, the next soldier was not keeping his mind full of God's word and was not being watchful. Only when the enemy approached and came closer did he rise up to fight. It was more difficult for him to shoot the enemy with his arrows, and the enemy was able to do some damage. The last soldier we saw was asleep. He only fought against sin when it disturbed his rest and threatened to kill him."

"What about the south side, where there was only the black flag?"

Teacher sighed. "The enemy has taken that territory and planted his flag. There is no need for the enemy to attack because it occupies that person's mind continuously and can do whatever it wants."

Disciple grasped his Book. "I want to be like that first soldier on the north side. I want to keep my thoughts on the words of this Book, constantly watching for the temptations of the enemy, so that I may defeat them before they get near enough to do damage."

Teacher patted Disciple on the back. "That's very wise. That's all I have to show you for today, but I'll have more for you to see tomorrow."

"I really enjoyed learning things by seeing them in motion," said Disciple.

Teacher pointed to his Book. "God's word often uses word pictures and symbols. One of my favorite uses of symbols is in Psalms. The passage says that a man who meditates on the words of this Book is like a tree planted by a river. In my mind, I can see that tree as it is receiving constant nourishment from the river. It doesn't matter to that tree whether there is a drought all around because it will continuously be sustained."

Teacher stood up and pushed his seat in. "It's late, and we both should get some sleep."

The next morning Disciple came downstairs and ate breakfast with Teacher. He couldn't wait to learn more. "What are we going to see today?"

Teacher pointed to a room just off to the side. "First let's go into this room over here."

They walked into the room where a man sat at a desk, writing in a book.

"What is he writing?" asked Disciple.

"Go and look."

Disciple peeked over the man's shoulder. He watched for several minutes, and then walked back and stood next to Teacher.

"What was he writing?"

Disciple looked away. "He was writing all the sins I had done before I started this Quest, and all of the sins I have done since."

Teacher motioned toward the man. "And if you would have stayed longer, you would have seen him writing the sins you will commit in the future, but that is not to be known at the present."

"Why was he writing all those things?" asked Disciple.

Teacher faced the man at the desk. "Keep watching."

The man finished writing all the sins that Disciple had committed and ever would commit, and then laid the book on the floor. Disciple then saw an image of himself approaching the Hill of Calvary on the first day of his Quest.

Disciple grabbed Teacher's arm. "I will never forget that day. I felt so burdened by my sins as I took them up that hill, but when I laid them at the foot of the cross, I felt forgiven and cleansed."

As Disciple kept watching, he saw himself kneeling down at the cross, and this time he saw Jesus hanging on that cross. The book the man had just written in, was sitting beside him as he knelt. Then a drop of blood flowed off the brow of Jesus and landed on the book. The pages began to rapidly turn as if being blown by a great wind. The sins that had been written in the book were lifted off the pages and began to swirl in the air until they landed on the back of Jesus.

Then something else happened. Words flowed off the body of Jesus filling up the blank pages in the book.

A Voice boomed, "For He hath made Him to be sin for us, Who knew no sin, so that we might become the righteousness of God in Him."

The pictures stopped, but the book remained on the floor.

Teacher pointed to it. "Go look at what is now written inside, then come back here and tell me what you saw."

Disciple walked over and picked up the book. After reading it, he laid it back down.

Upon returning to Teacher, he said, "Now the book contains the works that Jesus did to fulfill all the righteous requirements of the law."

Teacher responded, "That is correct. For Christ is the fulfillment of the law in order to accomplish righteousness on behalf of everyone who believes."

The pictures started again, and Disciple saw the image of himself approaching the throne room of God. Jesus stood by, and as Disciple came forward, Jesus picked up the book and handed it to the Father. The Father opened the book and then motioned for Disciple to come closer. Disciple saw in the pictures that the Father looked at him the same way He looked at Jesus. The Father welcomed Disciple with perfect acceptance. Then the pictures stopped, and once again the book remained on the floor.

Teacher walked over and picked up the book then brought it back to Disciple. "Keep this on the inside of your Breastplate and always remember it is Christ's righteousness that has been applied to you."

Teacher led Disciple back to the table where they had been sitting.

When they reached the table, Teacher said, "Did you understand all that you saw?"

Disciple sat down and pulled his chair up to the table. "I know that my sins have been forgiven and that I've been given righteousness because of what Christ has done for me, but I'm not sure I understand all that is involved in the process."

Teacher shifted in his chair until he was comfortable. "When you knelt before the cross at the Hill of Calvary, you were turning from your sins and putting your faith and trust in Christ. The guilt of all your sins, past, present, and future, were laid on Him, and in return, all of His perfect works in fulfillment of the Law were placed on your account. So when God looks at you, He looks at you on the basis of this new record. He sees you as if you had never done anything wrong, and as if you had always done what is right. We refer to this process as imputation, and we call this doctrine — Justification by Faith Alone."

Disciple put his finger to his cheek. "So that is why God the Father can look at me the same as he does Jesus – because the record of Christ's perfection has become my record."

"Yes," said Teacher nodding, "you can approach the Father at any time with full confidence that you will not be rejected."

"But what happens when I sin? How does that affect all of this?"

Teacher stood up again. "We'll discuss that more after I show you what's next."

Teacher led Disciple down the hall and into a room that's only light came from a small candle in the corner. There they saw a sorrowful man, kneeling on the floor and chained to a large bucket of black slime. He was crying and rocking back and forth as he pointed toward the bucket. Directly in front of him was a door with a sign above it which read, "This way to the Throne of Grace," but the man remained on his knees, weeping and beating his chest.

They stepped back out into the hall, and Teacher led them into another room. This time they saw a man that was happily jumping around. He was also chained to a bucket of black slime, but it was hidden beneath a rug. In front of him stood the same door with the same sign, which read, "This way to the Throne of Grace," but he didn't go through the door either.

They stepped back into the hall, and Disciple shook his head. "What is the meaning of this?"

"The bucket of black slime that you saw represents their sin." Teacher motioned toward the first room. "The man who was weeping is very aware of his sin. He's sorry that the sin in his life is causing him problems, but he doesn't want to give it up."

Teacher pointed toward the second room. "The other man doesn't want to be aware of his sin. He thinks the rug that's covering it up is grace, but it's not. He too doesn't want to give up his sin."

Next, they went into a third room, and there they saw another man who was also kneeling down and chained to a bucket of black slime. Before him stood the same door leading to the Throne of Grace. After a few moments, he stood to his feet, picked up the bucket, and walked toward the door. When he opened it, a bright light emanated from a throne, and as soon as the man stepped into the room, fire shot out from the throne and engulfed him.

Disciple gasped, but then he saw that the man wasn't burned because he was being protected from the flames by a robe of righteousness. The fire swirled around him, burning up the bucket of slime and the chain that was attached to it. When he walked back into the room where Disciple and Teacher were standing, his face was full of joy, and the sin and the chain were gone. The man merrily strolled out of the house praising God.

Teacher led them back to the table where they were before.

Disciple sat down and glanced over his shoulder. "I believe I understand this one. The third man took responsibility for his sin and carried it to the Throne of Grace. He was not consumed by the fire because he was clothed in the Righteousness of Christ. The fire burned up all the sin and released him from the chain. By taking his sin to the Throne of Grace, he was freed from its bondage."

Teacher clapped his hands together. "Indeed! That's exactly what happened." He stood up from the table. "The next thing I would like to show you is a few miles from my house."

Disciple gathered up his backpack and followed Teacher onto a road, wondering what he would see next.

19

MOUNT SINAI

As Disciple walked with Teacher, he remembered an earlier time in his Quest when the subject of sin came up. "At one point in my journey I heard a group of people talking about how some are too obsessed with sin, and since we've been forgiven at the Hill of Calvary, we should not worry about sin afterward. They said that focusing on sin makes us depressed and that instead, we should only focus on our new identity in Christ. They also said if someone points out any sin in your life to just remind them that there is no condemnation to those who are in Christ."

Teacher stopped and turned toward Disciple. "It's certainly important to understand that we are in Christ and covered by His righteousness. But there are some who want to skip the entire process of dealing with sin, believing their sin doesn't matter because grace will cover it."

Disciple folded his hands. "But, they're right when they say there is no condemnation to those who are in Christ?"

Teacher held up his finger. "Yes, that's a correct statement, but often it's misunderstood and misapplied. The Greek word for condemnation was a legal term that meant a judgment against someone. Because we are in Christ and our sins have been wiped away, no legal judgment can be made against us."

"So," said Disciple, "since there's no condemnation to those who are in Christ, their sins cannot be held against them to keep them from being accepted before God."

"Yes," said Teacher nodding, "because there's no condemnation, we can always come boldly before the Throne of Grace, knowing we won't be rejected. Many times though when people quote the verse concerning 'no condemnation,' they think it means they don't have to feel any guilt about their sin, but that's not true. Feeling guilty because of your sin is a good thing. This causes you to realize that you need forgiveness and grace, and then you can take your sin to the Throne Room of Grace where you can be set free from it."

Disciple glanced back toward Teacher's house. "The man in the first room who was chained to his sin felt guilt."

Teacher brought his hands together. "He felt sorrow because his sin was causing him problems, but he didn't want to repent."

Disciple shook his head. "That second man did look happy as he was jumping around."

Teacher raised his eyebrows. "Well, if you go from being like the first man who was wallowing in guilt and shame, to being like the other one who was jumping around, then yes, you're going to be more happy, but you're not going to be any more free."

Disciple thought on this for a moment to let it sink in. "I understand. We aren't given grace so we can avoid our sin, but so we can approach God with our sin knowing that something can be done about it."

"Yes, but there's a reason both men in those rooms were avoiding the Throne Room of Grace. There's a certain amount of suffering that is involved with dealing with sin. Facing the All Consuming Fire of God as we're holding our sin, is not a pleasant experience. But, as we stay in that fire, He burns up our sin and its bondage. Then we can experience a true joy."

Disciple and Teacher traveled a little further when Disciple suddenly stopped as if something was bothering him. "Isn't it true that Satan is the Accuser of the Brethren, and it's his job to point out our sins and make us feel bad about them? And if so, how do we distinguish Satan's accusations from the conviction of the Holy Spirit?"

Teacher thought for a moment. "That's a good question. The accusations of our enemies are meant to beat us down so we'll quit. The conviction of the Holy Spirit reveals our sinfulness, while also pointing us to grace and hope as the answer."

As they walked a little further, the ground began to shake, and Disciple heard a loud rumble. "What's that?"

Teacher held out his hand. "We're almost there. You'll see."

After cresting the next hill, Disciple saw a tall mountain with the top engulfed by fire. The rumbling came from the mountain as if it was constantly being shaken.

Teacher stopped and pointed. "That's Mount Sinai which represents the Law."

Off to the right Disciple saw a trail that descended between two large rocks. A sign was placed at the entrance which read, "The Valley of Humility."

At the bottom of Mount Sinai was a sign that had a large arrow pointing toward the valley.

Teacher motioned toward the mountain. "Let's stand here and watch."

Two gentlemen dressed in nice suits started up Mt. Sinai while waving their hands to let everyone know they were beginning their climb. They made it about ten feet up the mountain, when the ground in front of them suddenly popped up, knocking them back to the bottom. They landed right in front of the sign, but instead of following the arrow and going to the Valley of Humility, they started climbing again. The same thing happened, and again they came tumbling down.

As Disciple watched more people try to climb the mountain, there were some, who after a few tries, followed the arrow and descended into the Valley of Humility, but others kept trying to climb Mount Sinai.

Disciple scratched his head. "I'm sure there's a great lesson in all of this. Please tell me what we're observing."

Teacher took a deep breath. "There's something in all of us that wants to climb that mountain. We want to do something to feel good about ourselves. Each time that mountain shakes and rumbles it emphasizes our sinfulness. Trying to climb that mountain makes us feel as if we're doing something about our sinfulness, but we aren't."

Disciple pointed toward the people trying to climb Mount Sinai. "But can't they see when they're knocked to the bottom that the sign clearly points to the Valley of Humility?"

"Yes, they see the sign, but they know if they stop trying to climb, they must surrender and cease from their own works. Surrender is a very difficult thing for a human to do."

Disciple looked out toward a road that ran in the middle. "I see that there's another way that runs between Mount Sinai and the entrance to the Valley of Humility. It looks like a smooth road where one could make a lot of progress in a short amount of time."

Teacher pointed beyond the road. "That's the Path of License. Those who travel it believe grace gives them a license to sin. It may look like you'd make good progress, but not too far in the distance that road starts to wind back around and ends up going in circles."

"Why do so many avoid the Valley of Humility?" asked Disciple.

"You'll understand this more once you're there, but descending into the Valley of Humility means giving up the praises of men. By taking this path, you're saying to everyone that you are completely reliant upon God to overcome sin and all other obstacles in life. You're saying that it is no longer you that lives, but Christ in you, and the life you now live, you live by faith in the Son of God who loved you and gave Himself for you."

Disciple faced Teacher. "Will you be going with me into the Valley of Humility?"

Teacher shook his head. "I've been there many times, but today you'll travel alone. I must go back, for there are many others that I need to instruct and bring to this point on their journey."

Disciple held out his hand to Teacher. "Thank you so much for all that you've taught me. I'll remember all of it for as long as I'm on this Quest."

Teacher shook Disciple's hand and then stepped back as he prepared to leave. "I know you will, and if you're ever by this way again do stop in and see me."

Disciple grasped Teacher's hand with both his hands. "I will."

Teacher left to go back to his house, and Disciple moved forward. As he stepped toward the valley, Mount Sinai began to shake and rumble as if it was calling out to him and challenging him to climb it. With each rumble, all of his sinfulness was crying out to do something to make the guilt go away. But he knew that while the Law could point out his sin, it could not set him free from it or relieve his guilt. For that, he would need grace.

As Disciple entered the Valley of Humility, a quiet somberness surrounded him. The only sound was that of some songbirds, softly humming a tune of reverent worship. Trees lined each side of a path that ran through the middle of the valley. At the beginning of the path, a piece of paper lay on the ground with a message at the top which read, "Read and Eat."

The paper appeared to be made of a rice type material, which smelled sweet. Written in the middle of the paper was a verse from his Book, 'There is no one who does good, not even one.' Disciple remembered reading this in his Book before going into the Building of Reflection. Of course, this pronouncement applied to him before he went up the Hill of Calvary, but did it still apply to him now? Then he remembered reading the words of Jesus, 'No one is good except for God.' Disciple understood that all of his goodness was by virtue of being in Christ. He ate the paper, and it was sweet as honey.

Disciple walked further, finding another piece of paper with the same title at the top. It read, 'I am what I am by the grace of God.' He ate this paper, and it too was very sweet. He went further and came to another piece of paper that read, 'For it is God who is working in you both the will and the ability, to bring forth His good pleasure.'

Disciple thought on these words, acknowledging that God was the one who gave him both the desire to do what was right, and the power to carry it out. But what was his part? Was there anything he could take credit for? It occurred to him that the only good that he could do was to admit that there was nothing good that he could do. Disciple ate this paper as well, and it was also very sweet.

Further along, his path Disciple saw another piece of paper. This one read, 'God sets Himself against the proud, but He gives grace to the humble.' These words now meant a great deal to him. He understood that grace was God doing for him what he could not do for himself, and this power did not go into effect until he humbled himself and admitted his need for it. He began his Quest with that same realization. For it was by grace through faith that he was saved, and that not of himself, but it was the gift of God. This salvation was not due to any of his own works so there was nothing in which he could boast. He ate this one, and it too was very sweet.

Up ahead Disciple saw a cross. Next to the cross was a piece of paper that read, 'Take up your cross daily and follow me.' Earlier in his Quest, he would have said that the cross was only for the beginning of his journey, but he now knew that the cross and the message of Gospel Grace was for every day of his journey. He ate this paper too while savoring the sweetness of the words.

Drawing near to the end of the valley, his path led to a narrow passage carved into a large rock. Disciple knelt down to go through, and saw written on the rock, 'Become humbled under the mighty hand of God.'

Disciple crawled out of the passage and started forward on the path that was laid out before him. The lessons of the last few days had been challenging and intense, but the results produced a tremendous respect for God. As he traveled through the Valley of Humility, his view of himself had decreased, but his view of God had greatly increased. He'd been stripped of confidence in himself, but in its place was a new confidence in God. This confidence felt much stronger and more solid than what he had before.

As Disciple strode along his path, he spotted a beautiful fruit tree out in the distance.

As he passed by, he heard a scurrying sound in the branches, then voices began to speak. "Look who is here today. It is the great Disciple. He defeated the Giant of Shame, he conquered the Mountain of Unforgiveness—"

Disciple shouted, "I am what I am by the grace of God, and anything that I've accomplished was not me but the grace of God working through me."

A high pitched hiss came from the direction of the tree as something fell to the ground and scurried into the woods. Disciple was determined not to allow pride to have a foothold in his life again.

After traveling for awhile, he stopped at a cafe to get something cold to drink. He ordered a tall glass of apple cider, then went over to a table and sat down.

Soon, a middle-aged man with worn clothes walked in and ordered a glass of ice water. He then headed over to where Disciple was sitting. "Mind if I join you?"

Disciple stood up and motioned toward the chair beside him. "Sure, it's always good to have company to pass the time."

The man reached out his hand. "My name is Samuel."

He shook Samuel's hand. "My name is Disciple."

Disciple and Samuel sat and talked about the things they experienced on their Quest, giving praise to God for all He had brought them through.

As they were talking, a young man rushed in, panting and out of breath. "I'm looking for someone by the name of Disciple."

20

FORTRESS OF DECEPTION

Startled that someone he had never seen before was looking for him, Disciple stood up. "That's my name."

The man hurried over to his table. "I've come a long way. May I have a moment of your time?"

Disciple pulled up another chair beside them. "Yes, sit down. I'm interested to find out how you know me and why you're looking for me."

The man introduced himself as Thaddeus. "Let me start at the beginning. From time to time, a fortress will appear out in the distance where everyone who is traveling by can see it. We call this the Fortress of Deception, but it doesn't appear as a fortress to all. If someone has areas of their heart that desire something more than God, then this fortress takes on the appearance of whatever they're seeking. For some it might be worldly wealth, to others, it might be fame, and to some, it could be positions of power. When we see someone going off their path toward the fortress, we try to warn them, but most don't listen."

A waitress cleared plates from a table nearby, and Disciple asked her if she would bring another glass of ice water to their table.

Thaddeus continued, "Recently we've seen several going off their path toward this fortress, and many of us have been praying about what to do. After much prayer, we've decided to lead an assault against it and rescue all those who wish to be free. We heard about a man named Disciple, who had done many great things on his Quest, and we decided to look for him to see if he would lead us into battle."

Disciple did not consider himself to be a leader. He had only recently learned how to travel consistently on this Quest by himself. Someone like Caleb was much more qualified for a challenge such as this.

Disciple stared out in front of him for a moment, and then shifted his gaze to Thaddeus. "I think it's great that you want to rescue these people, but I don't know if I'm the person that should be leading you."

Thaddeus leaned forward and scooted his seat closer to the table. "What we hear, is that you trust in God, and right now that's what we need."

A waitress brought the glass of ice water to the table, and Thaddeus took the glass and thanked the waitress.

Disciple leaned back and crossed his arms. "How do you know these people want to be rescued? If they went off to this fortress even after being warned, maybe they want to stay in their deception?"

Thaddeus took a long drink of his water, almost finishing it in one gulp. "That's a good point, but we feel we should make an assault on this fortress and give them a chance. After being imprisoned, some may realize their mistake and wish to get out. We believe we must try."

Disciple finished his apple cider and rose to his feet. He took a few steps toward the door then turned back around. "It looks like our paths are going in the same direction so I'll go with you. Once we arrive, I'll want to talk to the others from your group as well."

Thaddeus stood up and held out his hand. "Thank you."

Disciple shook Thaddeus's hand and nodded.

Samuel picked up his backpack. "If you don't mind, I'd like to come along too and see this for myself."

Thaddeus started toward the door. "Sure, you're welcome to come with us."

Disciple paid for the extra glass of ice water, then he and Samuel followed Thaddeus. The walk was long, but they made good time and arrived a few hours before sunset. The ones who were waiting on them, saw them coming from a distance, and a few ran out to greet them.

Everyone appeared excited that Thaddeus had found Disciple. God had been gathering them together for several months, and now they felt they had a leader. Some had heard about Disciple's adventures, and they asked him questions about everything he experienced.

After spending some time talking with those in the group, Disciple stood up and looked around. "I'm curious as to what this Fortress of Deception looks like. Can you show me where it is?"

Thaddeus and three others led Disciple up a hill and handed him a small telescope. Peering through it, Disciple saw a large structure that was round and made of stone, with no windows. Three guards patrolled on top of the roof and three much larger guards policed the grounds. There appeared to be only one door to the inside, and it was barred shut.

After Disciple studied the fortress through the telescope, they returned to talk to the others.

Disciple motioned for everyone to listen. "Rescuing the people in that fortress is not going to be easy. They have guards on the roof, so they can see anyone coming toward them from far off, and the guards on the ground are also keeping constant watch. I'll pray for God's direction, and then check my path in the morning. If I am to lead you on this mission, then we're going to need God's plan to succeed."

Everyone went to their tents to pray before going to sleep.

As Disciple entered his tent, he thought about what he had seen through the telescope. When he first looked toward the Fortress of Deception, he saw himself on top of a castle looking down on all those cheering for him. This only lasted for a few seconds, but it was enough to make him aware that sin was always looking for an opportunity to manifest. He had won battles against pride, but it would always be lurking and waiting for an opening to take advantage of. He recalled all the verses he had read in the Valley of Humility and meditated on them as he went to sleep.

The next morning Disciple examined his path and discovered that it was pointing toward the Fortress of Deception.

After gathering everyone around, Disciple said, "I accept the role of leading this mission."

There was lots of excitement about the prospect of helping to free the people inside the fortress. Several came up to Disciple to shake his hand and thank him for being willing to lead them.

As everyone became quiet again, Disciple held up his hand. "I need all of your input as we're forming this plan because in a multitude of counselors there is safety and victory. The first thing I noticed was that the guards on the roof would be able to see us coming from a long distance."

Samuel stepped forward. "I know I'm new here, but if I might make a suggestion, I would say that you should approach at night when it will be harder to be spotted."

Disciple nodded toward Samuel. "That's a good idea. They have torches that will reveal our positions once we're near, but the cover of night should allow us to get much further before we can be seen. Still, the guards on the roof will spot us sooner than the ones on the ground, and they'll be able to alert the other guards, giving them more time to get ready for our attack."

A nice looking young man by the name of Benjamin stepped forward. Benjamin was tall and slender with short, curly hair, and he looked to be agile and quick on his feet. Pointing toward the fortress, he said, "If I can get to that ridge of trees and up the hill overlooking the fortress, I can use my sling to knock out the guards on the roof."

Disciple said, "That's good, but we'll need two others who can do it at the same time."

Two stout young men stepped forward, and Benjamin agreed that these two could use a sling as well as he could.

Disciple handed the telescope to Benjamin. "Use this to study the movements of the guards on the roof. You're going to have to time this perfectly, so you knock out all three of them simultaneously. Determine how to best position yourselves to accomplish this."

Benjamin led the other two men to a place where they could view the roof of the fortress through the telescope.

Next Disciple needed to come up with a plan to attack the guards on the ground. These soldiers were much larger than the ones on the roof, so he wanted to find a way to subdue them without getting into a long battle. Disciple shared this with the group and asked for suggestions.

An attractive and athletic looking young woman named Sarah stepped forward. "I believe I know what will work. I have seen something used called a bola. You take eight leather straps and tie them all together at one end, and then you fasten a rock of the same size to all the other ends. We can throw these at their feet, and they will become all tangled up and fall to the ground."

Disciple pictured the weapon Sarah described. "This is exactly what we need. Sarah, pick out five others who can help you and make six of these. I want two people throwing at the legs of each of the guards on the ground. Even though they're big, this should bring them down. Once you've made the bolas, all of those who are going to use them should practice and be able to throw them on the run."

Sarah and five others went off to make the Bolas and to practice with them.

Disciple thought about all the planning that went into the preparation of this mission. At first, he wasn't sure how he was going to come up with a strategy to deal with every aspect of this attack. But after listening to the others, he understood that leadership wasn't about knowing all the right answers, but knowing how to ask all the right questions.

As both Benjamin and Sarah prepared for their parts of the mission, Disciple turned to the ones gathered around. "We'll need several who know their Books well and are skillful with their Swords. Once all the guards are down, we must storm the fortress quickly to rescue those who wish to be free."

Thaddeus and nine others saw that their paths were heading toward the castle, and they stepped forward. Disciple spent time talking with these about what they might encounter once on the inside, and they shared their insights as well. When a few hours had passed, Disciple checked on each group to see how they were doing with their preparations.

Benjamin and the two with him were still studying the fortress and discussing the best way to hit the guards on the roof. Sarah and those with her had all their bolas made and were practicing with them. They set up poles and ran at them from a distance, letting the bolas fly toward the bottom of the poles. With each attempt, they became more accurate.

When everyone stopped to take a break, Disciple called them all together. "As we get closer to the Fortress of Deception, it will have an affect on all of us. We must resist anything that tries to deceive us."

Disciple took out his Book and read, "The heart is deceitful above all things, and totally corrupt, who can know it? I the LORD search the heart, and I examine the mind, so that I may give every man according to his ways, and according to the fruit of his deeds."

Glancing from one to the other, Disciple continued, "Each of us can be led off in deception. As we go to rescue these people who are trapped, we must also examine ourselves, knowing that we can be tempted in the same manner. We have a few more hours before it will be dark enough to start toward the fortress. Take this time to pray and read in your Book. Ask God to show you any areas that you need to repent. When the sun goes down, let's gather together again for final preparations."

After a few hours of reading and praying, they gathered back around Disciple to go over the final plan one more time.

Disciple looked at Benjamin. "Are you ready?"

Benjamin handed the telescope to Disciple. "Yes, we're ready. Each of us knows where we need to be positioned, and I'll give the signal for the exact time to release our slings and hurl the rocks at the guards."

Disciple nodded. "That's great. If they start to wake up, then be ready to sling more rocks. You probably won't get a clean shot at them again, but you may be able to keep them busy long enough to give us more time to get out. Once you see us leave the fortress and head back toward here, then you three leave as well."

Disciple motioned to Sarah. "Do you feel your group is ready?"

Sarah held up one of the bolas. "Yes, we've practiced to the point that we can hit our targets while at a full sprint."

After Disciple examined one of the bolas, he nodded toward Sarah and the others in her group. "Once you bring the guards down, take some ropes and quickly tie their hands and feet. The rope may not hold them for long, but we should have enough time to get in and offer freedom to all those inside. If the guards get loose before we're back out, hold them off for as long as you can."

Everyone milled about, making final preparations for the mission. Walking past one another, Benjamin and Sarah exchanged a smile.

Samuel joined Disciple. "My path is heading to the fortress as well, and I now know why God had me stop at that cafe yesterday where I met you. I've battled deception in my own life, and through the grace of God, I've been victorious over it."

Disciple said, "Then you can accompany me and the others who will storm the fortress to preach to those who are imprisoned. Have your Sword ready because you'll need it. We can only see what is on the outside of that fortress. We don't know what awaits us once we get through that door."

Samuel nodded in agreement.

Just before sundown, Disciple gathered everyone together to pray, then they headed off toward the Fortress of Deception.

While they quietly marched along, Disciple whispered, "As we're approaching the fortress, meditate on this, since we've been resurrected with Christ, think on things that are above, where Christ is seated at the right hand of God; set your hearts and affections on things above and not on the earthly temptations to sin."

When they were almost to the fortress grounds, Disciple motioned for everyone to stop. It was time for Benjamin and the two others to head east and set up on the hill.

Disciple put his hand on each of their shoulders. "I know you'll do well. I'll see you all back here soon."

After they separated, Disciple continued leading the others toward the fortress. When they were almost there, Disciple held up his hand, and everyone stopped. He then called Sarah forward. "When I raise my Sword, that's the signal to get into position to rush the fortress. Once I go, follow closely behind, and when you see the guards charge us, have your group fan out and attack each guard in pairs. As soon as you're in range, let the bolas fly."

Sarah nodded and quickly huddled with the others who would be attacking with her.

Disciple took out the telescope and peered toward the roof. At one point, the guards stopped and inspected the grounds. When they did, three rocks headed toward them. Each rock connected with the guards, and all three staggered back a step before toppling over and lying still on the roof. Disciple quickly raised his Sword, and everyone took their positions.

After bowing his head and saying a quick prayer, Disciple charged toward the fortress, with the others following closely behind. The guards on the ground saw him coming and ran toward him. Sarah and her group fanned out in pairs, as she directed them to their targets. All six of them swung their bolas and released them while running straight toward the guards. The bolas sailed through the air, then wrapped around the big legs of each guard, causing them to trip and fall hard to the ground. This disoriented them just long enough so that Sarah and the others could take out the ropes and tie their hands and feet.

Disciple pointed toward the front door with his Sword. "Now we must get inside as quickly as we can."

He and the others rushed toward the door and lifted up the bar. Once inside they discovered that the fortress was dimly lit by a few torches erected on poles. The walls were dirty and moldy from top to bottom, and the air had a musty, rotten odor, making it hard to breathe. Small rooms were scattered throughout the fortress, but instead of having doors, thick black mist covered each entrance.

After quickly surveying the area, Disciple motioned to the others to stay put until he explored the first room. Once he had penetrated the black mist and was inside the room, Disciple saw a man staring toward the entrance. But the black mist was no longer visible, and in its place were pictures of stacks of gold bars and lots of precious jewels.

Disciple read from his Book. "But the ones who desire to be rich fall into temptation, and into a snare, and into many foolish and harmful lusts which plunge people into ruin and destruction. For the love of money is a root of all kinds of evils. It is through this craving that some have departed from the faith and have pierced themselves with many sorrows."

Disciple raised his Book until it became a Sword then thrust it toward the pictures. "Keep your way of life free from the love of money, and be content with the things you have, for He has said, I will never leave you nor forsake you."

When Disciple's Sword made contact with the pictures, they disappeared, revealing the black mist. The captive saw that he had been deceived and was in prison. Disciple kept his Sword pointed toward the mist and motioned for the man to follow him. The prisoner hesitated at first, but then stood up and followed him out of the room.

Disciple explained to those with him what he'd done to help free the man trapped in deception. He instructed them to find in their Books something to counter the deceptive pictures, and then strike the mist with their Sword, so the person could see it for what it was.

All of those who entered the fortress, spread out, quickly going to different rooms. Samuel entered a room where a man watched pictures of himself enjoying a grand banquet while receiving a medal from all the people in neighboring towns. He was being honored because he refused to take a stand on God's word if he thought others might be offended by it. This man appeared to enjoy being told how much more loving and tolerant he was than others on the Quest.

Samuel opened his Book. "Jesus described those who will not confess him openly saying, 'For they loved the approval and praise of men more than the approval and praise of God.' And the Apostle John wrote, 'Do not love the world or the things in the world. If anyone loves the world, the love of the Father is not in him.' "

Samuel raised his Book until it became a Sword and pointed it toward the pictures. "Do you not know that friendship with the world is hostility toward God? Whoever desires to be a friend of the world makes himself to be an enemy of God."

Samuel pierced the pictures with his Sword revealing the black mist. When the pictures disappeared, the man in the room stood up quickly and stretched his hands out toward the mist trying to make the pictures come back.

While keeping his Sword in the mist, Samuel put his left hand on the man's shoulder. "If you wish to remain here, I will withdraw my Sword, and the pictures will return."

The prisoner stared at the floor for a minute before looking back up at Samuel. "I wish to be free."

Samuel led him out of the room and into the hallway with the others who had also been freed.

At the same time, Thaddeus entered a room where a man was staring at pictures of himself being the leader of a large House of Instruction. Thousands adored him, and he commanded those around him like a general in an army.

After asking the Holy Spirit for wisdom, Thaddeus took out his Book. "The Apostle Peter said, 'Do not be domineering over those who are under your care, but be an example to them.' And Jesus said,

'For you know that the princes of this world exercise full dominion over those under them, and those who are great trample on top of them.' " Thaddeus held out his hand. "While the leaders of this world dominate those under their authority it should not be so among us."

Thaddeus took out his Sword and pointed it toward the pictures. "Jesus continued, 'Whoever desires to become great among you, let him be your servant. And whoever desires to be first among you, let him be your slave, just as the Son of Man did not come to be served, but to serve, and to give His life a ransom for many.' "

Thaddeus pierced the pictures with his Sword, revealing the black mist. The deceived prisoner hung his head and stared at the floor.

Thaddeus reached out his hand to him. "Now is not the time to beat yourself up. This is the time to get up and get back on your path."

The prisoner took Thaddeus's hand and followed him into the hallway with the others.

All those who came inside the fortress with Disciple continued going through the rooms, and when someone wished to leave, they led them out to the hallway to join the others. After thirty minutes of going room to room, Disciple heard a commotion on the roof. The guards must have regained consciousness. Disciple could hear rocks crashing on the roof, so he knew Benjamin was doing his best to keep them from attacking Sarah and the rest of those on the ground.

Disciple yelled out, "Have all the rooms been covered?"

Samuel rushed up from the end of the hall, panting and out of breath. "Yes, I've just come out of the last one."

Right then Sarah yelled from the outside, "They're getting free from the ropes!"

Disciple glanced at the freed prisoners. "Once outside, we must run from these grounds as soon as we can. These guards cannot go past the fortress boundaries. Once we're beyond them, we're safe. Let's go now."

Everyone hurried outside and began to run.

One of the guards on the ground was free, and Disciple ran toward him while motioning to the others. "Go! I'll hold them off."

Everyone else took off running as fast as they could. Disciple struck the guard on his side, and then on his right leg. Disciple didn't know it, but another guard was now free and running toward him. As this second guard closed in on him, Samuel appeared and slammed his Shield into the guard's stomach.

Disciple blocked the first guard's fist with his Shield. "Thanks! Are the rest almost to the end of the fortress grounds?"

Samuel swung his Sword, hitting another guard on the shoulder, then quickly glanced back toward the others. "Yes!"

Disciple ducked as the first guard swung at his head. "Then let's get out of here!"

The guards attempted to grab Disciple and Samuel to keep them from leaving, but they gave each guard one more strike and then ran. The guards pursued them, but those final blows had slowed them down, allowing Disciple and Samuel to safely get away. Outside the fortress perimeter, they caught up with the others, and then Disciple motioned for everyone to stop.

Benjamin and the two with him ran up and joined the rest. Disciple did a count to make sure everyone was there. He then counted the ones that were rescued, finding that twelve left the fortress, but fifteen didn't come with them.

Samuel stepped forward. "I was with one of those who didn't leave. Even after I struck the deception with my Sword, he still wouldn't come with me. In fact, he became angry and told me to pull my Sword back. When I did, the deception appeared again, making him happy. I'm grateful though that I was able to help free one of those who did leave."

All those who escaped kept thanking the others who came to rescue them. Disciple then led everyone back to the camp, and once there, they shared what happened with those who stayed behind praying. Everyone thanked God for the victory. They were sorry that not all wanted to leave, but they purposed to pray for them.

After a time of singing and rejoicing, everyone went to sleep. The next morning, all those in the camp were still buzzing with excitement. A great victory had been won, and they had all worked together well as a team.

Benjamin motioned for everyone to be quiet, then pointed toward Disciple. "We want to thank you for leading us to this great victory. We knew God directed us to find you. Now we'd like for you to stay with us and lead us for the rest of our journey."

Disciple saw the anticipation on everyone's faces. "I'm honored that you think so highly of me. I didn't realize it until last night, but I do want to be a leader of a group someday. It was an honor to go into battle with all of you, and anyone would be blessed to be able to lead such brave warriors as yourselves. I prayed last night before I went to sleep, asking God if His will was for me to stay with you. When I woke up this morning, I believe the Holy Spirit impressed upon me that you already have leaders."

Everyone looked around at each other wondering what Disciple was talking about.

Disciple called for Benjamin to step forward. "As I was praying, I believe God has shown me that Benjamin is called to be your leader."

Disciple then called for Sarah to step forward. "And I believe that Sarah is to be by his side."

Those in the group were amazed because Disciple didn't know that Benjamin and Sarah had been fond of one another for several months. And no one knew just how much closer they had become over the last three weeks.

Benjamin appeared nervous, as he started digging into his pocket and then brought out a small box. To everyone's surprise, he got down on one knee and held out a ring. "Sarah, for as long as I am on this Quest I wish for you to be by my side every step of the way. Will you marry me?"

Sarah smiled as she placed her hand on her heart. "Yes!"

Everyone let out a cheer. One by one, all those in the group congratulated them while also confirming that Benjamin was called to be their leader. After talking with all those in their group, Benjamin and Sarah approached Disciple.

Benjamin said, "Thank you so much for everything. I've wanted to ask Sarah to marry me for weeks, but I was trying to work up the courage."

Sarah smiled as she took Benjamin's hand. "Yes, thank you. I was wondering when he was going to ask."

Disciple let out a laugh and then hugged them both. As all those in the group continued to celebrate and talk amongst themselves, Disciple walked over to his tent and began packing up.

Seeing that Disciple was preparing to leave, Samuel ambled over to him. "This has been a very eventful two days. I'm so glad our paths crossed. Where will you go now?"

Disciple threw his backpack over his shoulders. "Wherever my path takes me. This group is in good hands, and they'll do many great things together. How about you? What will you do next?"

Samuel glanced over his shoulder as everyone was still celebrating. "I believe I'll stick around and join them."

Disciple nodded. "I think that's a great decision. They can use someone with your experience."

Disciple patted Samuel on the back, and then walked over and said goodbye to the rest of the group. They gave him the telescope to help him on his journey, and as something to remember them by.

A part of Disciple was sad to go. He enjoyed leading this group of travelers into battle, and the feeling of comradery that came with it. For the first time, he felt like he was becoming a part of a group, and he was going to miss that feeling. He hoped that soon he would be able to experience it again, but for now, it was time to move on to the next thing on his path.

SWAMP OF SUFFERING

Disciple traveled until sunset, then found a nice spot to set up camp and settled in for the night. As he started out on his journey again the next day, he reflected on his latest adventure. He would miss Benjamin, Sarah, Samuel, Thaddeus, and all the others, but he hoped to one day see them again.

As Disciple moved forward, he was in deep thought and didn't notice that his path was taking him in the direction of a swamp. When water began to rise past his ankles, he stopped and then backed up several feet to make sure he had not strayed from his path.

After inspecting the area, it was clear his path was leading him into the watery mire. Disciple continued on, thinking it shouldn't be too much further before he'd be back on solid ground. But after wading through the mud and sludge for some time, he could see no end in sight. He knew this was the right path, so he was determined to keep moving forward no matter how things looked.

As Disciple moved further into the swamp, the water increased up to his waist. Fog filled the air, making it difficult to see, and the atmosphere was unsettling and uncomfortable. Tension grew, and fear of the unknown gripped him. With each step, his feet sank into the mire of the swamp, and each stride forward required persistent effort. Disciple heard the water stirring out to his left, and as he turned, his eye caught something moving toward him. He took out his Sword and readied his Shield. Then suddenly a large seven-foot crocodile rose up out of the water.

As the crocodile opened its mouth Disciple heard, "It's your fault; it's all your fault."

The crocodile swished its large tail back and forth, as it picked up speed and moved closer. Disciple braced himself, preparing for an assault. The crocodile opened its large jaws and lunged toward him. As it attempted to clamp down with its long sharp teeth, Disciple thrust out his Shield, striking it on the nose. The crocodile swung its tail wildly and again opened its jaws trying to bite down even harder. Once again, Disciple blocked the attack, but the force of the bite sent vibrations through his Shield and down his arm. The crocodile let out a low growl and swished its tail before swimming off.

Disciple was relieved to have survived the attack, but then he thought, was this creature right? Was it his fault that he was going through this swamp? He tried to think of sections of his Book to bring him encouragement, but it was difficult to feel encouraged in these circumstances.

He remembered reading that he should rejoice in trials and afflictions, knowing that these would produce endurance. And this endurance would produce character, and character would produce hope. He also remembered where it said that he should consider it all joy whenever he encountered various trials, knowing that the testing of his faith produced patient endurance. But he should be letting this patient endurance thoroughly accomplish its work in him, so that he would be mature and complete, lacking in nothing.

But how could he rejoice and count it all joy when going through something like this? What was he lacking, that going through this swamp was going to help him with?

Disciple heard the water stirring to his right, and noticed out of the corner of his eye that his enemy was approaching him again.

"It's your fault; it's all your fault."

The crocodile appeared to be angry, as it forcefully opened and closed its large jaws, making a loud cracking sound each time its teeth came together. The fog was denser, making it difficult to judge how soon the crocodile would be within range. Disciple prepared for the next attack, but he was having a hard time maneuvering and constantly felt off balance. Then something happened that caused terror to radiate throughout his body. The crocodile dove under water and headed straight toward him.

While part of the crocodile's body had been partially visible, it was tough to track, but now that it was swimming beneath the water, he had no idea when or where it would attack. Disciple held his Shield at his waist while drawing back his Sword, ready to strike at a moment's notice. A glimmer of sunlight pierced the fog, illuminating the water below. Disciple peered beneath the surface, anxious to get a glimpse of his attacker.

All of a sudden, the white teeth of the crocodile reflected a small bit of sunlight, revealing its position. Disciple thrust his Shield into the water just as the crocodile was about to strike, stopping its momentum. He then plunged his Sword into the side of his enemy and struck it again with his Shield. The crocodile thrust its head up and attempted to bite him on the arm.

Disciple slammed his Shield into the crocodile's mouth and reared back with his Sword. "For I consider that the sufferings of this present time are not worthy to be compared with the glory which shall be revealed in us."

Disciple struck the crocodile on its head three times, and at last, it swam away.

As Disciple slowly trekked forward, the fog lifted just enough in one area, so that he could see others, whose path went around the swamp. These people appeared to be pointing toward him.

Stopping to see if he could hear what they were saying, Disciple heard one person say, "I wonder what sin that poor man committed to get himself trapped in that swamp?"

Another replied, "I'm not sure, but he must have done something horrible to get caught up in a mess like that."

This was extremely difficult for Disciple to hear. He had been following his path, and this was where it led him.

"It's your fault, it's all your fault."

The voice now appeared to be coming from all around him. Disciple quickly turned this way and that, trying to discover which direction the crocodile might be coming from. He then felt the water slapping up against his back. Turning around just in time, Disciple saw the crocodile opening its mouth and coming toward him. He quickly thrust out his Shield, as the crocodile lurched forward. The creature bounced off the Shield and then tried to circle behind him.

Emboldened and determined to defeat this enemy, Disciple raised his Sword. "Beloved, stop being surprised at the painful sufferings taking place among you in order to test you, as if something strange is happening to you. But rejoice knowing that inasmuch as you are participating in the sufferings of Christ, you will also rejoice and be glad when His glory is revealed."

Disciple struck the crocodile on the top of its jaws, and as it again prepared to bite him, he thrust his Sword straight into its mouth. The crocodile bit down, but Disciple quickly pulled his Sword out of its mouth and hit the creature between the eyes. The crocodile rolled over on its back, then recovered and swam away.

Disciple moved forward, finally coming to the end of the swamp. His trek through the quagmire of mud and water seemed to have lasted for hours, and while in the middle of the struggle, it felt as if it was never going to end.

As he made his way onto dry ground, Disciple's clothes dripped with residue from the swamp. Many of those who walked by stared at him with disapproval. He now understood that part of the struggle of going through the swamp was enduring how others looked at him, as he was going through it.

Disciple overheard someone say that the name of the place was the Swamp of Suffering. Many thought only those who had done something wrong were led into it. Disciple realized that he too might have come to that same conclusion before experiencing it for himself. He thought of those in his Book who experienced times of trial and suffering even though they were walking in obedience to God.

There was Joseph, who was sold into slavery by his brothers. This same Joseph was put into prison for refusing to sin with his master's wife. There was David, who had to run for his life because King Saul was out to kill him due to his jealousy. Many of the prophets suffered because they spoke in the name of the Lord, and of course, he thought of Jesus, who suffered tremendously both in His earthly life and His death.

Disciple moved on from the swamp and continued on his path. He wanted to get out of his wet and dirty clothes, but there was nowhere to get cleaned up and change, so he kept going. Soon he came to a bench where a man was sitting and staring out in the distance. He was middle-aged with slightly graying hair, and he was slumped over as if he was being weighed down by a heavy burden.

Disciple started to pass by, but then he felt he should stop and join him. After pausing in front of the bench, he said, "May I sit down with you for a little while?"

The man looked up. "Sure, go ahead."

Disciple sat down and introduced himself.

The man introduced himself as Josiah and then studied Disciple for a few moments. "I can see by your clothes that you've been through the Swamp of Suffering."

Disciple shook some of the mud off his shirt. "Yes, it was a challenging experience."

"I've been through my own trials as well," said Josiah.

"I don't want to pry, but I'd be willing to listen," said Disciple, as he set his backpack on the ground.

Josiah took a deep breath. "It's my son. There were problems throughout his teenage years, and when he was eighteen, he left home. I heard he was in the Camp of Sin at one point, but I don't know if he's still there or not. I also heard that he was telling others that I was the cause of his problems. I was certainly not a perfect parent, but I really tried. When he was going through stages of rebellion I had to confront him and let him know he was going in the wrong direction. He felt I was always against him, but he didn't understand that I confronted him because I cared about him and loved him. I saw where his choices were leading, and the pain and struggle that was ahead for him. Now that he's experiencing the problems I warned him about, I feel so helpless."

Disciple was not sure what to say to him. He had never been a parent, so he had no experience with this sort of thing. He quickly prayed that God would give him some encouragement to share with Josiah.

Disciple sat back and stretched his left arm over the bench. "I didn't have a perfect childhood, but once I was in my late teenage years most of my decisions had nothing to do with anyone else. I did the things I wanted to do because I wanted to do them. Each person has to take responsibility for their own decisions and their own life."

Josiah looked out at all those traveling by. "There's a lot of struggling involved with being a parent. When the children are younger, you can control everything in their life, but as they get older, you see that you have less and less control. You want to make their decisions for them so they'll avoid the dangers and pitfalls of life, but at a certain point, you no longer can. And it seems that the more you talk, the less they listen. I finally realized that I would have to do less talking and more praying."

Disciple put his hand on Josiah's shoulder. "You can spend a lot of time beating yourself up over things you wished you could've done differently, but that isn't going to do you or your son any good. What's important is that he returns to his path, and then you can talk with him about many things. What's your son's name?"

"His name is Mark."

Disciple leaned forward. "Before I go, I'd like to pray with you about Mark."

Josiah nodded and closed his eyes.

Disciple bowed his head. "Dear Lord, we pray for Mark wherever he is. We pray that he would see the consequences that sin is bringing into his life and that he would turn toward you in repentance. Let him know that You love him and that Your grace is always available if he will turn around and receive it. Amen."

Josiah looked up with a tear in his eye. "Thank you for stopping and talking to me today. It's so good to be able to share these kinds of things with others."

Disciple gave the man a hug and continued on.

After walking further, Disciple came upon another bench where another gentleman sat looking even more depressed than Josiah had. He appeared to be in his early thirties and had a look of anxiousness and helplessness on his face.

Disciple felt compelled to speak to this gentleman too. "May I join you?"

The man nodded while scooting over. Disciple introduced himself, and the man introduced himself as Patrick.

Disciple felt emboldened by his last experience. "Sir, I feel God has caused me to pass by this way today to listen to those who are going through challenges in their life. I don't mean to imply that you're one of them, but if there's something you've been struggling with, then I'm here to listen."

Patrick didn't say anything at first, but then after a few minutes, he looked up at Disciple. "I feel like a failure. I have a wife and two children, and recently I lost my job. We're barely getting by on what we've saved, and I don't know what's going to happen when that's gone."

Disciple sat back, pondering what to say. "I've never been married, so I've never had a family, but I can understand how difficult this must be. I do odd jobs to earn money as I'm traveling my path, but I only have to think about myself. I can see that if others were counting on me, I would feel a lot more responsibility."

Patrick nodded and shifted his gaze. "Yes, you feel as if you're letting everyone down. My wife and children love me, and they're being supportive, but I can't help but feel as if they think less of me."

Disciple turned sideways, facing Patrick. "I don't know what God is doing in your life right now, but I know He hasn't forgotten you. Jesus said, 'Look attentively at the birds of the air, for they do not sow, nor reap, nor gather into barns, and yet your heavenly Father keeps providing for them. You are of much more worth than they, are you not?' "

Patrick smiled, and an expression of relief washed over him. "I think I know what I need to do today. I need to go home and reassure my family that God has not forgotten us. My family needs to hear that, and they need to know that I believe it."

Disciple folded his hands together. "I'd like to pray with you before I go." Bowing his head, Disciple prayed, "Dear Lord, only you know what your plan is for this situation, but I know you keep constant watch over those who fear and trust in you. I thank you that your plan is being worked out in Patrick's life and that you have everything under control. Amen."

Patrick thanked him, and Disciple gave him a hug before continuing on.

A little further ahead was another bench. A younger man sat on it with his elbows on his legs and his head resting in his hands. By now Disciple knew what he was supposed to do, so he sat down with the young man and introduced himself.

The young man glanced up. "I'm Jason."

Disciple waved his hand in front of him. "All today, God has caused me to stop and talk to people who are struggling with different situations in their lives. If there's anything you'd like to talk about, I'd be glad to listen."

Jason kept his head in his hands and stared down at the ground. "I started on this Quest about a year ago, and it's been extremely challenging. My parents aren't pleased with what I'm doing, and most of the friends I had before don't even want to talk to me now. I was so full of zeal at the beginning, but one thing after another has seemed to weigh me down."

"What happened?" asked Disciple.

Jason sat up and turned toward him. "Not long after starting this Quest, I met a nice girl at a House of Instruction. We started spending a lot of time together, and we made plans to be married. I was so happy. And then one day she told me she no longer wanted to get married. I asked her what had changed, and she didn't give me an answer. I still don't know what happened, but I was devastated. As I'm walking my path, I don't have any confidence. It feels as if I'm now expecting things to go wrong."

Silently, Disciple prayed that God would give him some encouraging words for Jason.

Disciple took a deep breath. "I'm so sorry your hope for marriage with this girl came to an end. God has not placed a woman along my path that I felt I was supposed to marry, but I can see that what you experienced was heartbreaking. I could tell you that someone better will come along and that there are other fish in the sea, as well as several other clichés, but none of that would help you right now."

Jason nodded. "You're right. Others have already told me those things, and in fact, I've told myself those things, but they don't make me feel any better about what happened."

Disciple pointed to his Book. "The one thing in God's word that helps me the most with things like this is where it says, 'And we know that all things work together for good to those who love God, to those who are the called according to His purpose.' There are times when all you can do is trust that God is working out all things for your good. This doesn't lessen the pain of what you're going through now, but it gives you hope that things will work out in the future."

Jason sat back and crossed his arms. "Thank you for sharing that. It does help to think of things as a part of a much bigger picture. I've been so focused on this one small part of my life that I haven't thought about all the things God has for me in the future."

"Yes," said Disciple nodding, "when we're going through tough times it can seem as if all the negative things we're experiencing are huge, and as if they'll be with us forever. It can be difficult to do, but there are times when we just have to keep putting one foot in front of the other and move forward."

Jason smiled and reached down for the satchel that was beside him. "I can see that. I purpose that today I'll start moving forward again. The first thing I will do is take out my Book and spend time reading. It's been a while since I did that. As you were quoting from this Book, it made me realize how powerful the words are, and how much I miss reading them."

Disciple held up his Book. "God's word helps put things into perspective. I know your journey so far has been tough, but God is able to take the trials of your life and make you stronger. I believe you're going to go on to see many victories and successes."

Jason thanked Disciple for the encouragement, and then Disciple asked if he could pray with him before he left.

"Yes, please do," said Jason.

Disciple prayed, "Dear Lord, You know the hardships that Jason has faced since starting on this Quest. I pray that You would continue to assure him that You're for him and not against him. Help him to have confidence that the plans You have for him are for good and not misery, that You want to give him a future and a hope."

Disciple hugged Jason and then stood up to leave. He took a step and then turned around. "I'm curious about something. This is the third time that God has caused me to stop and talk to someone who is going through something difficult in their life. Each time the person has opened up and talked to me as if they'd known me for years. Do you have any idea why that is?"

Jason studied Disciple's shirt and pants. "Yes, I do. The residue on your clothes shows that you've been through the Swamp of Suffering. Because of that, I know you understand what it's like to experience difficulty in your life. I felt I could talk to you without being judged."

Disciple smiled and walked away. The comfort and encouragement he experienced from God while going through the swamp, enabled him to give out this same comfort and encouragement to others.

After traveling a few miles, Disciple stopped and prayed. "Dear

Lord, my clothes will not always have the residue from that swamp, but I ask that others continue to see me as a person who will listen to their struggles without being judgmental."

Disciple thought of all the exciting and adventurous things he had done on his Quest, but he also thought that times like today were just as important and victorious. He couldn't stop and talk to everyone, but he wanted to be sensitive to the leading of the Holy Spirit as to when he should stop and encourage someone along the way.

After arriving at a clearing and setting up camp for the night, Disciple reflected on what God had been doing in his life over the past weeks. He had learned to develop relationships with others while leading a group of warriors on a mission, and he was learning how to identify with people through their struggles. What was God preparing him for?

22

A NEW MISSION

Disciple traveled on for three months, and each day he continued to grow in his relationship with God. When he encountered others along his path, he was able to open up more about his life, and he was able to relate to others in a more personal way.

One morning Disciple came to a House of Instruction. He joined in with all those who were there, singing praises and listening to the teaching of God's word. After the service was over, some of the members invited him to stay for a picnic lunch. He enjoyed the food and fellowship and even participated in some of the games they were playing.

After a few hours, Disciple decided it was time to start out again. One of the people told him about a nice inn that was just a few miles ahead, so after seeing that his path was heading in that direction, he thought he would go there and stay for the night. When He arrived at the inn, a sweet older lady named Joyce welcomed him and led him to a comfortable and spacious room. After unpacking and settling in, he spent time reading in his Book before lying down to go to sleep.

When Disciple awoke, he went downstairs and enjoyed a nice breakfast. After he ate, he stepped outside to see what direction his path was taking him, but it hadn't moved. He went back inside and approached the service desk. "I would like to stay for another night. Is that ok?"

Joyce smiled. "Sure. A man stopped by earlier this morning and told us he would pay for however long you wanted to stay."

"Who was he?" asked Disciple.

"He said he met you the other day when you visited their House of Instruction."

Disciple was grateful for God's provision, and he spent most of the morning getting to know others who were staying at the inn. Then later that evening he met a group whose path was taking them to a distant land where the people had not heard about Jesus. He was fascinated as they described the culture of the people they were being sent to. Disciple admired the courage and commitment of this group, and as they were leaving, he gave them some of the money he had earned to support their trip. After this, he went back to his room to spend some extra time studying in his Book.

When the next morning arrived, Disciple's came downstairs and discovered that his path still had not moved, so he went back to his room. But as soon as he sat down to read in his Book, someone knocked on his door.

"Excuse me sir, but a gentleman is here to see you."

Disciple stood up. "I'll be right down."

As soon as he reached the service desk, he saw a familiar old friend. "Pastor Sinclair! What brings you all the way out here?"

"Hello Disciple," said Pastor Sinclair as he gave him a hug. "I've had quite an interesting journey. I'll tell you all about it, but first I want to hear how you've been doing since the last time I saw you."

"Sure thing. Let's go have a seat in the dining area."

Disciple led then led him over to a table toward the back, and they spent hours getting caught up on everything he had experienced since the last time they saw each other.

Pastor Sinclair said, "So many exciting things have been happening since I last saw you. God has been doing great things in your life, and I can see by talking to you that you've made much progress."

Disciple smiled, taking in the compliment. "Thank you. That means a lot coming from you. I'm curious though as to why you came all this way to find me, and even how you knew I was here."

Pastor Sinclair sat back and crossed his legs. "I came here to discuss an important mission that I believe God may have for you. After listening to all that you've told me, I feel even more that it may be so. A few days ago, after spending time in prayer, I set out to find you."

What was this new mission that Pastor Sinclair had for him? Disciple wanted to interrupt and ask precisely that question, but he patiently listened.

Pastor Sinclair continued, "After following my path for many hours, I started asking people if they had seen someone matching your description. I talked to several people, and finally, someone told me you had come by this direction. I knew there was a House of Instruction nearby, so I went there to ask if they had seen you, and a nice lady told me you were on your way to this inn. So here I am, and I'm so glad I found you."

Disciple leaned forward. "I'm curious as to what this mission is that you believe God has for me."

Pastor Sinclair smiled. "As you were telling me about how you led that group of people into battle against the Fortress of Deception, I could see that God was preparing you to be a great leader. I believe I know the next step in preparing you for that calling."

"What is it?" asked Disciple, more curious than ever.

Pastor Sinclair took a deep breath. "Recently I've been a guest speaker at a House of Instruction. The leader there, whose name is Gaius, introduced me to a young man named Peter. He's a tall, handsome young man, a top athlete in his town and very popular. He's also intelligent and well spoken. Gaius said that he felt Peter had tremendous potential and was destined to be used mightily for God if he could get his life together. Peter spent time at the Camp of Sin and then went from there to the Camp of Religion. When he finally returned to his path, it was only about six months before he was right back in the Camp of Sin again."

Disciple sat back and shifted in his seat. "It sounds like this young man has had a tough journey."

Pastor Sinclair nodded. "Yes, it does. Gaius said Peter had once again returned to his path and recently began attending his House of Instruction. But Gaius is concerned that although Peter has all this potential, he's not very stable and is in danger of straying off his path again soon. Gaius asked me if I had any suggestions. I prayed about it that night, and then I thought of you."

Disciple raised his eyebrows. "Why would you think of me? Was I really that bad?"

Pastor Sinclair laughed and put his hand on Disciple's arm. "Oh no, that's not what I mean. I thought that this young man needed someone like you to mentor him and guide him."

This was not what Disciple had been anticipating. He thought Pastor Sinclair must have some grand and exciting mission that he could undertake.

Pastor Sinclair could tell that Disciple was not enthusiastic about the prospect of being a mentor to a troubled young man. "I understand this is not what you were expecting."

Disciple sat back and looked out a window. "You're right. I wouldn't have guessed it would be something like this. I feel I've finally arrived at a place where I can take care of myself, and I feel somewhat ready to lead others who are strong, but what you're asking is something entirely different."

Pastor Sinclair leaned forward. "Yes, it is. When you're only responsible for yourself, things are much simpler. And if you're leading those who are already strong, then you can focus more on the mission and less on the people. But that's why I feel this may be important for what God wants to do with you in the future. When you're called to lead a group of people that you will spend years in close relationship with, not all of them are going to be strong. And even those who are strong, are going to go through times of weakness. There will be times when you'll be disappointed and frustrated with them, and there will be times when they're disappointed and frustrated with you. You'll need to know how to walk with people during their weakest times, and while they're on different stages of their journey."

Disciple turned toward Pastor Sinclair and sighed. "Those are some good points, and what you're proposing could help prepare me for leadership, but what you're proposing also sounds difficult. If Peter is having this much trouble, then you and I both know he's probably going to continue to have problems for some time before he finally becomes consistent."

Pastor Sinclair put his hand on top of Disciple's. "You're correct. This won't be easy, but please pray about it. I'll stay here with you for one more night, and if you don't see your path going in the same direction as mine, then I'll go back and let Gaius know he'll need to keep praying for another solution to help this young man."

Disciple agreed and spent a lot of time in prayer that night. This mission was not something he was looking forward to. It seemed like a lot of hard work, with a high risk of failure. The next morning he went downstairs to find Pastor Sinclair waiting for him. When they stepped outside, they saw that their paths were going in the same direction.

Pastor Sinclair put on his hat and smiled. "Are you ready?"

Disciple smiled and shook his head. "No, but let's go."

Pastor Sinclair laughed, and then they were on their way.

As they traveled, Disciple asked, "What do you feel is the best way to approach this? Does Peter know anything about what we've been discussing?"

"I told him that I was going away for a few days, and I may return with someone that could talk to him, and perhaps accompany him on some of his journey."

"How did he respond?"

Pastor Sinclair glanced away for a moment before turning back toward Disciple with a big grin on his face. "He was about as excited as you were when I first told you about it."

Disciple laughed. "This is going to be interesting."

After they had walked for a few hours, Pastor Sinclair stopped and took out a canteen full of water. "Gaius has some rooms ready for us to stay a few days. I've left a very capable fellow in charge of my House of Instruction, so I can stay until you and Peter are ready to start out on your journey again."

Disciple looked behind him. "It feels as if I'm going backward now. I've spent so much time going forward and making progress."

Pastor Sinclair took a drink of water and returned his canteen to his backpack. "You're not going backward. I've been up and down many of the same paths with several different people over the years. Each time I do, I learn even more."

"I wonder if we'll be led to all the same places I've already traveled."

Pastor Sinclair adjusted his backpack, preparing to move forward again. "I don't think so. Almost no one walks the same path in the same way. There may be similarities, but it will be different. I'm sure you'll have some new adventures and experiences."

They traveled on for a few more hours and then arrived at Gaius' House of Instruction. It was built on a lovely piece of property which had several dogwood trees and a vegetable garden. Horses were kept on the property, and there was a big stable with lots of space for the horses to run around.

Gaius was waiting as they walked up. "Welcome back Pastor Sinclair, and I see you didn't return empty-handed."

"It was a rewarding journey," said Pastor Sinclair. "This is Disciple."

Gaius held out his hand. "Nice to meet you. Pastor Sinclair has told me a lot about you."

Disciple shook his hand. "I'm not sure how I feel about that."

They all three laughed and walked inside.

Gaius welcomed them into a small office where he introduced Disciple and Peter to one another, and then they all four sat down together to talk. Disciple didn't say much. He wanted to listen to what Peter would say and how he would respond to different questions and topics.

After talking with everyone for a while, Peter looked over at Disciple. "I'm grateful you've come all this way to spend some time with me. I'm sure there are things I can learn from you, but I don't think I'll need someone to accompany me on my journey. I know where I made mistakes in the past, and I feel I'll be able to avoid them this time."

Disciple could tell this was not what Pastor Sinclair and Gaius wanted to hear. "I'm here to offer whatever help I can. Meet me tomorrow morning out back near the stables as soon as you've had breakfast."

Peter nodded and stood up. "Well gentleman, it's been a great time of fellowship. I think I'll go get some sleep."

The three of them also stood to say goodnight to Peter, but then sat back down at the table.

Gaius turned to Pastor Sinclair. "Do you see what I mean?"

Pastor Sinclair looked over his shoulder. "Yes, I do see a lot of potential, but I also see a lot of warning signs."

Disciple tapped his fingers on the table. "If he doesn't want me to accompany him, then I can't and won't try to force that. I'm willing to do whatever God says, but Peter is going to have to want my help."

Pastor Sinclair nodded. "I agree. We'll take it one day at a time. Do you know what you're going to do tomorrow?"

Disciple looked as if he was in deep thought. "Not yet. I hope to have some direction before I meet him in the morning."

Pastor Sinclair stood up to leave. "Yes, I hope so too."

They all said goodnight and agreed to pray for direction for the next day.

23

BASIC TRAINING

Disciple woke up early the next morning and spent time reading in his Book and praying. After a quick breakfast, he went out to the stables to look for supplies to make a wooden sword and shield. He found what he needed and quickly constructed two of each.

Peter came out about an hour later. "So what is it we're going to do today?"

Disciple picked up one of the wooden swords. "We're going to do a little bit of sparring."

Peter examined the wooden weapons. "So we're not going to use our regular Swords and Shields?"

Disciple picked up a wooden shield and then motioned with his sword for Peter to do the same. "No, these will serve our purpose for now."

Peter picked up a wooden shield and a wooden sword and examined them closely. "If we used our regular armor, you'd have a tremendous advantage. You're much more experienced at using those than I am, and I'm sure yours is stronger. But if we're going to use these wooden ones then I'm afraid you're at a terrible disadvantage."

Disciple tilted his head to the side and shrugged. "Why would you say that?"

Peter scanned his own body and then Disciple's. "Well for one thing look at us. I mean you're not a scrawny guy, but I'm bigger than you are. I'm also younger and faster. Are you sure you want to do this?"

Disciple stood in a fighting stance. "I'll do my best to keep up with you."

Peter smiled. "Well okay, but I did try to warn you. When do you want to start?"

Disciple held his wooden sword out in front of him. "Whenever you're ready."

Peter smiled again and then rushed at him, but Disciple darted out of the way as Peter flew past him. Peter turned around, thinking he should take this more seriously. He stepped back and then carefully approached Disciple. First, he aimed a blow at Disciple's chest and then at his head, but Disciple blocked each one with his shield.

The smile on Peter's face vanished. He raised his sword again and attacked Disciple's right side as hard as he could, then followed by swinging at his legs to try to knock him off his feet. Disciple blocked the first blow and then jumped to avoid the swipe at his legs.

Peter lunged with his sword straight at the center of Disciple's chest, but Disciple blocked the attempt with his shield. Peter quickly countered with blows aimed at Disciple's thigh and waist, but once again Disciple blocked each one.

Peter threw down his shield, then grabbed his sword with two hands, and tried to bring it straight down on top of Disciple's head. Disciple dodged out of the way and shoved him to the ground. Peter quickly jumped to his feet, and letting out a yell, he rushed at him. Disciple sidestepped the attack, then gave Peter a kick on his backside, sending him face down in the dirt.

Disciple put down the wooden sword and shield and started to walk off. "That's all for this session."

Peter stood up and dusted himself off. "What do you mean that's all!"

Disciple turned around. "Here is what you need to learn. Your problem is that you're arrogant. You think you already know everything, and you believe whatever you do will succeed. While we were sparring, it was easy for me to see what you were going to do and avoid it. As soon as things started to go wrong, you got angry and wanted to lash out, which made you predictable. When your enemy sees this, he laughs because he knows he has you."

"Is there anything else?" Peter said sarcastically.

"Yes, I could tell from listening to you last night that you had a hard time receiving instruction. As soon as Gaius or Pastor Sinclair would offer advice, you acted as if you already knew it. That told me you don't like to listen. I could have started today in many different ways, but I knew that anything I said would just be a waste of time. I needed to show you what was wrong."

Peter threw down the wooden shield and sword. "You know what, I didn't ask for you to come here and help me. I went along with it because Gaius has been so nice to me, and he asked me if I would talk to you. I don't need a lecture from the Great Disciple. I'll be just fine on my own."

As Peter stormed off, Disciple called out, "How has that worked out so far in your life?"

Disciple glanced up toward the house and saw that Gaius and Pastor Sinclair had been watching the whole time. He walked up to where they were and stood next to them.

"I see that went well," said Pastor Sinclair.

Disciple leaned up against the fence. "It went about the way I expected. Before Peter can receive help, he has to be willing to admit that he needs it."

Pastor Sinclair stared toward the stables as Peter disappeared out of sight. "So what's next?"

Disciple shook his head. "I'm not sure. I'll let him cool off before I approach him, but if he doesn't come around soon, then you both know this isn't going to work."

Gaius nodded.

Pastor Sinclair said, "I agree with that. It's best to find out sooner rather than later if he's willing to cooperate. He has some difficult challenges to overcome, and he has to be willing to be honest with himself to have any chance of success."

Disciple prayed for about thirty minutes and then set off to see if he could find Peter. He walked alongside a river and came to a shaded area where Peter sat against a tree.

When Disciple stopped, Peter looked up and then looked away. "Did you come here to criticize me some more?"

Disciple paused while taking a deep breath. "No, there's nothing more I can say. The rest is up to you."

Peter picked up a rock and threw it in the river. "People think my life has been easy just because I've always been popular and didn't have to work hard for things. But what they don't realize is that when you're popular, you always have to maintain a certain image for everyone. You're not allowed to mess up or make mistakes. There's constant pressure to be what everyone expects you to be."

For the first time, Disciple saw a glimpse of Peter's true heart that lay beneath all the arrogance and pride he had seen so far. Disciple walked over and sat down next to him.

Peter gazed at the river. "One day someone came to my town and told us about how we owed this great debt of sin and how Jesus paid the price for our debt. I didn't think too much about it, but as days passed, I became more and more convinced that I owed this debt. When I went to the Building of Reflection I truly saw myself for the first time. It was difficult to see all those awful things."

"Yes, that's a humbling experience," said Disciple.

Peter continued. "At the same time though, it felt so freeing. I didn't have to be anything for God. He already saw me for who I was, and yet He was still willing to accept me with all my sin. I went up the Hill of Calvary that day and repented of my sins. I asked Jesus to be my Lord and Savior, and I felt like a new person."

Disciple gazed out toward the river. "I remember that feeling too. It's a wonderful experience."

Peter nodded. "Yes, it is. When I first started on this Quest, everything was wonderful. I was enjoying my fellowship with God and others. I was even offered a position of leading youth at a House of Instruction, after only having been a Christian for three months. I took the position, and things went well at the beginning, but then I started focusing on all the attention and approval I was getting."

"I see," said Disciple.

Peter picked up a small stick, trying to break it as he talked. "People were telling me that I was destined to be a leader one day, and I started to let all of this talk go to my head. Soon I found myself being critical of the leader of that House of Instruction because I thought I would be better. I was so full of myself, making it real easy for the enemy to trick me. I saw the Orchard of Vanity, and I was drawn to it. I could have sat there for days listening to what those voices were saying."

"I understand," said Disciple, "I fell for that too."

Peter looked a little surprised because he hadn't heard that part of Disciple's story. "It was then easy for Rebellion to lead me down to the Camp of Sin. I knew I shouldn't be there, but it reminded me of my days of being popular and well liked in my old life. For a while, I was extremely popular at the Camp of Sin, but when I was all used up, I was taken to the garbage dump."

"What happened after that?"

Peter paused for a moment and drew on the ground with his finger. "While I was there, some people from the Camp of Religion came and preached at us, telling us how bad we were. I wanted to be one of them. I wanted to be the one yelling at the people in the garbage dump instead of being there in the middle of it. So I followed them, and within a few weeks I was working my way up and doing quite well."

Disciple sat up. "I've never been there. What's it like?"

"Advancing in the Camp of Religion is simple once you get the hang of it. You figure out what it is they want you to do, and you just do it. They don't care about your motives. As long as you're going through the motions, everything is just fine. I heard them often say, 'Hey if you don't feel it, just do it, and the feelings will come later.' Well, the feelings never came. I just kept doing what I thought I was supposed to do."

"So what made you want to leave?"

Peter shook his head. "It all felt so empty. I looked around and saw everyone else going through the motions, and I thought, this was not why I started my Quest. I could have gone through the motions of life back in my hometown if that's all I wanted to do. I started this Quest because I was tired of that life, and I wanted something different. I wanted the kind of life that Jesus died for me to have."

Disciple held out his hands. "So after those experiences why did you end up back in the Camp of Sin again?"

Peter shrugged and threw another rock into the river. "That's a great question, and I've asked myself that many times. I mean the first time you end up in the Camp of Sin you can say you were deceived, but after that, you should know what's coming, right? Well, I learned the Devil always has new levels of deception. I didn't see it coming until it was too late."

Peter stopped and stared at the ground. Disciple could tell that

Peter was still angry with himself over what happened. He figured the best thing to do was just wait until he was ready to continue.

After a few minutes, Peter sighed. "I guess after I got back on my path, I still had a lot of the Camp of Religion in my system. At first, I was just glad to be making progress, but it didn't take long before once again I thought I knew everything. I decided to go back to my hometown, thinking I was going to win over all my friends and convince them to join me on the Quest, but instead, they ended up influencing me."

Disciple nodded. "I think it's great to go and talk to your old friends about becoming a Christian, but you must be on steady ground yourself, and you have to know where to set the boundaries."

Peter stared out as if he was visualizing what happened. "When I arrived back at my hometown, I visited my old friends, and they were all glad to see me. I decided to take things slow, so I didn't say anything at first. Not long after arriving I accepted their invitation to a party. I knew what was going to happen there, but I told myself I could handle it. When I arrived, one of my friends offered me something to drink. I thought to myself it's just one drink. Well, one drink turned into two which turned into four and then more, until I ended up getting drunk. I never got around to telling them about how I started my Quest or anything about it. Soon I realized that if I did say anything I'd look like a hypocrite."

Disciple shifted around toward him. "Why didn't you immediately start back on your path after that?"

Peter looked away. "I don't know. Once I gave into guilt, it's like I just dove further into my sin. I spent two more days with my friends going around to different parties, and after that, I felt even more guilty. I eventually tried to make my way back toward my path, but on the way, I saw a group of people camping. They looked like they were having a good time so I joined them. Not long after being there, they offered me something to drink. I got drunk again, and after a few days I stumbled back into the Camp of Sin."

Peter shook his head and then continued. "I don't remember a lot that happened after that, but it wasn't long before I found myself back in the garbage dump again. I wanted out of there so bad, but I was determined not to go back to the Camp of Religion, so I called out for grace. A heavenly being put me back on my path and led me to the House of Instruction where I met Gaius. That was about a month ago."

Disciple said, "It doesn't sound like you've ever gotten a good foundation in your Christian faith. How much time do you spend in your Book?"

Peter's gaze shifted to the stream and then back at Disciple. "Not a lot. I've always thought I knew what I needed to know."

Disciple removed his Book from his satchel. "You're going to have to change your attitude toward this Book and start spending more time studying in it. That's the only way you can expect to make progress. Change is not going to be easy. I believe I can help you, but it's going to be a lot of work. What do you think about that?"

Peter shrugged his shoulders. "I don't think I have a choice because I've not been able to do it on my own. When Gaius first suggested I have someone mentor me, I was offended because I didn't think I needed it, but now I realize I do. It's humbling having to admit that."

Disciple nodded. "You're going to find that humility is the key to everything."

"So what happens next?" asked Peter.

"We stay here until our paths move again," said Disciple. "While we're here we study, we talk, we pray, and we do whatever it takes to get ready to go back out there on our journey. Gaius is here and so is Pastor Sinclair, and we'll be listening to everything God has to say through them as well."

Disciple stood up and held out his hand.

Peter took Disciple's hand and climbed to his feet. "I will do whatever it takes."

24

PETER'S FIRST BATTLE

Disciple spent the next two weeks working with Peter. They read daily in their Books and prayed, then they talked about the different challenges Peter would face once he started his journey again. Each evening after dinner they would meet with Gaius and Pastor Sinclair, receiving teaching and instruction from them.

One day after a long training session, Pastor Sinclair approached Disciple and stood next to him. "Do you think he's ready?"

Disciple glanced toward Peter, who was walking back into the house to get ready for dinner. "I don't know. It's one thing to follow God when you're in a sheltered environment, but it's going to be different once we're back out there traveling our path and facing various challenges. I'll know more once I see how he does in his first battle."

"Gaius and I have been talking, and we sense that you'll be leaving soon."

Disciple nodded. "I've been feeling the same way. We'll check our paths in the morning, but I believe soon it's going to be time for us to head out."

The next day when he awoke, he checked his path and saw that it was moving away from the House of Instruction. Disciple knew this was where the hard part really began.

He walked over and put his hand on Peter's shoulder. "It's time to get back out there and continue on our path."

Peter tapped his chest twice revealing his armor. "I feel I'm ready."

Everyone had breakfast together followed by one last time of studying together in their Books. Afterward, they all prayed for one another, and then Gaius and Pastor Sinclair hugged them and wished them well.

Disciple and Peter started out on their path, traveling farther and farther away from the House of Instruction. Peter was enthusiastic and excited as they walked along, but Disciple was more subdued. He didn't know what was ahead, but he thought Peter would face some kind of challenge soon.

Their first day was quiet. They camped that night, then continued on the next day. They made good progress that morning, and then right after lunch Disciple heard a familiar metallic clanging sound in the distance. He peered through his telescope and spotted a wave of Black Knights charging toward them. He knew these were coming to face Peter.

Disciple pointed toward the enemy with his Sword. "You're about to face the Black Knights of Lust. Remember the portions of this Book that I gave you to memorize and keep your mind focused on the words. There are going to be flashing pictures on the front of their armor that will try to stir up lust. Keep your focus on God's words and don't get distracted by those pictures."

Peter held out his Book until it became a Sword, and marched out to face the Black Knights. Peter appeared ready for battle, but as his enemies came closer, it was as if he fell into a trance. The Black Knights stormed toward him and ran him over. Peter made a weak attempt to get back on his feet, but they pinned him to the ground and beat him. Disciple ran out and attacked the Black Knights, clearing them off of Peter, and driving them away.

Disciple helped him to his feet. "What happened?"

"I don't know," said Peter, picking up his Sword. "I thought I was ready, but when I saw all those pictures, I just froze."

Disciple examined the scrapes and bruises Peter received from the Black Knights. "Did you try to think about the verses you had memorized?"

Peter returned his Book to his satchel. "Well, sort of."

Disciple glanced back up at Peter, attempting to make eye contact with him. "What do you mean sort of? You've been memorizing and meditating on them haven't you?"

Peter looked away. "I guess not as much as I should have been."

Disciple pointed toward the side of his head. "What have you been fixing your thoughts on?"

Peter shrugged. "Sometimes I just let my mind wander. It takes a lot of energy to fight off thoughts of lust all the time. I mean, I am a single young man, and you can't expect me not to think about such things."

Disciple didn't know how to respond to that. He shook his head and gave Peter a stern look. "What do you mean? Do you realize that the person who wrote most of the verses about the lust of the flesh was a single man? Can you show me where this Book ever excuses giving into lust just because you're single?"

Peter stood there silently while avoiding making eye contact.

Disciple threw out both his hands. "You told me that you hadn't looked at any pictures that would tempt you to lust since we started training. Is that true?"

Peter didn't say anything.

Disciple let out a short quick breath and shook his head. "I'll assume that your silence means you've not been truthful about that."

Peter hesitated and then walked over to his belongings and pulled out a picture. "It's my last one, and I was going to give it up soon."

Disciple took the picture and tore it up. "How did you think you could face the Black Knights of Lust when you've been letting your mind be consumed with thoughts of lust? You may as well have worn a big sign out to the battle today that said 'Please Beat Up On Me!' " Disciple shook his head. "I just don't understand."

Peter yanked off all his armor and threw it on the ground. "I didn't think this was going to work. You expect me to be perfect, and I can't be perfect." He turned and walked away.

Disciple called after him, "I don't expect you to be perfect, but I expect you to be honest, and I expect you to try. Is this what you're going to do? When things get hard are you going to quit?"

Peter kept walking until he was out of sight. Disciple wasn't sure what to do. He set up his tent, and then read in his Book and prayed. He wondered if he had been too hard on him. But Peter had to start taking things more seriously, or he was going to end up right back at the Camp of Sin again.

Disciple realized this was another reason it had been much easier to remain alone. Relationships could get messy. But then he remembered what Pastor Sinclair said about walking with people through difficult times. As uncomfortable as this was, it was something he needed to go through and learn from.

The day passed, and the sun was beginning to set. Disciple had just started a fire when out in the distance, he saw someone lumbering toward the camp. As the person drew closer, he recognized it was Peter. He trudged into the camp and sat by the fire with Disciple. Neither of them said anything for several minutes.

Peter threw a small stick in the fire. "When I left here, I didn't know where I was going, and I didn't care."

Disciple stared toward the fire. "Why did you come back?"

Peter leaned against a stump. "Once I had traveled for a few hours, I saw a group of people that reminded me of my friends back home, so I joined them for a little while. They offered me something to drink, but I didn't take it. I made up an excuse. While I was there, they kept drinking more and more, and it was the first time I had been around a group of people getting drunk when I was still sober. I saw all the dumb things they said and did, and I saw how they all thought it was so funny. As I kept watching and listening, I realized this was the lifestyle Jesus delivered me from. I saw that giving into sin was an insult to all that God has done for me, so I left and started back."

Disciple took a deep breath and turned toward Peter. "I'm glad you came back. If you're ready to become more serious, then I'm ready to do whatever it takes to help you, but there's one thing you need to know. If you ever walk off and leave again, I won't be here when you get back."

Peter looked over at Disciple and nodded. "I'm ready to work hard. When we were back at Gaius' House of Instruction, I thought I was doing fine and didn't need to focus as hard as you wanted me to. I figured you were being extra demanding, but now that I've been in battle, I see you were trying to prepare me for what was ahead. Today was the first time I think I've been in a battle. All of the other times, I just gave in before a battle even started."

Disciple put another piece of wood on the fire. "Once you set yourself to make progress against your flesh, there's always going to be a struggle. Sin is like a river flowing downstream. As long as you're moving with the current, you don't realize how strong it is, but once you start to swim upstream, you find out just how strong that current is."

Peter looked back toward the field where the battle had taken place. "So what do we do now? Earlier today was a disaster."

Disciple reached into his satchel for his Book. "We get ready. God has brought you this way for a reason. He wants you to face these Black Knights as your first test. We have a few hours to read and study."

Peter agreed, and they spent the next few hours studying and memorizing words from their Books.

As they were finishing up for the night, Peter set his Book down and turned to Disciple. "There was something else that caused me a problem when facing the Black Knights. The moment I saw those pictures, I felt guilty and defeated."

Disciple nodded. "Something we all have to learn is that there's a difference between the temptation to sin and sin itself. Temptation by itself is not a sin. The world, our flesh, and the devil can present pictures of things that might tempt our minds. What makes it sin, is when we begin to interact with those pictures. Everyone gets tempted. Jesus was tempted. Satan presented ideas and pictures to Jesus of different types of enticements, but Jesus gave no place to them and immediately answered these temptations with words from this Book."

Disciple read out loud where Jesus was led into the wilderness by the Holy Spirit to be tempted by the devil.

He then looked back up at Peter. "When pictures are presented to our minds, we are to immediately fight them off with God's word and not interact with them. One major difference between Jesus and us is that He did not have a sinful flesh, so there was nothing in Him that desired what He was being tempted with. On the other hand, we do have the flesh that wants to interact with temptations as soon as they are offered to us. So if we are presented with a picture, and we do nothing to fight it off, then our flesh is going to latch onto it and begin interacting with it. It's at this point that temptation turns into sin."

Peter said, "I need to remind myself of this often. As soon as I see a picture of sin in my mind, I feel I've already sinned. Then once I feel defeated, it seems I don't even try to fight."

"That's something we all have to remind ourselves of," said Disciple nodding. "Satan will first present sin to our minds, and then immediately try to beat us up for it. Sometimes the guilt from being tempted is more successful than the temptation itself."

"Another problem I have," said Peter, "is that I don't think I take sin serious enough when it's just in my mind."

Disciple pointed to his head. "The battle against sin is won and lost in our minds. A person that is surrendering to sin in their thoughts will soon surrender to that same sin in their actions. God's word says that those who think according to the flesh, live according to the flesh, and those who think according to the Spirit, then live according to the Spirit."

"That makes sense," said Peter, "because whenever I've given into sin, I've always been thinking about it first."

Disciple clasped his hands together and leaned forward. "That's why we have to be vigilant in the very first moments of temptation. We must fight aggressively against allowing sin to have any space in our thoughts. We must not tolerate it for a moment. We must fight these thoughts of sin as if they're coming to take our very life away. Remember that one of our primary verses against the lust of the flesh is, 'Beloved, I plead with you as foreigners and pilgrims, to refuse to give into fleshly lusts, which wage war against your soul.' "

Peter said, "Thoughts of lust start out feeling really pleasant, but now I understand why I feel as if I was run over by a horse afterward."

Disciple nodded. "That's right. Lust or any other sin seduces us by promising pleasure, but what it's really doing is making us numb, so we don't feel the damage it's causing until it's through beating on us."

Disciple and Peter talked for a little longer and then settled in to get some rest. Peter spent time meditating on all the verses he had memorized as he lay down to sleep. The morning came, and after a quick breakfast of berries and nuts, Disciple tried to prepare Peter for what today's battle was going to be like.

Peter lowered his head. "I don't know if I'm ready."

Disciple put his hands on the side of Peter's shoulders. "That's the best thing you could say. We're never ready. It is only through the grace and strength of God that we can triumph."

Disciple and Peter prayed together, and then Disciple watched as Peter trekked toward the area where the battle took place the day before. He hadn't gone far until the sound of clanging metal echoed nearby. The Black Knights rushed toward Peter, as once again pictures enticing him to lust were flashing on the front of their armor. This time Peter was determined not to allow his mind to fixate on the pictures. He took out his Sword and quoted the verses he had memorized. It wasn't a perfect quote, but it was close.

Several Black Knights charged at Peter, attempting to overwhelm him before he could get any momentum. As the enemy approached, Peter dug in the ground with his Shoes and leaned forward with his Shield. When the knight's spears crashed into his Shield, his whole body vibrated from the collision. There were so many of them, and the pressure seemed so strong that Peter felt the urge to lie down and quit.

He lifted his eyes toward heaven, as he strained to hold off his enemies. "The Lord God alone is my rock and my salvation. He is my strong defense. I shall not be moved."

Peter felt a surge of energy and thrust his Shield outward, knocking several of the Black Knights backwards. Two knights charged him from different directions, and just as they were upon him, he stepped back so that they crashed into one another. He then slammed his Shield into one and slashed the other with his Sword.

Three fierce Knights rushed him all at once with one to his left, one in front, and one to the right. Peter thrust his Shield into the one on the left, and then quickly pierced the one in front with his Sword. At the same time, he kicked the one to the right, knocking out all three.

Peter kept battling, and even though he went down to one knee a few times, he was never knocked on his back. The battle lasted over two hours, and when Peter cleared away all the Black Knights, he collapsed in exhaustion. Disciple hurried out to him and helped him back to the tent. When Peter had recovered, they spent more time reading and memorizing from their Books. The next day was much like the day before, but Peter was doing better.

Over the next few days, the battles persisted, but Peter continued to grow stronger. When the fifth day of battle arrived, Peter marched out to the battlefield with a determined look on his face. He was tired of sin prevailing in his thoughts, and he was ready to do whatever it took to take back control of his mind. The first wave of Black Knights came pouring over the hill, but this time Peter did not wait until they got closer.

Charging toward the Black Knights, he shouted, "How shall we who are dead to sin live any longer under its domination!"

Peter took aim at the closest knight and pierced it straight through its chest. "Therefore I will no longer serve the old nature which is corrupt according to sinful lusts, but I will be renewed in the spirit of my mind."

With the knight still attached to his Sword, Peter swung it up into the air. When the knight crashed to the ground, it shattered into pieces and disappeared.

Fifteen Black Knights surrounded him, but he did not lose his poise. He spun around, striking out at the knights to keep them at a distance.

As some moved closer, Peter forcefully swung his Sword. "I will fix my thoughts on things that are true…"

He knocked out two knights with one blow, and then took aim at two more. "I will fix my thoughts on things that are honorable…"

Peter knocked three to the ground with his Sword and then slammed his Shield into the heads of two more. "Whatever things are righteous and pure…"

He drew back his Sword and prepared to strike again. "Whatever comes from love and is of a good report, if there is anything that is virtuous and deserving to be praised, it is these things that I will think on!"

Peter swung his Sword so hard that he sliced five knights in half. As their bodies bounced to the ground, they instantly disappeared.

God's word was taking root in Peter's thoughts and giving extra strength to his Sword, enabling him to clear out all the Black Knights that had tried to surround him. A few more tried to attack, but they were no match for Peter any longer.

The last knight came charging toward him at full speed.

As it got close, Peter wound up with his Sword. "I will consider myself to be dead to sin, but alive to God through Christ Jesus my Lord!" He then struck the knight so hard that it went flying into a tree and instantly disappeared. Peter had defeated all the Black Knights.

Disciple ran up to Peter and smiled. "Congratulations on your first victory! No matter how tough things became, you didn't quit."

Peter let out a sigh of relief. "Thanks. This has been a tough few days, but it feels good to have persevered."

Disciple nodded and patted him on the shoulder. "You've discovered that when you stand up against sin with the power of God's word, while relying on the Holy Spirit, sin cannot dominate you. It's not going to be a perfect victory every day, and it's not always going to look pretty, but when we walk by the Spirit, we will not give into the lusts of the flesh."

Disciple and Peter packed up their camp and followed their path. Peter was excited about his victory over the Black Knights of Lust, but he understood that in order to keep this victory, he could not allow thoughts of lust to dominate his mind again.

Disciple and Peter talked and laughed as they traveled, but Disciple knew that even more difficult challenges lay ahead.

25

PETER BATTLES THE GIANT

For the next few weeks, things were quiet, and Disciple and Peter were able to spend a significant amount of time studying and discussing things together. As they were traveling one day, Disciple noticed that their path joined a dirt road that appeared to be well traveled. As they went further, Disciple recognized where they were at, seeing a sign he remembered all too well.

The sign read, "All those on this Quest must defeat the Giant of Shame and enter the River of Healing. Once you do, the Giant must let you come back and forth as you wish, but you must first bring him to his knees."

Disciple knew Peter was in for a tough battle. Before they went further, he told him the strategy the Giant would use, and how to defeat him. Having conquered the Black Knights, Peter felt confident he was ready to face this enemy as well. Soon they reached the area where the people were waiting to face the Giant of Shame.

A young man had just stepped up to battle the Giant. As Peter watched the Giant of Shame mercilessly taunting the young man, he became angry. When the young man tried to fight the Giant, he was beaten back quickly and then mocked. Peter felt it was time someone taught this enemy a lesson, so he marched toward the Giant of Shame.

Disciple called out to Peter. "Remember, be humble."

As Peter drew closer, the Giant of Shame started laughing. He didn't say anything, but he just kept laughing. Peter was confused and

189

frustrated.

Finally, Peter said, "What are you laughing at?"

"Why, I'm laughing at you of course." The Giant then laughed some more.

Peter's anger grew, and he raised his Sword. "What are you laughing about?"

The Giant of Shame smiled at Peter. "I can't believe you're even trying to face me. You've been a complete mess since you started your Quest. You've only won one battle, and that's because you had a lot of help. I see they've even had to assign you a babysitter, so you don't make an even bigger mess of your life."

Peter was now enraged, and he rushed toward the Giant with all his strength, trying to strike him with his Sword. But the Giant grabbed him by the hair and pushed his head down. Peter kept swinging his Sword back and forth, but his blows found only air. Then the Giant of Shame turned him around and swatted him on the backside with his club, sending Peter tumbling toward the ones who had been watching on the side. Peter crawled over to where Disciple was sitting and put his head down in his hands.

Disciple sat quietly for a few minutes. At last, he said. "What happened?"

Peter kept his head in his hands, shaking it side to side. Disciple saw this wasn't going to get done in a day, so he started to set up camp. Peter helped but continued to be silent. As evening drew near, Disciple built a fire and took out his Book to read. When others learned that he had already defeated the Giant of Shame, they came to ask him questions about how he did it.

Disciple taught those who were gathered around the strategy for defeating shame. They all listened intently, vowing to go back and study more in their Books before challenging the Giant again.

When the others left, Peter came out of his tent and sat by the fire. "Why do you think he was able to get to me so easily?"

Disciple pointed toward the Giant. "He knows your greatest weakness. He knows that you still want to prove that you're better than what you have shown thus far on your Quest. What you must realize is you're not any better at all. You're just as messed up now as you were when you were in the Camp of Sin."

Peter looked confused. "What do you mean? I'm doing much

better now than I was then."

"You're *doing* better, but it's not because you *are* better. When have you made progress since we started this time together?"

Peter thought for a moment. "I guess it's when I realized I needed help and reached out for God's grace."

Disciple held up his index finger. "That's right. We all start on this Quest calling out for grace because we realize we aren't able to pay our own debt. It's too big, and we are utterly incapable. Then as we go along, we think it now depends on us. That's not true. We need that same grace each and every moment. We are what we are by the grace of God, and anything good that we do is God working through us. Our job is to get out of the way."

Peter thought this over, reviewing his times of failure. "So I've always been my own worst problem?"

Disciple nodded. "Yes, that's true of all of us. We all want to prove that there's something good in us. It's a tough thing to admit that we're the problem. We have been crucified with Christ and identified with His death, so that it is no longer we that live but Christ who lives in us. And the life that we now live, we live by putting our faith and trust in the Son of God, who loved us and gave Himself for us."

"I have a lot to think about tonight," said Peter.

Disciple fixed the fire while Peter spent a little more time reading. After that, they lay down to go to sleep. As Peter was drifting off, he continued to meditate on what he had learned.

When the morning came, Disciple noticed there was someone else who was teaching others how to defeat the Giant of Shame. He walked up to the young woman. "My name is Disciple."

She introduced herself as Elizabeth.

Disciple said, "How long have you been here teaching others?"

Elizabeth looked around at all those waiting to fight the Giant. "I've been here about two months. A very nice woman named Overcomer was helping us to learn how to defeat the Giant of Shame. After I won my battle, Overcomer saw that her path was to continue on, but I felt I should stay and continue what she started. I'm sure one day I'll leave too, but for now, I'm glad that God is using me here. Will you be staying and teaching others as well?"

Disciple shook his head. "I don't think so. I'm accompanying a young man on his journey, and I believe that once he has defeated this enemy, we'll be moving on."

Elizabeth thought about the impact Overcomer had on her life. "Being a mentor to someone is a great thing. We all need someone to help us at times."

"Yes," said Disciple, "I've had many people come into my life to help me along the way."

Elizabeth said, "I'm glad I was able to meet you. It will be nice to have you here, even if it's just for a day. There are so many who need help overcoming their shame."

After shaking hands, Disciple and Elizabeth both continued to talk to those who were waiting to fight the Giant. After his conversation with Elizabeth, Disciple thought about his role as a mentor in Peter's life. For the first time since he had started this new role, Disciple realized what God was doing with him right now. He'd had many mentors, like Caleb, Pastor Sinclair, Teacher, and others who helped train him along the way. Now God was asking him to play that same role in someone else's life.

The Holy Spirit brought to Disciple's remembrance the passage in his Book where the Apostle Paul wrote to Timothy. "And the things which you have learned from me in the presence of many witnesses, present these to faithful men so that they may be able to teach others also." Paul spent time pouring into Timothy's life, and Paul wanted Timothy to pour into other's lives as well.

Disciple returned to Peter and sat down. "Do you think you're ready to face the Giant again?"

Peter stopped reading and looked up. "No, I think I need at least another day to get ready."

Disciple patted Peter on the back. "Keep studying, and as you do, listen to the Holy Spirit while you're reading. He'll cause you to understand more than what seems to be on the surface. There are many layers of wisdom in God's word."

Peter looked down at his Book. "I'm starting to discover that."

Disciple stood up. "I'm going to go talk to some others, and when I come back, we'll discuss what you've read."

Peter nodded and went back to reading. Disciple walked off, asking God to lead him to those who needed help. As he ambled through the cluster of people, he saw a group of young men standing in a circle engaged in serious conversation.

One young man whose name was Jacob said, "I've never felt good enough for God. I'm so thankful He saved me, and even if I never defeat this Giant, my life is still better than what it was before I started this Quest."

Disciple approached the group and introduced himself then turned to Jacob. "I overheard what you said, and I'm curious as to why you don't feel like you're good enough for God? What do you think would make you good enough?"

Jacob lowered his gaze and shook his head. "If I could just get to where I was more consistent and living in victory, then I would feel worthy."

"What do you feel has kept you from being consistent?" asked Disciple.

Jacob shrugged. "It seems like whenever I start to do better, I commit some kind of sin, and then I feel terrible. After that, I don't want to read my Book, because I don't feel worthy to read in it. I don't want to pray because I feel I've disappointed God. Then after a few days, I desperately want to feel close to God again, so I start reading and praying, only to have the cycle repeat itself."

Disciple noticed that the rest of the group was nodding as if they had the same experience.

Looking intently at Jacob and the others, Disciple said, "Do you all realize that you're not any more right with God on your worst day than you are on your best day?"

Jacob gave Disciple a puzzled look. "What do you mean? That can't be so. God hates sin. How could He look on us the same way when we've committed sin, as when we've been faithfully living for Him?"

Disciple said, "The reason you're having a hard time finding a solution is because you don't understand your problem. You're trying to achieve something that's impossible. Here in this Book, it says, 'If we claim that we have no sin, we deceive ourselves, and the truth has no place in us.' We constantly have sin in us because we are sinful. We are not sinful because we commit sins, but we commit sins because we are sinful. Even on your best day you are still unworthy and fall short."

Seeing that Jacob and the others were trying to grasp what he was saying, Disciple said, "Here's what I want all of you to do. Close your eyes and imagine what you think a perfect day would look like."

Disciple waited a minute and then continued. "Now, I want you to think of yourself approaching God based on how you've done on your perfect day, and then I want you to see yourself being rejected."

He could see from the expression on their faces that some of them were starting to understand. "You see, even if you could live what you would consider a perfect day, it would still not be good enough. You stand before God as completely holy and without blame because of what Christ did. It has nothing to do with you."

Jacob looked around at the others in the group. "Then do our actions matter? Are we wrong for wanting to do better?"

Disciple quickly shook his head. "No, you're not wrong. We should all want to see improvement in our lives, but the question is why do you want to do better? If you want to do better for the sake of making up for your guilt and shame, then all you're going to do is add more guilt and shame, because it will never be good enough. You have to see that your acceptance with God is based on the finished work of Christ. Put your faith and trust in that. Instead of working to feel approved, you work because you are approved."

All those who had been listening decided that they were going to spend the rest of the evening studying in their Books together. They planned to be ready to fight the Giant of Shame the next day.

Disciple went back to check on Peter. He thought to himself that another reason God placed him on his current path was so he could go back over some of the same ground, teaching others who were going through the same things.

Disciple reached their camp and sat down. "How's it been going?"

Peter smiled and pointed toward his Book. "I feel as if I finally understand this. Since I began my Quest, I've been focused on me and what I could do. Now I realize it's all about Christ in me. I've been used to people admiring me because of my strengths, and I didn't realize how much I was relying on their approval. I read where Paul said that he had a lot of things he could take pride in. At one point he was a zealous Pharisee, exceeding many of those of his own race and age. And as far as the outward standards of the law, he was considered blameless. Paul was a star in the religious world, but he counted all those accomplishments as mere trash. He wanted nothing to do with a righteousness that he could help achieve, but he only wanted the righteousness that is found through faith in Christ."

Disciple smiled. Peter was reading and understanding things for himself. He was getting into his Book, and as he did, the Holy Spirit was teaching him.

"I feel you'll be ready to face the Giant of Shame tomorrow."

"I hope so," said Peter. "I'm going to try."

After others stopped by to ask questions, Disciple and Peter continued to talk through the rest of the evening. At last, they lay down to go to sleep.

When the next day arrived, anticipation could be felt all through the camp. Several people planned to battle the Giant that day, but no one wanted to be the first one. Then Peter stepped forward and headed toward the Giant of Shame. The Giant looked at him and started laughing again. This time though Peter stood before his adversary unfazed.

The Giant realized laughing was not having the same effect on Peter. "So I see you've tried to prepare for your battle against me today. Do you really think you're ready? Do you know how few ever get by me? Much better men than you have tried and failed."

Peter looked over to the side, and Disciple nodded confidently toward him.

The Giant stomped his foot. "Everyone thinks you're a walking disaster, but they won't tell you to your face. They smile when they talk to you, but laugh as soon as you walk away."

Was this true, Peter thought? Had it always been true? He always feared that as fake as he had been in trying to keep up his image, others were just as fake in making him think he had succeeded. The Holy Spirit reminded Peter that Jesus was to be his example in humility. Jesus did not hold on to all the outward privileges of being God, but he emptied Himself and became like a man. Jesus did not care what others thought. He came to the earth to do the will of the Father.

The Giant stomped his foot again. "What happens when Disciple stops holding your hand? You and I both know you'll head straight back to the Camp of Sin. Michael says he misses you as his drinking buddy, but he's saved a special tent just for you because he knows you'll be there soon."

Normally, Peter would have crumbled under this kind of accusation, but he realized this wasn't about him. He looked down at his Breastplate and was reminded of Whose righteousness it symbolized. It was the righteousness of Christ. His righteousness was Jesus Himself.

The Giant of Shame then said, "You cannot fight me. You will never be good enough."

Peter raised his Book until it became a Sword. "You're right. I'll never be good enough, but I don't come at you today based on my goodness but on the Goodness of Jesus Christ. He is the LORD our Righteousness!"

Running straight up to the Giant, Peter struck a blow into his gut. The Giant staggered, but after regaining his footing, he lifted his club above his head and brought it down with force in an attempt to crush Peter's skull. Peter saw it coming and rolled out of the way.

As the Giant tried to hit him while he was still on the ground, Peter held out his Shield. "It is no longer I that lives, but Christ in me!" The Giant's club bounced off Peter's Shield.

After blocking another blow, Peter jumped to his feet and struck the Giant on the left shoulder with his Sword. The Giant of Shame yelled out in pain and swung wildly at Peter's legs, trying to knock him off his feet. Peter jumped, as the massive club swept underneath him.

Moving to his right, Peter pulled his Sword back as far as he could. "I will not trust in any righteousness I can achieve, but I will only trust in the righteousness that is by faith in Christ."

Peter then connected with a blow to the Giant's right leg knocking him down to one knee. The Giant tried to recover, but Peter quickly landed a strike on his right shoulder.

He shouted at the Giant of Shame, "I am not perfect, but there is one thing that I do. Forgetting those things which are in the past, I press forward to the things which are ahead, to the high calling of God in Christ Jesus."

With one knee already on the ground, the Giant desperately tried to get back on his feet, but Peter was determined to finish him. Peter dodged a last futile blow and positioned himself directly in front of his adversary.

Peter raised his Sword above his head. "Not by MY might, and not by MY power, but by the power of YOUR Spirit, Oh Lord God Almighty!"

Peter then brought his Sword down on top of the Giant's head, bringing him to his knees.

Looking toward heaven, Peter raised his Sword high in the air and shouted, "Glory to God!"

Disciple raced over and grabbed Peter's arm. "Congratulations!"

All those who had watched the battle stood up in recognition of Peter's triumph over the Giant. Disciple and Peter walked toward the River of Healing together. Once in the water, Peter closed his eyes and lifted his hands toward heaven in thanks to God who gave him the victory. He relaxed into the water as it flowed all around him, washing away the residue of guilt and shame.

Disciple held out his hand to Peter. "That was a great battle."

Peter shook Disciple's hand. "Thank you for being patient with me, and thank you for helping me to see my weaknesses."

"I know it's been a tough few days, but you kept pressing forward and didn't quit," said Disciple. "And I'm even more proud of the fact that you learned to listen to the Holy Spirit as you read your Book. The ability to read and understand God's word is the key to any victory over our enemies."

Excitement radiated through the camp, as others prepared to fight the Giant of Shame. One after another, those who had been in the group with Jacob the day before rose up and won their victory. Also, several who Elizabeth had taught also defeated the Giant. It was a joyous day.

Disciple and Peter approached Jacob and those with him and congratulated them as well.

"Thanks," said Jacob as he splashed some water on his face. "After we spoke to you yesterday, I think we all started to understand better what our problem was."

Disciple smiled. "I'm glad I could be of help. So where are you all heading now?"

Jacob glanced around at the other guys. "We attend a House of Knowledge, so we're heading back there."

"What's a House of Knowledge," asked Disciple.

"It's a place where you can be taught God's word along with other subjects and earn a degree," answered Jacob. He paused for a moment then said, "Hey, why don't you guys come back there and visit with us. It looks like your paths are heading in the same direction as ours."

Disciple glanced at Peter. "Sure, sounds like a great idea."

They visited with Jacob and his friends at their House of Knowledge for two days. It was a great time of fellowship, and when they were ready to leave, Disciple encouraged Jacob and the others to continue studying and praying together. Disciple and Peter said goodbye and then started back on their path.

26

INSTRUCTION IN RIGHTEOUSNESS

As they were walking along, Peter said, "I've noticed that the words from my Book are having much more of an impact on me now than they did in the past. I and others used to talk about how we were always encouraged to read in our Books, but it didn't seem to help us in our struggles."

Disciple stopped and opened up his Book. "Reading is not enough. We're told that we should meditate on the words in this Book day and night. We should commit them to memory and think about them throughout the day."

Peter put his hand to his chin. "Yes, that makes a lot of sense. In the past, I would read in my Book, but afterward, I would let my mind wander onto anything my flesh wanted to think about. Since battling with the Black Knights, I've been fighting to keep God's word in my thoughts instead of thoughts of sin."

Disciple turned the pages in his Book. "In the parable of the sower, the words of God are compared to seed. When we meditate and study on these words, they are planted within us, and then sprout up to produce fruit. James wrote, 'For this reason, put aside all uncleanness and abundance of evil, and in humility receive the implanted word, which is able to transform and save your souls.' We must receive God's words into our hearts with humility so that these words go beyond just our intellects. Once the words of God take root in our souls, they work changes in our lives so that we bear fruit for Him."

Peter said, "I remember once in a House of Instruction we were taught we should be doers of the words of this Book and not hearers only. I honestly tried to be a doer, but I couldn't seem to do it consistently."

Disciple pointed to his Book. "In the same place where it says we are to be doers and not hearers only, it goes further and tells us how to become a doer. The difference is that a doer continues to look into the words of this Book and keeps these words before his eyes, meditating continuously on them in his thoughts. Remember, these words are like seeds, and it's the seeds that produce the fruit."

Peter responded, "For the first time, I've seen real consistent changes in my conduct. I've learned that you can't play with sin while trying to obey God, and you can't obey God without His grace."

Disciple closed his Book and nodded. "Yes, learning that alone will cause someone to make much more progress on this Quest."

They returned to their journey and eventually arrived at another House of Instruction. A sign out front asked for help with repairs on the roof and around the building. Disciple thought they'd enjoy helping out with a project like this, and since they were getting low on supplies, it would be an opportunity to earn some money.

They spent the next three days replacing roof tiles, hammering loose boards in place, and painting walls. At the same time, they got to know many of the members who attended that House of Instruction. Most were elderly and very much appreciated the work being done to restore their place of worship. After finishing the repairs, they stayed one more day, as everyone gathered to hear the preaching of God's word. The singing was lively and vibrant, while the preaching was uplifting and encouraging.

At the end of the service, the leader asked Disciple and Peter to stand in recognition of their work on the building. Afterward, they shared a meal with some of the members then prepared to travel on. As they were leaving, one elderly couple gave them a little extra money in appreciation for their hard work.

On their way, Disciple and Peter talked about how nice it was to be able to help those in need while earning extra provision.

After they traveled for two hours, Disciple thought he recognized the surrounding area. Within a few minutes, he saw that they were near Teacher's house.

Disciple stopped. "There's someone I would like for you to meet. I hope he's home. He travels a lot, but when he's here, he takes people in, helping them understand many things about the Book. His name is Teacher."

"That sounds great," said Peter.

When they came to the house, Disciple walked up to the front door and knocked. They waited a minute, and then as they were about to leave Teacher opened the door.

"Hello! It's so nice to see you again Disciple, and I see you brought someone with you."

"Yes, this is Peter. We were traveling this way, and I recognized that we were going right by your house."

Teacher stepped to the side and motioned for them to come in. "Please do come inside. I can't wait to hear about all your adventures."

Disciple and Peter stepped into the house. Peter surveyed the majestic paintings lining the walls and the beautiful mural on the ceiling. After a few minutes, Teacher led them to a long table with tall chairs. They sat and spent hours talking about all that happened since the last time Disciple was there.

When the conversation tailed off, Disciple stood, and strolled around, remembering all the things he had seen the last time he was here. "I've told Peter about all the wonderful things you're able to show people to help us understand more about the Book. Do you have time to share some of these things with us now?"

"Yes, yes I do have a few days before I must travel again." Teacher stood up from the table. "The first thing I'd like to show you is something new. Let's go to the field that's just outside the house."

Teacher led Disciple and Peter to a nearby field that looked like it had been freshly cleared. On each side of the field, the ground sloped upward, making it look as if it was in the middle of a valley.

Teacher put his hand on Peter's back and pointed toward the center. "Watch this."

Peter saw an image of himself coming out onto the middle of the field as if he was about to compete in an athletic event. "This reminds me of the days when I was an athlete in my hometown. I always felt as if I was a mighty warrior stepping onto the field of battle."

Teacher nodded. "Continue watching."

The sloping sides began to fill with people who were booing Peter and yelling insults at him.

Peter said, "That was what it was like to compete in another town. They treated me and the other members of our team as if we were enemies."

Teacher held out his hand toward the field. "While we're on this Quest, it's as if we're always competing in hostile territory. Jesus told His disciples that if they were of this world, then the world would love them, but because they were not of this world, that was why the world hated them."

Peter continued watching, as the crowd yelled and called him names. "That's part of what makes this Quest hard for me. I don't like being booed. We're called intolerant if we don't accept sinful behaviors. We're labeled as judgmental if we take a stand for what this Book teaches, and we're called narrow-minded if we hold to it as the very words of God."

Teacher nodded, as he looked toward the field. "Yes, all of that is true, and that's part of the suffering we're called to go through during this time of our Quest. We'll never be popular with the world. Jesus never was, and we won't be either. But there is something more that I want you to see in this picture. Look above the field, and look above where all the people are cursing and screaming."

Peter shifted his gaze to the air above the field. A great number of people appeared, whose faces shone like the sun, and each was clothed in beautiful white robes. Angels were among them, blowing their trumpets, while these white-robed individuals cheered for Peter. As Peter watched his image down on the field, a change took place. Earlier he appeared slumped over and saddened by the reaction of the crowd. But now, with the appearance of these new people in the air surrounding him, he stood up tall, marching with confidence around the field.

Teacher smiled as he gazed up into the air. "God's word says we are surrounded by a great cloud of witnesses. The world will never praise us, but there is an invisible cheering section that surrounds us and applauds as we move forward on our Quest. Rather than watering down what we believe to try and soften the boos from this world, we should press onward and upward, seeing the approval of those we will be with for eternity."

"I see," said Peter. "I've been focused on the approval of those who are destined to perish, and I haven't realized that what really matters is the view of those with whom we will spend eternity, and especially God."

Disciple stepped forward, looking at the great crowd of onlookers in the air. "It's easy to get caught up in how the world sees us, forgetting that we are just traveling through on our way to our ultimate destination. Someday we'll travel on a new earth, where things will be very different than they are now."

Teacher turned back toward his house. "Yes, that will be a glorious time. The hardships we go through now are nothing compared to the glory we will experience during the billions of billions of years of eternity. Every moment we spend battling sin and living for God will be worth it."

Teacher led them back to the house, where he spent the next two days showing Peter all the things he had shown Disciple when he was there. He showed him the lion that was seizing the sheep, reminding him that people aren't aware of how strong sin is until they start to fight it.

Peter then learned a valuable lesson, as he observed the soldiers on the roof battling sin. He paid careful attention to the first soldier who kept the ground saturated with God's word. This caused Peter to understand even more why he should keep his mind full of thoughts of the Book as a barrier against sin. Teacher helped him understand that actions start as thoughts, and if he could defeat sins while they were still thoughts, then they wouldn't become actions.

As Teacher led them downstairs, Peter said, "I saw how hard the first soldier was working to defeat sin, but when the others continued to fall under attack, why didn't they change their tactics?"

Teacher replied, "Some eventually do learn, but sometimes it takes getting beat up many times before someone will change."

Teacher then showed Peter the room where the man wrote down all of his sins in a book, and Peter saw an image of himself at the Hill of Calvary. He witnessed all the words representing his sin being lifted out of the book and onto Jesus as He was on the cross. Peter also saw where the record of Christ's perfection was then written in the same book. Then he saw the most wonderful thing of all. Jesus handed the book to the Father, and the Father looked at the book and motioned for Peter to come forward.

Peter whispered, "I understand much better now how God can accept me even though I'm still sinful. God does not see my record of sin, but He sees Christ's record instead. I am counted as righteous because of Christ."

Teacher picked up the book and handed it to Peter. "Keep this on the inside of your Breastplate and always remember it is Christ's righteousness that has been applied to you."

When Teacher was finished showing them all these things, he invited them to stay for one more day. The next morning they all had breakfast together and talked about what they had seen the previous two days.

When they were finishing up, Teacher turned to Peter. "The reason I asked you to stay one more day is that I feel there is something else I can show you that will be of benefit to you."

"I would be grateful for anything you can show me to help me on my Quest," said Peter.

Teacher settled back in his chair. "As we've been talking these last couple of days, you mentioned that your biggest battle has been with pride. I want to help you understand how this played a part in your being attracted to the Camp of Religion, and how it can trip you up in the future. Later today I'm going to take you to Mount Sinai. Your sinful flesh will experience a strong pull from this mountain, and I want you to understand why."

Disciple turned to Peter. "Yes, Mount Sinai will draw you to it. You think you can climb it, but your efforts are worthless."

Leaning forward, Teacher said, "There's a legalist in all of us that wants to achieve right standing with God based on our own efforts."

"Why is that?" asked Peter.

Teacher sat back and sighed. "Because we know that we fall short of what God expects, and we want to do something about it."

"But that's why Jesus came to this earth and died for us," said Peter.

Teacher nodded and folded his hands. "True, but our old nature drives us to try and achieve right standing with God based on our works."

He pushed his chair away from the table. "Let's all go into that room over there where you see the light shining under the door. When we come back out, we'll talk some more."

Teacher led them over to the room next to the bookcase. Once inside they saw a man with a scruffy beard and tattered clothes digging at the dirt walls looking for gold. It seemed the man had been working a long time because the room looked like the inside of a mine. Sitting beside the man were a few pieces that looked like they could be gold.

Teacher leaned over and whispered, "That's all he's dug up so far."

Out to the left, was a huge pile of pure gold, which was so large that a thousand men could not have mined that much gold in a thousand years. In the back of the room was another person who looked like a strict schoolmaster. He held a long wooden rod in one hand, and with the other hand, he wrote a number on a board. Each time the other man started digging, the schoolmaster would erase the previous number and write an even bigger number.

Peter whispered to Teacher, "Can I talk to the one who is digging?"

Teacher nodded.

Peter walked over to him. "Sir, why are you doing all this, and why is that schoolmaster writing those numbers on that board?"

The disheveled man continued to dig but looked up quickly. "That number is my sin count, and I'm digging to find enough gold to make up for it. But it seems like the more I dig, the higher that number goes, so I have to keep working even harder."

Peter pointed to the other side of the room. "But look over there at that huge pile of gold. It has to be enough to pay the sin count for anyone who has ever lived. Why don't you just use that?"

The man stuck his nose into the air, as he continued to dig. "I don't believe in charity. I earn my own way."

Teacher then whispered for them to leave, so they went back out and sat down.

Peter stared anxiously at Teacher. "Please tell me more about what we just saw."

Teacher settled into his chair. "The man digging represents legalism. Legalism insists on working to make up for sins and looks down on anyone who relies on grace. The schoolmaster represents the Law. The more you try to follow it in order to make up for your sin the more in debt you become."

"Why is that?" asked Peter.

Teacher read from his Book. "For whoever tries to keep the whole Law but stumbles in just one point, has become guilty of breaking all of it."

Teacher looked up at Peter. "When we try to follow a set of rules to feel right with God, we always end up committing more sin because even the good things we do aren't perfect. Some catch on and turn to grace, but others keep trying harder, and this eventually leads them to the Camp of Religion."

Peter said, "I heard those at the Camp of Religion say Jesus was quite clear that if we loved Him, we would prove it by obeying His commandments."

Teacher then turned in his Book and read the portion in the Gospel of John where Jesus taught about the Vine and the branches.

Teacher pointed to his Book. "What came first? Did the branches bear fruit first or were they first united to the vine?"

Peter held out his hand. "They had to be united to the Vine first of course."

Teacher leaned over his Book. "Further down we read that He told His disciples to abide in his love, and then He told them to keep His commandments. Keeping His commandments is the result of remaining in Him, it is not the cause. That's what the Camp of Religion twists around."

Disciple turned in his Book and read, "But whoever is keeping His word, in him the love of God has truly been perfected. This is how we know that we are in Him."

Looking up, Disciple said, "Without the love of God already having been perfected in us, we would not be able to keep His word. If we are trying to follow the commandments in order to earn God's love and approval, then it is a work of rebellion."

Peter replied, "Those at the Camp of Religion would say their way is the only way to produce results."

Teacher sat up, putting his palms flat on the table. "The Camp of Religion can teach people how to produce a lot of wood, hay, and stubble, but their way will not produce any gold, silver, or precious stones."

They continued to talk for another hour, and then Teacher suggested that it was time to leave and go to Mount Sinai.

MR. LAW KEEPER

Disciple, Peter, and Teacher traveled toward Mount Sinai, and when they reached the base, they felt the rumbling of the mountain. Peter understood how the reverberation called out to his sinful flesh, challenging him to climb the mountain.

Disciple stopped and turned toward Peter. "The pull from that mountain is strong, but I learned that only Jesus could climb it. Jesus came in the likeness of sinful flesh and did for us what we could not do for ourselves. All the righteous requirements of the law have been fulfilled by Jesus and have been placed on our account. God sees us as always having kept all of the Law perfectly because He sees us as in Christ."

Teacher smiled and patted Disciple on the back. "You've learned many things from this Book, and I know that you'll continue to teach others also."

Teacher hugged them both. "I must go back, but I know that you both will continue to make progress and do well on your Quest."

Disciple and Peter told him goodbye, and then Teacher left to return to his house. As they watched him walk away, the mountain rumbled with a loud roar. Jarred by the sudden shaking, they spun around toward Mount Sinai. Some were trying to climb the mountain only to be quickly beaten back down. Many more then tried to climb it but failed as well.

This reminded Peter of himself earlier in his Quest. He could see his stubborn pride first prodding him to keep going up the mountain, and then when he couldn't do it, this same pride prodded him to get mad and quit. But Peter knew he was at a much different place in his life now.

Disciple showed Peter the entrance to the Valley of Humility, and they both entered. Lying on the ground were all the papers with the verses on them that Disciple had eaten before, but this time there were two papers for every verse. They each read and ate all the verses they came across.

When they came out of the Valley of Humility, Peter sensed that he had a confidence that he did not have before, causing him to feel he could be successful on this Quest. It wasn't because he felt better about himself, but because he understood where his strength truly came from.

As they traveled forward, they saw a man up ahead who was shouting. He was overweight and dressed in a tight black suit that was one size too small. He had an angry look on his face, and he scowled at those who walked by.

Peter said, "I know him. People call him Mr. Law Keeper. He was one of the main leaders in the Camp of Religion. I wanted to be just like him."

As Disciple and Peter came closer, they could hear Mr. Law Keeper shouting. "You must become holy to be acceptable to God, and you must keep these rules in order to be holy."

Disciple saw that Mr. Law Keeper was giving out a list of rules, so he walked up and asked if he could have one. After receiving the list, he walked back over to show it to Peter.

Peter studied the paper. "Yes, I remember that list. Different leaders in the Camp of Religion had different lists. Sometimes the leaders would argue about whose list was better or which list was more holy."

Disciple carefully read each item on the list. "Some of the things on here are good suggestions, and I can see how they would help someone stay away from sin, but others seem to be mere opinion. What really concerns me though is the attitude that keeping a list of rules is what makes you holy and acceptable to God. Let's go talk to him about this."

Disciple marched up to Mr. Law Keeper. "May I ask you a few questions?"

Mr. Law Keeper stuck out his chest and cocked his head back. "Sure, I'd be glad to answer any questions."

Disciple pointed to the list. "Why does keeping your rules cause someone to be holy and acceptable to God?"

Mr. Law Keeper cleared his throat. "Well, keeping this list of rules shows that you're dedicated to obeying God."

"But I don't see most of these rules in my Book," said Disciple.

Mr. Law Keeper pointed his finger at him. "That's because you're not looking hard enough. Everything on this list is based on a principle from that Book."

Disciple replied, "But it would appear that you're getting into an area of opinion. Are you aware that the Pharisees had many traditions which they expected people to follow even though they were not commanded by God? Jesus told them that they were teaching the opinions of men as if they were the commandments of God, and this was wrong."

Mr. Law Keeper waved his hands in the air. "Do you not see how many there are on this Quest committing sins every day? If they kept the rules on my list, there would be less sin."

Disciple shook his head. "I don't think so. You cannot combat sin with a set of rules. Sin will just find a different way to manifest itself. A person must be changed from the inside out."

Mr. Law Keeper smirked, as he leaned forward. "You're probably one of those who talks a lot about grace. I see them all the time, and I see how much sin they commit."

Disciple raised his hand. "A true understanding of grace causes someone to commit less sin, not more."

Mr. Law Keeper held up his list of rules. "I've heard that kind of talk before. When people have left our group and stopped following our rules, most of them end up in the Camp of Sin. Clearly we were keeping them on the right track with our rules."

Disciple frowned at Mr. Law Keeper. "I don't think that proves anything. They just traded in one form of rebellion for another."

Mr. Law Keeper threw up his hands and turned away. "I don't have time for this. When you're ready to live a holy life, you have my list. Come back when you're ready to show me that you're following it. Until then I have nothing else to say."

There was a part of Disciple that wished to stay and continue the conversation, but he knew it was time for them to leave.

As they walked away, Peter glanced back at Mr. Law Keeper who continued to hand out his rules. "During my time at the Camp of Religion, I liked having a set of rules. It made things simpler, and it was a way for me to feel like I was making progress. The more rules I kept, the more approval I got."

Disciple placed his hand over his chest. "The problem though is that the heart is deceitful. We can be following rules on the outside, while our heart is still far from God. It says in this Book, 'That all the ways of a man are pure in his own eyes, but the Lord weighs the thoughts and intentions of the heart.' "

"Isn't it true though that a lot of people today have no standards at all and are doing whatever they feel is right?"

Disciple replied, "Yes, that's true. Grace should not be used as an excuse for sin, and when it is, it's not true grace that they're speaking of. True grace teaches us to refrain from sin, not to continue in it."

They walked a little further, and then Peter stopped. "Why are so many attracted to legalism?"

Disciple said, "As Teacher shared, there is a legalist in all of us because we know we fall short of God's expectations. God gave us the Law to show us that we fall short. The Law shows us what our conduct is supposed to look like so we can run to God's grace to make it happen. But rather than turning to grace, our sinful flesh would rather turn to rules, so it doesn't have to die. When God gave the Law, He wanted all of the children of Israel to come closer to Him, but they told Moses that he should go talk to God for them, and they would do whatever God said to him."

Peter had a confused look on his face. "Why didn't they want to get close to God?"

Disciple clasped his hands. "They felt that if they came close to God, they would die, so they stood afar off. It's the same way with many people today who don't want to have a direct relationship with God. They only want someone to tell them the rules, so they don't have to die to their fleshly desires. God doesn't want just our conduct – He wants all of us."

Peter said, "So you're saying that God gave us rules knowing that we couldn't follow them? Why?"

"Because," said Disciple as he held out his hand, "God wanted us to see our shortcomings so that we would turn to Him for help. The Law can show us what our problem is, but it has no power to bring about a solution. The Law shut us up into one big courtroom and declared us guilty, but it did this to point us to Christ. God knew that a set of rules could not set us free, and He spoke through the prophets that He was going to do something new."

Disciple took out his Book and read, from Jeremiah. "But this is the covenant that I will make with the house of Israel after those days, says the LORD: I will put My law in their minds, and write it on their hearts; and I will be their God, and they shall be My people."

Then Disciple read from Ezekiel. "I will give you a new heart, and I will put a new spirit within you. I will take the stony heart out of your flesh and give you a heart of flesh. I will put my Spirit within you which will cause you to walk in my commandments, and you will keep my just decrees and do them."

Disciple looked up from his Book. "The law of sin, our sinful flesh, is an inward principle, and an outward set of rules cannot defeat it. God knew it would take an even more powerful inward principle to defeat sin, and that is what He did in the New Covenant. He caused us to be born again and have a new nature that was created after His image in righteousness and true holiness. Surrendering to this new nature by the power of the Holy Spirit truly defeats sin in our lives and causes us to become holy."

Peter said, "I can see that. All that time I was trying to keep rules, my conduct may have been different, but my heart was not any better. Now that I've been surrendering to God's word in my life and relying on His grace, I've seen real change."

"Exactly!" said Disciple as he grasped Peter's shoulder. "You've been presenting all of yourself as a living and continuous sacrifice to God, which caused your conduct to be holy and acceptable to Him. By receiving His words into your heart you stopped conforming yourself to the ways of this world, and you've become transformed by the renewing of your mind."

Disciple and Peter both praised God for all His wonderful works. They desired to follow all of God's commandments, and since it was God who was working in them the desire and ability to do what was right, then He was the One who was due all the glory.

TRAIL OF DISCOURAGEMENT

Disciple and Peter spent the next four weeks traveling their path. Disciple saw much progress in Peter, and he saw a great deal of progress in himself as well. Being a mentor in someone's life was a lot of responsibility, but God was using it to teach him many things.

One day as they were walking, Disciple noticed something off their path in the distance. He peered through his telescope to see a giant rock in the shape of a cylinder, rising high into the air. Positioned on top of the rock was a large castle, with dark grey clouds hovering above.

The castle was black as coal as if it had been burned at one time by a great fire. Lightning shot out of the clouds, and thunder boomed against the castle walls. Iron bars covered each of the windows, and a prisoner with a look of dejection and misery appeared at one of the windows grasping the iron bars.

Disciple handed Peter the telescope, pointing toward the towering rock.

Peering through the telescope, Peter said, "I've never seen anything like it."

A group of travelers stopped to gaze at the curious structure.

Disciple motioned for Peter to follow him, as he approached the newcomers. "Do any of you know what this is?"

One of the members of the group named Jim said, "That's the Castle of Despair. People who have become extremely discouraged on this Quest go there and are trapped. They wander off their path and go through the muddy terrain to the base of that rock. The owners of the castle throw down a rope to pull them up, but they must leave behind their armor and their Book."

"Has anyone ever escaped?" asked Disciple.

Jim looked up at the castle. "I've seen people go there, but I've never seen anyone leave."

"Hasn't anyone ever tried to help the people in there?" Disciple asked.

Jim's eyes widened, as he shook his head. "Oh no, no one has found a way to get into the castle, unless you're willing to leave behind your armor and your Book. And if you did that, you'd be just as trapped as the ones there."

Disciple took out his telescope again, and after looking around some more, he noticed that something appeared to be hidden behind the dark grey clouds hovering above the castle.

"What's beyond those clouds?" Disciple asked, as he handed Jim his telescope.

Jim peered through the telescope and then handed it back. "That's the Mountain of Hope."

Glancing down at his path, Disciple said, "I don't know how, but I believe God is going to use me to help the people in that castle. I see that my path is leading me to that mountain behind it."

Jim nodded. "I'll pray for you. In order to get to the Mountain of Hope, you must first go up the Trail of Discouragement. That will be hard just by itself, and even if you did make it to the top of the mountain, I don't see how that helps you get to the castle."

Disciple put his telescope back in his satchel and glanced over at Peter. "I'm not sure either, but I know that's where we're supposed to go. We'll stay here tonight, and then we'll start out tomorrow."

Jim wished them well, and he and the rest of his group left.

Peter rolled out his tent and began setting it up. "I don't know how we're going to get to that castle, or even what we'll do if we're able to get there, but I know that if God is leading us in that direction, He must have a plan."

"Yes," said Disciple as he hammered in his last tent spike. "We must be patient and wait on Him to reveal that plan to us."

Disciple stood up and put his hands on Peter's shoulders. "So far,

I've watched as you fought the battles God has given you. I've been there to encourage you and pray for you, but now we'll be fighting this one together. No matter what we may face, I know I can count on you."

Peter glanced down, before looking back up at Disciple. "I can do all things through Christ because He is the one who strengthens me."

Disciple and Peter spent time reading and praying and then went to sleep. When they awoke the next morning, they thought they heard familiar voices outside their tents. They came out to find Jacob and the five others with him that they had visited after their battle with the Giant of Shame.

Disciple shook their hands. "It's so good to see all of you. What are you doing so far from your House of Knowledge?"

Jacob said, "We're on break from our classes, and we all felt we were being guided to go on an adventure. We've been traveling for several days, and today we ended up here."

Disciple handed Jacob his telescope and pointed toward the giant rock and castle on top. "We're about to embark on an adventure to assault that castle."

After looking through the telescope, Jacob handed it to one of the others. "I've never seen anything like that. It looks impossible to get up there. What's your plan?"

Disciple told them as much as he knew about the Castle of Despair, and how they planned to go to the Mountain of Hope.

Jacob motioned for the others with him to go off to the side, where they spent a few minutes talking together. Next, they looked toward the Mountain of Hope.

Jacob returned to Disciple and said, "We believe we've been brought here to accompany you on this adventure."

Disciple glanced at Peter. "It will be great having all of you join us."

Jacob set a large duffel bag on the ground and started opening it. "In our spare time, we've been working on perfecting something that might be of some help."

He then pulled out a large crossbow from the bag. The steel arrow it shot was three feet in length and attached to a long rope.

Jacob picked up the crossbow. "Watch this."

Pointing toward a large tree about a hundred yards away, Jacob aimed the crossbow about twenty feet up the tree and squeezed the trigger. The arrow shot out, taking the long rope with it before sinking into the tree. The other end of the rope lay at Jacob's feet.

Disciple asked if he could see the crossbow. "I believe we can use this in our assault on the Castle of Despair."

Jacob climbed the tree to pull out the arrow and then climbed back down. Disciple asked everyone to find a smaller piece of rope that was about three feet long and to find strong pieces of cord they could use to tie up any guards that might be inside the castle.

After packing up all their supplies, Disciple pointed to the trail at the base of the mountain. "To get to the top, we must climb the Trail of Discouragement."

They gathered together for prayer, then headed out. As they started up the trail, there was an immediate feeling of oppression. The air itself seemed to be pushing down on them, making each step more difficult. After traveling about a hundred yards, they all began to hear whistling in the trees, and then the whistling turned into whispering voices. What they would discover later was that each one heard something different. The whispering spoke to each person concerning the thing they were most insecure about.

Disciple heard, "You will fail as a leader. You will lead these people to their doom."

Peter heard, "You're not ready for this. You're going to let people down. Just quit and go back."

Jacob heard, "You're not as good as Disciple and Peter. You will only drag them down and cause them to fail."

The others heard different things as well.

After praying for God to give him wisdom, Disciple asked everyone to stop and gather around. "The whispering voices are telling me that I'm going to fail."

The others nodded and shared that the voices were saying similar things to them as well.

Disciple scanned the trees. "I perceive this whistling is the voice of Self Doubt. We must keep our focus on the Lord. He is the one who goes before us and gives us the victory."

Disciple bowed his head. "Lord, You said that You would keep us in perfect peace as our mind stays steadfast on you."

Everyone started forward again. While the whistling continued for a little longer, the voices stopped. The group marched on, and soon they began to hear sad and depressing music, which seemed to rise up out of the ground. As they listened, the tune reminded them of all the times they had failed and wanted to quit.

Disciple quickly took out his Book and read, "Why are you cast down and discouraged, Oh my soul? Why are you disturbed within me? Hope in God! For I shall still praise Him for the saving help of His presence."

He then led the others in praises to God. As they continued to worship, the disturbing music began to fade. They traveled forward wondering what was going to happen next.

Soon they saw hyenas lined up along the trail who were calling out all the foolish things each person had said and done while on their Quest. The hyenas laughed at Disciple because of all the arrogant things he said before he entered the Orchard of Vanity. They laughed at Peter because of all the dumb things he said and did while at the Camp of Sin. The hyenas reminded Jacob and those with him of the times they had been judgmental and condemning of others only to fall into sin themselves a few weeks later.

Peter turned toward Disciple. "All the things these hyenas are saying about me are true. I've done a lot of dumb and stupid things."

Disciple looked around at the others. "So have I. There were times when we thought we knew everything, but having learned from our mistakes, we should forget those things which are behind and press forward to the things which are ahead."

After traveling further, everyone began to hear the piercing sounds of deep anguish and agony. It was the type of sorrowful crying one would hear from a parent who lost their child in a tragic accident, or a spouse, who lost a husband or a wife to a terrible disease. Everyone stopped and listened. The sounds were almost unbearable because each of them was reminded of all the suffering and heartbreak that exists in the world.

One of the young men, whose name was Stephen, fell to his knees and started crying. "I can't take this! It's too much."

Everyone gathered around him, and he shared how his father died when he was a young boy. He spoke of how hard it was for his mother as well as himself and his sister.

Stephen looked up and shook his head. "I just don't understand. Why us? My father wasn't a bad person, and our family loved God."

Another young man who had come with Jacob named Jack kicked at the ground. "I think of all the horrendous suffering that's going on in the world, and I wonder where God is."

Disciple replied, "Sometimes I feel the same way, but I have to remind myself that God did not create evil or suffering. It is the result of the curse, because of man's sin. While Jesus was on the earth, He promised to leave us with His peace. Jesus didn't promise there would be perfect peace around us, but He promised to give us His peace on the inside of us."

Peter knelt beside Stephen. "I wish I could tell you something that would make sense of what happened with your father, but I can't. As Disciple said, God gives us peace to sustain us through all the hardships that come with this life. One day this part of our Quest will be over, and we'll see God face to face. At that time, things will make a lot more sense than they do now."

Everyone prayed for Stephen, and he began to slowly stand to his feet.

Stephen raised his hands toward heaven. "Lord, I don't understand why this tragedy came to our family, but I won't murmur and complain against you. I know that the things we suffer while on this earth are producing for us an eternal weight of glory which is beyond comparison. Because we do not look at the things which we can see, but to the things which we cannot see. For the things which we can see are only temporary, but the things we cannot see are eternal."

Jack knelt down and raised his hands. "Lord, forgive me for complaining. Help me to rejoice in all things, and in all things to give thanks. Even as Job said, even though you slay me, I will still trust in you."

After a few minutes everyone continued, and eventually, the sounds of wailing and crying stopped. The trail began to slope upward, while the ground became slippery, making each step all the more difficult. Everyone felt their energy being drained to the point of exhaustion.

"Let's stop for a minute," said Disciple, "and get some water."

Jack sat down and opened his canteen. "This reminds me of so many times where it feels like nothing I do is ever good enough. I fight and push to make some progress, but at the end of the day I remain disappointed with my efforts."

Disciple nodded. "I know how you feel. I have those days too. What I've learned is that when I feel that way, it's a sign that I'm still operating in my own strength and not resting in God's."

Jacob sat down and wiped the sweat from his forehead. "Sometimes the struggle is so hard that you wonder when it's finally going to end and start to get better."

Peter sat down next to them and took a drink of water from his canteen. "I know that I often have to remind myself to keep going and not quit."

Disciple pulled out his Book and read, "Let us not become weary in doing good, for we will reap in due season if we don't quit."

Everyone stood back up and persevered through the steep climb. When they were nearing the top, the trail seemed to stop, and a tall rock wall stood before them. Disciple approached the wall and discovered it was slick as glass. After everyone examined the rock, they all concluded there was no way to climb it.

Disciple looked at Jacob. "Do you think your crossbow and rope could help us get to the top of this?"

Jacob ran his hands over the rock wall, then shook his head. "No, the arrow would have to have something to attach to, and I can't see anything up there to aim at. We'll have to find a different way."

Some in the group became discouraged, wondering if they had come all this way for nothing. They all walked around the bottom of the wall searching for a way up but found none. Disciple knew though that if God had brought them here, there must be a way, so he gathered them together and prayed for wisdom.

Motioning to Peter and Jacob, Disciple marched over to the rock wall. "Give me a boost so I can get higher up."

After being lifted up, he began to feel around on the rock.

At last, he looked down and smiled. "Okay, let me go."

Peter and Jacob stared at him as if he was crazy, but he said it again, so they let him go. To their astonishment Disciple did not fall. He seemed to be hanging from something, but they couldn't see what it was.

Laughing, as he held on with one hand, and waved with the other, Disciple said, "I'm hanging onto an invisible ladder, a ladder of hope. Hope that is seen is not hope at all, but we hope in the things we cannot see because we've been promised them by God." He let go and jumped to the ground. "God didn't call us here to fail. This rock wall is a test to see who will look for a way up, or who will use it as an excuse to quit and go back."

Disciple and Peter helped boost the rest up the ladder, and then Disciple helped Peter up. Peter grabbed onto the ladder with his hands and let his legs dangle so that Disciple could grab his ankles. Peter then climbed the ladder using just his arms until Disciple could grab onto the ladder and start climbing himself.

Once everyone was up, they found themselves at the top of the Mountain of Hope. Things looked much different from the top of the mountain than they had from the Trail of Discouragement. Peering out over the mountain-side, the group could get a small glimpse of how God was moving people along their different paths, working out all things for His glory. They could see how God was using tragedy, failure, and even one's sin for the purpose of bringing people to their destinations. They marveled at the wonderful work of God and his Sovereignty.

Disciple said, "Now we must find a way to the Castle of Despair."

29

MOUNTAIN OF HOPE

Disciple studied the castle through his telescope and discovered that the roof was not being guarded. He thought the keepers of the castle probably didn't think the roof was vulnerable to attack. The castle appeared to have two levels. The top level contained all the prisoners while the ground level housed the guards. These guards resembled rhinos that were standing upright. Their bodies were covered with plated armor, and they each carried long sharp spears.

Disciple handed the telescope to Jacob. "If you shot the crossbow toward that roof, would the rope be long enough to reach it?"

After looking through the telescope, Jacob handed it back to Disciple. "It's possible, but it's going to be close. What do you have in mind?"

Disciple pointed toward the top of the castle. "We're going to create a zip line. We'll tie one end of that long rope to that tree over there and then shoot the arrow, which is attached to the other end of the rope toward the roof. We'll then each take the smaller ropes we brought, wrap them around the long rope and glide down to the castle roof."

Peter held out his hands. "It's going to be hard to maintain a grip all the way down."

Disciple knelt and pulled out a jar from his backpack. "I know. I found this grease before we left, so we'll grease up the rope, making it easier to slide down. We're going to need at least five days to get ready, so for the first three days I want all of us to begin building up our strength."

Disciple held up one of the small ropes they brought with them. "We need to place these around a tree limb, and practice pulling ourselves up several times while seeing how long we can hold our arms at a ninety-degree angle."

Each of them took out a small rope, tying a big knot at each end so they could grip it better. They swung it around a tree branch and began to try and pull themselves up. Some did better than others, but it was clear they were all going to need to build up their strength.

Peter turned to Disciple. "Even if we can pull this off and set those prisoners free, how are we going to get away?"

Disciple stepped toward the edge of the mountain and looked down at the castle. "Remember the ropes they use to pull people up? We'll use those same ropes to get down."

Disciple approached Jacob. "Take this telescope and see if you can find a place on that roof to aim your arrow."

Jacob took the telescope and walked over to the edge, while Jack started exploring the mountaintop.

Suddenly, Jack shouted, "Come here everyone!"

They discovered that Jack had found several large keys lying on the ground.

Disciple picked one up. "These must unlock the prison cells in the Castle of Despair. We'll all take as many as we can hold. If someone does not wish to be free when we get there, then we can at least give them a key, so they can use it later."

It was getting late, so Disciple suggested everyone set up the camp. When they were done, they prepared a meal and gathered around the fire.

Jacob finished roasting a piece of fish and sat down. "What is it we can say to those in the Castle of Despair to persuade them to come with us? They must have experienced a lot of hardships and problems to cause them to go to that castle. How do we convince them that things will be different if they begin their Quest again?"

Disciple took a drink of water. "That's a good question. That's why we need these days to prepare. We must come up with a strategy to defeat the guards, but we must also have a strategy to convince the prisoners to use their keys and get out. We need to be searching our Books for what God says about those trapped in despair, and about how He has given all of us hope to continue our journeys."

They spent the next three days studying the movements of the guards and doing strength exercises, including pull-ups and push-ups, to prepare their bodies. But most important of all, they spent time studying in their Books about hope, then discussing with one another what they learned.

One night Jacob said to the group, "Our instructors at the House of Knowledge talked to us about burnout. They said that leaders could take on too much, wearing themselves out physically. They said these leaders could also become worn out emotionally, by taking on God's role in people's lives. I'm sure some in the Castle of Despair were leaders on this Quest at one time."

Disciple took out his Book and read, "Come to Me, all you who labor and are heavy laden, and I will give you rest. Take My yoke upon you and learn from Me, for I am gentle and lowly in heart, and you will find rest for your souls. For My yoke is easy and My burden is light."

Disciple closed his Book and looked around at the others. "Jacob makes a good point, and it's something all of us should pay attention to. There's an endless amount of good things that need to be done on this Quest, but that doesn't mean we as individuals should try to do them all. We must find out what God has for us to do, trusting that He has others to do what we can't. Also, as we minister to others what God lays on our hearts, we must then leave the results to the Holy Spirit. We cannot assume the responsibility for the results of our teaching and preaching. If we do, we will be worn out emotionally and spiritually."

Disciple then read from his Book, "Be humbled under the mighty hand of God, so that He may exalt you in due season, having cast all your care upon Him, because He cares for you."

He tapped the page with his finger. "We cannot cast our cares upon the Lord, until we have first humbled ourselves before Him, acknowledging that He alone is able to carry our burdens."

Everyone continued to talk for another hour, and then spent the rest of the day searching their Books for verses to defeat despair.

When the next day arrived, Disciple told them not to do any more exercises so they would be rested. Later that night, they would attack the castle. Each of them had grown stronger and was ready to hang onto their ropes all the way down to the roof. Jacob had found a spot to shoot the steel arrow so it would hold firm, and the crossbow was in place.

Disciple looked over at Jacob. "Did you bring some extra Books?"

Smiling as he held up several, Jacob said, "Sure, we always do."

Disciple received three Books from Jacob and put them in his backpack. "We'll give all the prisoners a Book. The ones who use their keys to get out can convert them to Swords. They won't have armor, and they'll be rusty in the use of their Sword, but it will help."

"We'll have to think quickly once we're there. There's only so much we can see from here," said Peter.

Everyone agreed. They knew the guards went in and out from the first and second levels, but they didn't know how many guards would be waiting for them when they arrived. Contemplating the dangerous task that lay ahead, they each went about preparing what they would need for the mission.

Disciple walked over to Jacob. "I guess this was a little more adventure than you all thought you were going to have when you set out several days ago."

Jacob laughed. "Yes it is. If we make it through this, we'll have quite a tale to share with everyone back at our House of Knowledge."

Jacob and Jack spent some time greasing the long rope, and everyone else gathered the supplies they would need. Disciple let everyone know they would attack about an hour before sunrise because that seemed to be when more guards were asleep. If all went as planned, they should be descending the castle wall as the sun was rising.

When everything was ready, they lay down to get some rest. Everyone drifted off to sleep – everyone but Disciple. He remained awake, praying throughout the night. When it was close to the time to begin the assault, he began waking up the others. Each person quietly prayed to themselves as they broke camp, then they gathered around Jacob and his crossbow.

Disciple took out his Book and read, "Fear not, for I am with you; Be not dismayed, for I am your God. I will strengthen you, Yes, I will help you, I will uphold you with My righteous right hand."

Disciple bowed his head. "Dear Lord, this task seems too big for us, but nothing is too big for You. We submit ourselves to You, and put our trust in Your strength."

Everyone said, "Amen!"

Disciple took out his telescope and peered toward the castle. "It's time."

30

CASTLE OF DESPAIR

After Peter tied one end of the rope around the tree, Jacob placed his right hand on the crossbow trigger. He squeezed slowly but firmly, shooting the arrow toward the castle. The arrow, with the long rope attached, flew through the air, making a whirring sound as it traveled. Then as the arrow reached the roof, they heard a faint thump.

Peter checked the rope to make sure it was tight. Disciple peered through the telescope, verifying that the roof was still clear. After confirming that no guards had come up to the roof, he motioned that they could depart. Each of them started in front of the tree where the rope began, placing their small ropes around the slippery, long rope. Then tightly gripping their ropes, they ran toward the side of the mountain and jumped off when they reached the edge.

One by one, they sailed toward the castle, until Jacob and his group were safely down. Peter then took off, followed shortly by Disciple. As Disciple sped through the air, he felt as if he was flying. The ground below whizzed by, as the crispness of the night air struck him in the face. His arms began to ache, but he was determined not to lose his grip. When he reached the edge of the roof, he lifted his legs and glided safely next to the others.

Once everyone gathered around, Disciple pointed toward the door leading to the second level. "I'm going to barely open this door, and throw a small rock down the steps. Hopefully, this attracts the guard that is closet to the door to come up to the roof. Once he does, we'll knock him out and tie him up."

Disciple opened the door ever so slightly, then gently tossed the rock down the stairs. They could hear it bouncing off each step until it finally came to a stop. At first, there was silence, then they heard a guard start up the stairs. As soon as the guard cleared the door, they jumped him and wrestled him to the ground. They then gagged him and tied him up. After pulling the guard away from the door, Peter knocked him out with a blow of his Sword.

After everyone regrouped in front of the door, Disciple said, "Now we should be able to get into the room and surprise the rest. Let's go!"

Disciple and Peter were the first ones down the stairs, and when they entered the room, some of the prisoners stood up to see what was happening. The guards were shocked that intruders had broken into the castle. The nine guards stared at each other a moment and then rushed toward the invaders.

Disciple and Peter were instantly engaged in battle. Jacob and the others barreled into the room, and Jacob immediately realized they needed to block the door leading to the ground level. The last thing they wanted was more guards coming to join the fight. He found an old chair and fought his way over to the door. The guards saw that Jacob was trying to keep re-enforcements from coming up the stairs, so two of them charged him. But before they could reach him, Jacob shoved the old chair underneath the doorknob, jamming the door.

The two guards tried to outflank Jacob, with one approaching from the left, and the other from the right. As they drew near, he jumped into the air, kicking out with both legs and landing a solid kick on each of the guards. They fell back but quickly righted themselves and charged again. Jacob fought with a stubborn determination, blocking one guard with his Shield while attacking the other one with his Sword.

Jacob yelled to the others, "I could use a little help!"

Disciple ducked as one of the guards swung at him with their spear. "We'll get to you as soon as we can."

Disciple fought one guard, as another one quickly closed. The first guard managed to knock Disciple off his feet, and then plunged his spear downward, trying to pin him to the floor. Disciple reacted quickly, rolling to the side, just as the spear stuck in the wooden floor next to him. Disciple swung at the spear with his Sword, cutting it in half. The guard angrily tried to kick him, but he grabbed the guard's leg and pulled him off his feet.

The second guard aimed his spear at Disciple's head, trying to pierce him while he was still on the ground. Disciple struggled to one knee and blocked the spear with his Shield, then struck the guard on the legs with his Sword. The guard was off balance but tried to swing at him with his spiked claws. Disciple quickly jumped to his feet, slammed his Shield into the fist of the guard, and kicked him in the stomach.

The guard tumbled to the floor, but by now the first guard was back on his feet. Disciple backhanded him with his Shield and then gave him a forearm to the face, knocking him to the ground again. The other guard struggled to get to his feet, but Disciple swung his Sword at his legs, sending him crashing to his back. While Disciple had both guards on the ground, he landed a knockout blow to each of them with his Sword and Shield.

Peter was in the midst of a fight with the biggest and fiercest guard who towered a full foot above all the others and carried a large spiked hammer instead of a spear. The giant guard swung his hammer at Peter so hard, that even though he blocked the blow with his Shield, the force of the attack knocked him backward and onto the ground. He jumped back to his feet just in time to block another assault from the guard. This attack also knocked him back, but he managed to maintain his balance. The guard was determined to beat Peter into the floor, and kept pounding down on top of him with his hammer. Peter blocked every one of the strikes, but each one caused his knees to buckle.

The guard could see that Peter was on the defensive, and he gave Peter a little smile as he reared back with his hammer. Just as the hammer plummeted toward him, Peter darted to the side. The huge guard's momentum carried him forward and caused him to go down to one knee. Peter immediately struck him on the back of his neck with his Sword, then followed up by slamming his Shield into his head and knocking him out.

Peter grabbed the large hammer lying on the floor and fastened it to the back of his breastplate. "This might come in handy."

While Disciple and Peter were tying up the guards they had defeated, Jacob was still having a hard time with the two guards he was fighting. He was at a disadvantage because he was defending a small space, while the two guards he was battling kept constant pressure on him. Jack, Stephen, and the others were holding their own against the guards they were facing.

Disciple yelled over at Peter, "Once your guard is tied up, go help the others. I'll help Jacob."

Disciple ran to the corner where Jacob was fighting, and as he drew near, one of the guards turned to confront him. Disciple lunged at him with his Sword, stabbing the guard in the left shoulder. The guard swung wildly at him with his spear, but Disciple ducked and stabbed the guard in the right shoulder. With both shoulders injured, the guard attacking Disciple could barely raise his spear. Disciple blocked a weak attempt of the guard to thrust his spear into his midsection. He then landed an uppercut to the guard's chin with his Shield and followed it with a blow to the side of the head with his Sword. The guard stumbled and fell down unconscious.

While Disciple had the other guard occupied, Jacob unleashed a flurry of blows on the one in front of him. He swung his Sword at the side of the guard, and then spun around and landed another blow on the other side. The guard doubled over in pain. Jacob then brought his Sword down on the back of the guard's head knocking him out.

All the guards on this level were now defeated, and Peter, Jack, and the others finished tying them up.

The prisoners in the cells were astonished at what was happening. None of them had seen anyone since they arrived at the castle. They could only hear the cries and weeping of the others in their cells. Now they were watching strangers, seemingly come out of nowhere, defeating several of the creatures who had been tormenting them.

Disciple scanned the room. "Quickly, let's get Books and keys to each of these prisoners. If they won't come with us then perhaps they can use them later."

Jacob glanced at the door as the guards from the ground level were trying to force it open. "That door isn't going to hold for very long. We've got ten minutes at the most."

They quickly went around and gave a Book and key to all the prisoners.

Some of the ones imprisoned said, "What does it matter? It will just be the same as it was, and I'll end up right back here again. I might as well not even try."

Disciple lowered his Sword until it became a Book. "We have come here to bring you hope. You have your Book, and you have a key. If you don't come with us today, then know that God is always willing to set you free when you turn to Him. It is written, 'Blessed is the one who has the God of Israel for his help, who places his hope in the LORD his God.' "

Jacob opened his Book. "Our hope must be anchored to something beyond what we can see in this present life. 'If we who are in Christ have hope only in this life, then we are of all people most miserable.' "

Peter took out his Book and read, "Waiting for our blessed hope, the glorious appearing of our great God and Savior, Jesus Christ."

Disciple marched from cell to cell making eye contact with each of the prisoners as he spoke. "We place our hope in the ultimate triumph and victory that will be revealed at the return of Jesus Christ, our Great God and Savior. I can't tell you that if you start your Quest again, you won't face adversity, discouragement, failure, or even tragedy. All of these things happen every day on this earth. But staying in these prison cells is not the answer. There is an enemy out there that is trying to cause as much destruction as possible, and as long as you are trapped in here, you can't do anything about it. There will be a time when all of this suffering is no more, but until then we must fight every day to make a difference. Listen to what God says, 'For I know the thoughts that I think toward you, says the LORD, thoughts of well-being and not of misery, to give you a future and a hope.' "

Some of the captives took their keys and unlocked their prison doors. Those who were not leaving hid the keys and Books they had been given.

Disciple told all those who were released to hold up their Books until they became Swords. "Since you don't have armor, stay near someone who does, and help them as much as you can.

Jacob glanced over at the door he had blocked with the chair. Seeing that it was bulging inward from the strain of the guards pushing on it, he shouted, "That door is about to give. Quickly roll one of those guards that's tied up over here and let's kick him down the steps to clear a path for us."

Jacob rammed his foot against the door, then yanked the chair out of the way. Disciple rolled one of the guards into position, and Jacob flung open the door. Disciple launched himself at the guards at the top of the steps while holding out his Sword, moving them back just far enough, so Peter had room to kick the guard down the steps. As the guard rolled down, the other guards backed up, clearing enough room for Disciple and Peter to jump downstairs. Ten guards instantly surrounded them. They each thrust out their Shields to create space for Jacob and the others who sprinted down the stairs, followed by the escaped prisoners.

Disciple yelled out, "We have to get outside!"

Disciple, Peter, Jacob, and the others fought fiercely, striking at the guards, trying to clear a path to the door. Disciple swung his Shield back and forth to create some space, while Peter launched himself at five guards pushing them backward. Jacob and Jack repeatedly jumped into the air and kicked out at any guard that came near. Stephen and the others swung furiously with their Swords, striking at anything that moved. Finally, they had cleared enough space to see the doorway, but two large guards stood in front of it blocking their escape.

Reaching behind his back, Peter said to the others, "Hold them off and give me some room."

Peter pulled out the large hammer he had taken from the giant guard. He placed both hands firmly around the handle and began swinging his whole body around in a circle with the hammer out in front of him. After turning several times, Peter released the hammer toward the guards blocking their exit. The hammer flew through the air, crashing into the guards, and knocking them completely through the doorway.

"That's one way to open a door," said Disciple smiling.

Everyone rushed from the room to the outside, where more guards were waiting. Disciple knew their only hope was to fight their way to the edge of the castle wall, then hold off the guards long enough for the escaped prisoners to climb down.

Disciple shouted, "Do as much damage to them as you can and remember our plan."

Each of them fought valiantly, as they all faced multiple enemies.

Those who had been released from the castle were regaining some skill with their Swords and helped with the combat. Everyone fought in groups of three with their backs toward each other, ensuring that none of the enemies could surprise them from behind.

After an intense battle, they finally fought their way to within twenty feet of the edge. The guards became more ferocious in their fighting, now aiming to knock them off the castle. Disciple, Peter, Jacob, and the rest formed a wall to give those who were released space to let down the ropes and begin climbing down the castle. All of those forming the barrier extended their Shields while digging in with their Shoes. They all knew what was at stake. They must hold steady to give the prisoners time to climb down the wall. The guards also knew what was at stake, and after they quickly regrouped they charged toward them.

Disciple shouted, "Get low and lean forward. As they get close, thrust out your Shield to stop their momentum."

The guards slammed into the wall of Shields, but they weren't able to knock Disciple and the others back. The guards retreated about twenty-five feet and then charged toward them again. Once again Disciple and the others held firm. Disciple looked back to see that all of the ones who were released were safely down the ropes.

Peter then yelled out, "What now? As each of us attempts to climb down, that's fewer people to hold off the guards."

Digging in with his Shoes, Disciple yelled back, "It's what we have to do. Jacob, get your men over that wall and do it quickly."

Two of those who had been forming the Shield barrier stood up and grabbed a rope to climb down. As they did, the guards realized that with fewer people, the rescuers would have a harder time holding them off. The guards charged toward them even more vigorously. This time as the guards made contact, they knocked Disciple and the others back five feet, leaving only fifteen feet between them and the edge of the castle.

As the guards regrouped to make another run, two more from Jacob's group left the battle line and headed toward the ropes to climb down. The guards charged at them again and knocked them back to within five feet of the edge. The guards were stunned by the impact and had to back up and regroup before attempting to charge again.

It was now only Disciple, Peter, Jacob, and Stephen who remained to form the barrier.

Jacob said, "I don't want to leave you two."

Forcefully motioning toward the ropes with his Sword, Disciple said, "We'll be just fine. You and Stephen get down that wall now."

Disciple knew that he and Peter were not climbing down the ropes. There was no way they would be able to hold off another charge. As soon as Jacob and Stephen were over the wall, Disciple stood up.

Peter stood up as well, seeing that the guards were about to rush them. "Any suggestions on what to do now?"

Disciple adjusted his helmet and gripped his Shield. "Yes, we fight until there's no strength left."

Peter cocked back his Sword. "I was kind of hoping for a better plan."

Disciple looked at Peter and smiled. "So was I, but this one will have to do."

As the guards came closer, Disciple and Peter jumped up into the air, kicking out at them. They each knocked down three guards, and five others behind them toppled over as well. Disciple and Peter swiftly jumped to their feet and blocked several spears thrust toward them. Disciple swung his Sword in a circle, stunning six guards with one strike. Peter knocked back two with a combination of blows from both his Sword and Shield.

Disciple and Peter fought bravely, but there were just too many guards. Slowly their adversaries backed them up to the edge of the castle wall.

The guards held their spears at Disciple and Peter's chest. One of them smirked. "This isn't how you thought it was going to end is it?"

Disciple looked defiantly at the guard. "It doesn't matter. The captives have been set free!"

The guards yelled as they forced both Disciple and Peter off the edge, sending them toward the ground below.

As they were falling with their backs to the ground, Disciple glanced over at Peter, and yelled, "We have fought the good fight, and I wouldn't have wanted to fight it with anyone else."

Disciple tightly closed his eyes, stiffening his body, as he prepared to strike the ground. He instantly flashed back, seeing himself as he went through the Building of Reflection, and then up the Hill of Calvary. He saw the brightness of the sun shining through the trees when he was baptized. He saw all of his adventures, The Valley of Doubt, The Forest of Fear, The Giant of Shame, The Mountain of Unforgiveness, The Fortress of Deception, The Swamp of Suffering, along with the battle that just took place in The Castle of Despair. He had lived a full life, even if it was to end right here.

Disciple was ready to meet his Savior face to face.

Knowing he was about to crash to the ground, Disciple reached out his hand toward heaven...

THUD!

Loud cheers erupted, as Disciple opened his eyes to see they had landed on a large tarp being held by several different people.

Disciple and Peter rolled off the tarp and onto their feet. They didn't have much time to celebrate though because the guards up at the top started throwing their spears at them.

"Raise your shields and walk backward," shouted one of the men.

They all held up their Shields as they backed away. When they were safely out of range, Disciple looked around and saw that fifteen of those who had been imprisoned escaped with them.

As they were making their way through the muddy terrain, those who escaped found the armor they had left behind. It needed to be cleaned up and strengthened, but they were glad to have it back again. When they were clear of the thick mud, they all stopped and rested.

One of the men who were holding the tarp approached Disciple. "Hello, I'm John. Earlier, just as the sun was coming up, I saw the prisoners climbing down the side of the castle rock, so I called out to some others, and we ran over and began helping them. Someone had brought a tarp to catch anyone who needed to jump, so when we saw you two backed up to the edge, we quickly spread it out and held it tight."

Disciple smiled. "Thanks. I believe we're going to be having a celebration soon, and you're all welcome to join us."

"I think I'll do that," said John.

They started back toward the camp, and all along the way, those who had been released from the Castle of Despair were thanking God for their deliverance. After they arrived back at the campsite, they started preparing a meal for everyone to share together. John took charge of grilling some fish from a nearby stream, and soon they put together a feast for everyone to enjoy. Afterward, they sat around the fire for the rest of the day and well into the night singing praises to God.

As the night was winding down, Disciple walked up to Jacob, Jack, Stephen, and the others. "I want to say thanks to all of you for joining Peter and myself on this adventure. I don't believe we could have done it without you. You each overcame hardships on the Trail of Discouragement, and you fought bravely as we set these people free from the Castle of Despair."

Disciple shook each of their hands and then rejoined the others who were still sitting around the fire. He thought of all that God had done over the last several days. Lifting his eyes toward heaven, he thanked God once again. After a little while longer, everyone began settling into their tents for the night. Some of the passersby had donated tents and supplies for the escaped prisoners, so everyone had a place to sleep.

As Peter was about to go into his tent, Disciple held out his hand. "You were a tremendous asset on this mission. Through our time together, I've watched you grow to become a mighty warrior. I'm grateful to have you by my side."

Peter reached out to shake Disciple's hand, and for maybe one of the few times in his life, he was at a loss for words. "I don't know what to say. I know it's me that's doing all these things, but at the same time, I know it's not me. I can't explain it, but that's all I can say."

Nodding his head, Disciple said, "I understand completely. It is no longer we that live, but Christ in us."

After a peaceful night's rest, Disciple woke to see that his path and Peter's was continuing on.

Disciple called Jacob over. "It's time for Peter and me to leave."

"This has been a great adventure," said Jacob. "I hope to see you two again sometime in the future."

Disciple looked around, as everyone was packing up and preparing to leave. "I trust that you and the others will take care of the people who were rescued from the castle."

Jacob glanced over at Stephen and Jack. "We have a few more days before we have to be back for classes. We passed an inn on the way here that's next door to a House of Instruction. It's a perfect place for them to go before they start out on their journey again."

Taking some gold coins out of his pocket, Disciple said, "Take this and use it for their stay at the inn."

Disciple and Peter said goodbye to everyone and then started on their way.

31

A NEW ADVENTURE BEGINS

As Disciple and Peter continued their journey, Peter said, "I can't believe all that's happened since I first met you. You know, on that first day of training, I really didn't like you, and honestly, there were some days after that where I wasn't that fond of you either."

Disciple glanced at him and smiled. "I could tell you I've loved every minute of it, but you wouldn't want me to lie now would you?"

They both laughed and traveled on.

After a little while, Peter stopped and turned to Disciple. "Thank you. I'm not sure if I've ever said that to you, but I mean it. My life was a mess. If God hadn't placed you in my life as a mentor, I don't know what would have happened."

Patting him on the back, Disciple said, "You're welcome. God sent people to walk with me along my path as well. When a person is truly ready to be done with serving sin, God will give them what they need to succeed."

Peter smiled and shook his head. "I look back now, and I wonder what took me so long. I think about why I had to waste all of that time learning the lessons that I did."

"Yes, I know," said Disciple, "but it's knowing that we wasted all that time that pushes us to make sure we don't do it again. We can also tell others about our experiences. Hopefully, some of them will be willing to learn by listening, so they won't have to go through the hard times that we did."

Gazing toward heaven, Peter said, "I'm so thankful that God

never gave up on me. I think of all the times I persisted in sin, and yet He never left me. He was always right there waiting for me to turn around. That's what drives me more than anything. It's because of His goodness and great love toward me that I want to serve Him for the rest of my life."

Disciple prepared to move forward. "Very well said."

Disciple and Peter spent the next week traveling together. On the sixth day, they noticed that their path was taking them further away from the others on their Quest. They seemed to be traveling on ground few had walked on before. By the seventh day, they did not see anyone else the entire day. The next day their paths took them to a slope that overlooked a large valley.

As they approached the slope, they heard a raucous noise coming from the valley below, so they edged closer and stopped behind some trees. Disciple peered out over the valley through his telescope and spotted a large camp of ogres and giants. He estimated there must be at least a hundred of them, but there could be more because they were constantly moving in and out.

Disciple and Peter pulled back from the edge to make sure they couldn't be seen from the valley and began to set up camp. They prayed through the night anticipating what the next morning would bring. When they awoke, they saw that their paths had not moved. They stayed another night, and the next morning was the same.

Disciple said, "It looks like we're going to need more people to arrive before God causes our paths to move toward that valley."

"What do we do until then?" Peter asked.

Disciple gazed out at the terrain that had led them here. "We wait."

****

Disciple is right. God is preparing more Warriors to join the battle!

DON'T STOP READING! Disciples Quest 2: The Adventures of Jeremiah & Zeal IS NOW AVAILABLE ON AMAZON!

Also Now Available on Amazon:

Disciple's Quest 3: Esther & Overcomer, Women of God

Disciple's Quest 4: Warriors of God

Join me on Facebook:
https://www.facebook.com/DisciplesQuestBooks

ABOUT THE AUTHOR

I have a passion for teaching God's word and making it relatable to anyone who wants to learn. I believe that understanding and applying God's word is the key to success in all areas of life.

Walter Cantrell

SCRIPTURE REFERENCES

Some of these quotes are only partial quotations from Scripture, and some are loose paraphrases designed to fit the dialogue.

Chapter 1

Witness said that because Adam disobeyed God, it was counted as if all human beings had sinned along with him, and this was why we all had this debt of sin. (Romans 5:12, 18, 19)

For all have sinned, and fallen short of the glory of God. (Romans 3:23)

We have been brought forth in iniquity and conceived in sin. (Psalms 51:5)

Witness says to study, meditate on, and discuss the words from his Book throughout his Quest. (Deuteronomy 6:6-9)

Chapter 2

Disciple read, "All Scripture is God-breathed and is beneficial for teaching, for reproof, for correcting faults, and for instruction in righteousness." (2 Timothy 3:16)

Disciple read, "There is no one who is righteous, not even one. There is no one who understands. There is no one who seeks after God." (Romans 3:9-11)

Disciple told Mr. Enlightenment "But you don't understand. This Book was written by God Himself. It says that He worked within the men who wrote it in such a way that it was His words." (2 Peter 1:20,

21)

Mr. Good Works is referring to something he heard, "Oh wretched man that I am!" (Romans 7:24 NKJV)

Chapter 3

Disciple realized that all of his thoughts were exposed and visible to God. Nothing was hidden from His sight. (Hebrews 4:13)

Falling to his knees, he cried out, "God be merciful to me, sinful man that I am!" (Luke 18:10-14)

Disciple cried out, "All my works are completely rotten!" (Isaiah 64:6)

Disciple looked down at the floor. "I am undone and completely sinful!" (Isaiah 6:5)

The Holy Spirit said, "Yes, the wages of sin is death." (Romans 6:23 NKJV)

The Holy Spirit said, "You must look to the cross and receive what Jesus did for you, putting your trust in Him." (Numbers 21:5-9)(John 3:14, 15)

Chapter 4

A Voice thundered from heaven. "You are a new creation. Old things have passed away, behold all things have become new!" (2 Corinthians 5:17 NKJV)

Disciple realized that even as he was counted as sinful because of Adam, he could now be counted as righteous because of Christ. (Romans 5:19)

Teacher said, "You see here, it says that your old sinful nature was crucified on the cross with Christ." (Romans 6:6)

Teacher places two bookmarks. One is in the Gospel of John, and the other is in 1 Corinthians 15.

Chapter 5

Pastor Sinclair says, "This is wonderful. For even the angels in heaven rejoice each time someone goes through the Building of Reflection and up the Hill of Calvary." (Luke 15:10)

Pastor Sinclair says, "The Gospel of Christ is such good news. It is the power of God to bring salvation to all those who believe." (Romans 1:16)

Pastor Sinclair says baptism symbolizes a new life in Christ by identifying with His death, burial and resurrection. (Romans 6:4, 5)

All verses referred to by Pastor Sinclair regarding communion. (1 Corinthians 11:23-26 NKJV)

All verses referring to the armor given to Disciple by Pastor Sinclair. (Ephesians 6:10-18)

Pastor Sinclair says that the Sword (the word of God) is able to separate between soul and spirit. (Hebrews 4:12)

Pastor Sinclair says "All Scripture is God-breathed, and is profitable. It will teach you sound doctrine, correct you when you need it, and teach you how to conduct yourself while on your Quest." (2 Timothy 3:16)

Pastor Sinclair says "You are welcome. You're equipped and ready to begin your journey." (Ephesians 4:11-13)

Pastor Sinclair says, "Also, as you continue to study that Book, you will notice that your path will be lighted, as if a lamp were constantly at your feet." (Psalms 119:105)

Chapter 6

Disciple shouted, "Thanks be to God, Who always gives us the victory in Christ." (2 Cor. 2:14 NKJV)

Disciple shouted, "Blessed be the LORD my Rock, Who trains my hands for war, And my fingers for battle!" (Psalms 144:1)

Disciple remembered a verse which read, "The one that has died, has been set free from sin." (Romans 6:7)

Disciple cried out, "LORD, those who patiently look to you will regain their strength. They shall soar on the wings of eagles. They shall run and not grow weary. They shall walk and not be faint." (Isaiah 40:31)

Chapter 7

The story of Jesus crossing the lake with his disciples: (Matthew 8:23-

27)

A reference to John the Baptist experiencing doubts: (Matthew 11:1-11)

When Disciple lay down to go to sleep, he meditated on "We do not look at the things which we can see, but we look at the things which we cannot see. For the things which we can see are temporary, but the things which we cannot see are eternal." (2 Corinthians 4:18)

Verses that Disciple used in his battle with the Vultures of Doubt: (Romans 10:9, 13 NKJV) (John 10:28) (Romans 8:16)

Chapter 8

Disciple advanced toward the wolf. "Even though I walk through the valley of the shadow of death, I will fear no evil, for You are with me. Your rod and Your staff they comfort me." (Psalms 23:4 NKJV)

Disciple proclaimed, "The LORD is my light and my salvation; Whom shall I fear? The LORD is the strength of my life; Of whom shall I be afraid?" (Psalms 27:1 NKJV)

Disciple said to the wolf, "It is the Lord that helps me, therefore I will not fear." (Hebrews 13:6)

Disciple shouted, "Though an army encamp against me, my heart shall not fear. Though war may rise against me, even in this I will be confident." (Psalms 27:3 NKJV)

Disciple said to the wolf, "Through my God I shall do valiantly, for it is He who will tread down my enemies." (Psalms 108:13 NKJV)

The Scriptures that Disciple read to Mark and his siblings in the Forest of Fear: (2 Timothy 1:7 NKJV) (Psalms 34:4 NKJV) (Psalms 91)

In the Forest of Fear, Disciple observed that as the others read and meditated on God's truth it set them free. (John 8:31, 32)

The story of the twelve spies and the Promised Land (Numbers 13 and 14)

Pastor Bill turned several pages. "Another writer in this Book says that they were not able to enter in because of their unbelief and their refusal to trust in God." (Hebrews 3:16-19)

Pastor Bill read to them, "It is the LORD who will go before you. He will be with you, and He will not leave your side nor abandon you. Do not fear or be discouraged." (Deuteronomy 31:8)

God told Joshua to be strong and of good courage. (Joshua 1:9)

Do not fear bad news or live in dread of what might happen. (Psalms 112:7)

Chapter 9

There are no Scripture references in chapter 9, but think about the many verses where the Bible talks about how pride comes before a fall.

Chapter 10

There are no Scripture references in chapter 10, but think about the many verses where the Bible talks about the consequences of sin.

Chapter 11

Verses about sowing and reaping: (Galatians 6:6-9)

The story of the Prodigal Son: (Luke 15:11-32)

Pastor Sinclair says, "No, a person that comes through the Building of Reflection and takes his sin up the Hill of Calvary cannot end up in the Lake that Burns Forever because he is kept in the hands of both the Father and the Son. He can never perish." (John: 10:28, 29) *Note: The Greek that is usually translated "will never perish" is a specific grammatical construction that uses a double negative with an Aorist Subjunctive and means that not only will it not happen, but it is impossible.*

Sin grieves the Holy Spirit who lives inside us. (Ephesians 4:30)

If we do not have the Holy Spirit then we are not God's child. (Romans 8:9)

Pastor Sinclair said, "He has promised that for those which He has begun a good work in, He will surely complete it." (Philippians 1:6)

Chapter 12

Disciple remembered reading in his Book that we were to forget those things that were behind and press forward to those things that were ahead. (Philippians 3:13, 14)

Focusing on today and letting tomorrow take care of itself. (Matthew 6:33, 34)

We Walk by Faith and Not by Sight. (2 Corinthians 5:7)

The story of Peter walking on the water. (Matthew 14:22-33)

Calling out to God, Disciple shouted, "Whenever I am afraid, I will trust in you." (Psalms 56:3 NKJV)

Disciple thought of the words he had read in his Book: "Trust in the LORD with all your heart, And lean not on your own understanding; In all your ways acknowledge Him, And He shall direct your paths." (Proverbs 3:5, 6 NKJV)

Chapter 13

Disciple said to the Giant of Shame, "God does not deal with me according to my sins, nor does he punish me according to what my iniquities deserve." (Psalms 103:10)

Disciple said to the Giant of Shame, "There once was a great man who said, 'For a day in Your courts is better than a thousand anywhere else. I would rather be a doorkeeper in the house of my God than live in the tents of the wicked.' " (Psalms 84:10)

Disciple realized that God had adopted him into His family and made him an heir with Christ. (Galatians 4:4-7) He did not need to fear rejection by God, because God was the one Who chose him. (John 15:16)(Ephesians 1:4, 5)

Verses referenced just before Disciple raises his Sword to fight the Giant of Shame: (Psalms 103:14-16) (James 4:14) (Isaiah 53:1-6) (Ephesians 1:3-8)

Disciple said, "There is no one that does anything good, and that includes me." (Romans 3:12)

Disciple said, "There is none that seeks after God, and left to my own decisions, I never would have either. Everything I am or ever will be is because of His grace." (Romans 3:11) (1 Corinthians 15:10)

Disciple said, "There is no one who is righteous, and I know that the only righteousness I have is of Christ. (Romans 3:10) (2 Corinthians 5:21) It is no longer I that live, but Christ that lives in me. (Galatians 2:20) I don't care what people think of me. I only care to show people Christ in me!" (Colossians 3:3)

Disciple said, "If the LORD kept a record of our sins and held them against us, who could stand before Him? But with Him there is forgiveness that we might fear His Name." (Psalms 130:3)

Disciple said, "For as far as the east is from the west, so far has He removed our sins away from us." (Psalms 103:12)

Overcomer said, "There is no condemnation for those who are in Christ, and that includes me!" (Romans 8:1)

Overcomer shouted, "My sinfulness is always before me, but the answer to my sinfulness, the Lord Jesus Christ, is always before the Father on behalf of me." (Psalms 51:3)(Romans 8:34)(1 John 2:1)

Overcomer said, "I have become the righteousness of God in Christ!" (2 Corinthians 5:21)

Overcomer said, "It is the Lord My God that helps me, therefore I will not be disgraced. I have set my face like flint, determined to do his will, therefore I will not be put to shame." (Isaiah 50:7)

Overcomer said, "I will set my focus on Jesus, Who is the author and the perfecter of my faith, Who endured the cross and despised the shame that went with it, because of the joy that was set before Him." (Hebrews 12:2)

Overcomer said, "I have boldness to enter into the Most Holy Place because of the blood of my Lord Jesus. Because of His sacrifice I am able to draw near to the Throne of God, with full assurance of faith, and receive cleansing from all the guilt and shame that assaults my thoughts." (Hebrews 10:19-22)

Overcomer said, "I realized that we do not overcome the Accuser of the Brethren by denying his accusations, but by the blood of the Lamb and the word of our testimony in Christ." (Revelation 12: 10, 11)

Chapter 14

The story of the unforgiving servant: (Matthew 18:23-35)

Disciple said, "God, give me the ability to love my enemies, to do good to those who hate me, and to pray for those who spitefully use me." (Luke 6:27, 28 NKJV)

Caleb said, "Hatred stirs up strife, but love covers up all offenses." (Proverbs 10:12)

Charlotte shouts, "Love is not easily offended, and it does not keep a record of suffered wrongs." (1 Corinthians 13:5)

Disciple read, "Be angry and sin not, do not let the sun go down on your rage, and do not give such place to the devil." (Ephesians 4:26, 27)

Disciple said, "Help us to be kind to one another, tenderhearted, forgiving one another, even as God in Christ forgave us." (Ephesians 4:32 NKJV)

Charlotte said, "Help us to bear with each other, and forgive one another. If any of us has a complaint against someone; even as Christ forgave us, so let us do also." (Colossians 3:13 NKJV)

The men imprisoned said, "Lord, forgive us of our sins as we also forgive those who have sinned against us." (Matthew 6:12)

The men imprisoned said, "Vengeance belongs to the Lord. It is His place to repay and not ours!" (Romans 12:19)

Chapter 15

Disciple remembers a verses about confessing his sins. (1 John 1:9)

Disciple said, "Stop being deceived; God is not mocked, for whatever a man sows, this will he also reap. For he that sows to his flesh shall of the flesh reap destruction, but he that sows to the Spirit shall by the Spirit reap eternal life." (Galatians 6:7, 8)

Chapter 16

Disciple said, "I discovered that the moment I think I am standing, I should take heed lest I fall." (1 Corinthians 10:12)

Elder Jenkins said, "For I acknowledge my transgressions, and my sin remains continually before me. Against You, You only, have I sinned, and done this evil in Your sight, so that You may be justified when You give your sentence, and be blameless when You judge."(Psalms 51:3, 4)

Elder Jenkins said, "The Apostle Paul pressed toward his goal and calling as if he was continuously straining forward." (Philippians 3:14)

Chapter 17

Disciple read, "Search me, Oh God, and know my heart. Examine me, and know my thoughts. See if there is any wicked way in me, and lead me in the way everlasting." (Psalms 139:23, 24)

The three primary verses that Disciple used against the Black Knights (Romans 12:1) (Romans 13:14) (1 Peter 2:11)

Disciple said, "I present my mind and my body as a continuous sacrifice to God." (Romans 12:1)

Disciple said, "I will not surrender to the lusts of my flesh which wage war against my soul." (1 Peter 2:11)

Disciple said, "I will not make any provision in my thoughts for the lust of the flesh." (Romans 13:14)

Disciple said, "The Lord is my portion, so therefore I will put my hope in him." (Lamentations 3:24)

Disciple shouted, "I will not live according to my flesh by setting my mind on things of the flesh, but I will live by the Spirit and set my mind on things of the Spirit." (Romans 8:5)

Disciple shouted, "Those who belong to Christ have crucified the flesh along with its cravings and lusts." (Galatians 5:24)

Disciple shouted, "I have been raised with Christ and seated with Him in heavenly places. Therefore I will seek those things which are above where Christ is sitting at the right hand of God." (Colossians 3:1) (Ephesians 2:6)

Disciple shouted, "I will set my mind on things that are above and not the sinful desires of this world." (Colossians 3:2)

Disciple shouted, "I will walk by the Spirit so that I will not fulfill the lusts of my flesh." (Galatians 5:16)

Disciple declared, "I will keep a constant watch over my heart, for out of it flows the well springs of life." (Proverbs 4:23)

Disciple said, "The LORD is my strength and song, And He has become my salvation; He is my God, and I will praise Him; My father's God, and I will exalt Him." (Exodus 15:2 NKJV)

Chapter 18

Teacher pointed to his Book. "God's word often uses word pictures and symbols. One of my favorite uses of symbols is in Psalms. The passage says that a man who meditates on the words of this Book is like a tree planted by a river." (Psalms 1:1-3)

A Voice boomed, "For He hath made him to be sin for us, Who knew no sin, so that we might become the righteousness of God in Him." (2 Corinthians 5:21)

Teacher said, 'For Christ is the fulfillment of the law in order to accomplish righteousness on behalf of everyone who believes.' " (Romans 10:4)

Teacher quoted, "If we say that we do not have any sin, we deceive ourselves, and the truth has no place in us. If we confess and turn from our sins, he is faithful and just to forgive us of our sins, and to cleanse us from all unrighteousness." (1 John 1:8, 9)

Teacher said, "This Book teaches that if someone has truly turned to Christ, then their lives will show the results of this change. John clearly instructs us in his first letter that if a person is born of God, they will not go on practicing sin." (1 John 3:8, 9)

Teacher said, "Once you are God's child, He will not let you sin without discipline." (Hebrews 12:7)

Chapter 19

Teacher said, "There is a certain amount of suffering that is involved with dealing with sin. "(1 Peter 4:1)

Teacher said, "Facing the All Consuming Fire of God as we are holding our sin, is not a pleasant experience. But, as we stay in that fire, He burns up our sin and its bondage. Then we can experience a true joy." (Hebrews 12:28, 29)

Teacher said, "You're saying that it is no longer you that lives, but Christ in you, and the life you now live, you live by faith in the Son of God who loved you and gave Himself for you." (Galatians 2:20)

Verses on the papers in the Valley of Humility in order: (Romans 3:12) (Mark 10:18) (1 Corinthians 15:10) (Philippians 2:13) (James 4:6) (Ephesians 2:8, 9) (Luke 9:23) (1 Peter 5:6)

Disciple shouted, "I am what I am by the grace of God, and anything that I have accomplished was not me but the grace of God working through me." (1 Corinthians 15:10)

Chapter 20

Disciple said, "I need all of your input as we're forming this plan because in a multitude of counselors there is safety and victory." (Proverbs 24:6)

Disciple read, "The heart is deceitful above all things, and totally corrupt, who can know it? I the LORD search the heart, and I examine the mind, so that I may give every man according to his ways, and according to the fruit of his deeds." (Jeremiah 17:9, 10)

Disciple continued, "Each of us has the capacity to be led off in deception. As we go to rescue these people who are trapped, we must also examine ourselves, knowing that we can be tempted in the same manner." (Galatians 6:1)

Disciple whispered, "As we're approaching the fortress, meditate on this, since we have been resurrected with Christ, think on things that are above, where Christ is seated at the right hand of God; set your hearts and affections on things above and not on the earthly temptations to sin." (Colossians 3:1-5)

Disciple read from his Book. "But the ones who desire to be rich fall into temptation, and into a snare, and into many foolish and harmful lusts which plunge people into ruin and destruction. For the love of money is a root of all kinds of evils. It is through this craving that some have departed from the faith and have pierced themselves with many sorrows." (1 Timothy 6:9, 10)

Disciple said, "Keep your way of life free from the love of money, and be content with the things you have, for He has said, I will never leave you nor forsake you." (Hebrews 13:5)

Samuel said, "Jesus described those on this Quest who will not confess him openly saying, 'For they loved the approval and praise of men more than the approval and praise of God.' (John 12:42, 43) Do not love the world or the things in the world. If anyone loves the world, the love of the Father is not in him.' " (1 John 2:15 NKJV)

Samuel said, "Do you not know that friendship with the world is hostility toward God? Whoever desires to be a friend of the world makes himself to be an enemy of God." (James 4:4)

Thaddeus said, "Do not be domineering over those who are under your care, but be an example to them.' (1 Peter 5:3) And Jesus said, 'For you know that the princes of this world exercise full dominion over those under them, and those who are great trample on top of them.' " (Matthew 20:25)

Thaddeus said, "Whoever desires to become great among you, let him be your servant. And whoever desires to be first among you, let him be your slave, just as the Son of Man did not come to be served, but to serve, and to give His life a ransom for many." (Matthew 20:26-28 NKJV)

Chapter 21

The two verses Disciple remembered when he first entered the swamp: (Romans 5:3, 4) (James 1:2-4)

Disciple said, "For I consider that the sufferings of this present time are not worthy to be compared with the glory which shall be revealed in us." (Romans 8:18 NKJV)

Disciple said, "Beloved, stop being surprised at the painful sufferings taking place among you in order to test you, as if something strange is happening to you. But rejoice knowing that inasmuch as you are participating in the sufferings of Christ, you will also rejoice and be glad when His glory is revealed." (1 Peter 4:12, 13)

Disciple quoted, "Look attentively at the birds of the air, for they do not sow, nor reap, nor gather into barns, and yet your heavenly Father keeps providing for them. You are of much more worth than they, are you not?" (Matthew 6:26)

Disciple quoted, "And we know that all things work together for good to those who love God, to those who are the called according to His purpose." (Romans 8:28 NKJV)

Disciple's prayer for Jason: (Jeremiah 29:11)

Disciple discovers his ability to comfort others: (2 Corinthians 1:4)

Chapter 22

There are no Scripture references for this chapter.

Chapter 23

There are no Scripture references for this chapter.

Chapter 24

The temptation of Jesus (Matthew 4:1-11)

Disciple said, "God's word says that those who think according to the flesh, live according to the flesh, and those who think according to the Spirit, then live according to the Spirit." (Romans 8:5)

Disciple instructs Peter. "Beloved, I plead with you as foreigners and pilgrims, to refuse to give into fleshly lusts, which wage war against your soul." (1 Peter 2:11)

Peter said, "The Lord God alone is my rock and my salvation. He is my strong defense. I shall not be moved." (Psalms 62:6)

Peter said, "How shall we who are dead to sin live any longer under its domination!" (Romans 6:2)

Peter said, "Therefore I will no longer serve the old nature which is corrupt according to sinful lusts, but I will be renewed in the spirit of my mind." (Ephesians 4:22, 23)

Peter quotes this verse in parts as he fights the Black Knights: (Philippians 4:8)

Peter wound up with his Sword. "I will consider myself to be dead to sin, but alive to God through Christ Jesus my Lord!" (Romans 6:11) *I would strongly urge anyone to study and meditate on all of Romans 6 in their battle against sin. The Amplified Version does a particularly good job in bringing out all the subtleties of these verses.*

Disciple tells Peter, "When we walk by the Spirit, we will not give into the lusts of the flesh." (Galatians 5:16)

Chapter 25

Disciple said, "We have been crucified with Christ and identified with His death, so that it is no longer we that live but Christ who lives in us. And the life that we now live, we live by putting our faith and trust in the Son of God, who loved us and gave Himself for us." (Galatians 2:20)

Disciple thought on this verse about being a mentor: "And the things which you have learned from me in the presence of many witnesses, present these to faithful men so that they may be able to teach others also." (2 Timothy 2:2)

Disciple said to Jacob, "If we claim that we have no sin, we deceive ourselves, and the truth has no place in us." (1 John 1:8)

Disciple said, "You stand before God as completely holy and without blame because of what Christ did. It has nothing to do with you." (Ephesians 1:4)

Peter quoted from this when describing to Disciple what he'd been reading: (Philippians 3:3-9)

Peter's first quote to the Giant of Shame: I don't come at you today based on my goodness but on the Goodness of Jesus Christ. He is the LORD our Righteousness!" (Jeremiah 23:5, 6)

Peter said, "It is no longer I that lives, but Christ in me!" (Galatians 2:20)

Peter said, "I will not trust in any righteousness I can achieve, but I will only trust in the righteousness that is by faith in Christ." (Philippians 3:9)

Peter said, "I am not perfect, but there is one thing that I do. Forgetting those things which are in the past, I press forward to the things which are ahead, to the high calling of God in Christ Jesus." (Philippians 3:12-14)

Peter said, "Not by MY might, and not by MY power, but by the power of YOUR Spirit, Oh Lord God Almighty!" (Zechariah 4:6)

Chapter 26

Disciple's instruction to Peter about the word of God at the beginning of the chapter: (Joshua 1:8) (Deuteronomy 6:6-9)

The parable of the sower: (Matthew 13:3-23)

Disciple read, "For this reason, put aside all uncleanness and abundance of evil, and in humility receive the implanted word, which is able to transform and save your souls." (James 1:21)

How to be a doer of the word: (James 1:22-25)

Teacher said, "Jesus told His disciples that if they were of this world then the world would love them, but because they were not of this world, that was why the world hated them." (John 15:19)

Teacher shows Peter the great cloud of witnesses: (Hebrews 12:1)

Peter said, "God does not see my record of sinfulness, but He sees Christ's record instead. I am counted as righteous because of Christ." (Romans 5:19)

Teacher read from his Book. "For whoever tries to keep the whole Law but stumbles in just one point, has become guilty of breaking all of it." (James 2:10)

Teacher reads about the Vine and the branches: (John 15:1-8)

Disciple turned in his Book and read, "But whoever is keeping His word, in him the love of God **has truly been perfected**. This is how we know that we are in Him." (1 John 2:5) *Most English Translations use the wording "is perfected," but the Greek Verb being used is in the Perfect Tense. Using this verb tense places emphasis on the fact that it is the ones who have already been perfected in love who are able to keep His word. Keeping God's words are important, but we should always understand that the power to keep these words originates with Him and not in our own desires and abilities.*

Teacher said, "The Camp of Religion can teach people how to produce a lot of wood, hay, and stubble, but their way will not produce any gold, silver, or precious stones." (1 Cor. 3:12-15)

Chapter 27

Disciple said, "All the righteous requirements of the law have been fulfilled by Jesus and have been placed on our account. God sees us as always having kept all of the Law perfectly, because He sees us as in Christ." (Romans 8:3, 4)

Teaching the opinions of man as the commandments of God: (Matthew 15:1-9)

Disciple said, "The problem though is that the heart is deceitful, and we can be following rules on the outside, while our heart is still far from God. It says in this Book, 'That all the ways of a man are pure in his own eyes, but the Lord weighs the thoughts and intent of the heart.' " (Proverbs 16:2)

Grace teaches us to refrain from sin. (Titus 2:11, 12)

The Israelites standing afar off from God: (Exodus 20:19-21)

Disciple said, "The Law shut us up into one big courtroom and declared us guilty, but it did this to point us to Christ." (Galatians 3:22-26)

Disciple read, "But this is the covenant that I will make with the house of Israel after those days, says the LORD: I will put My law in their minds, and write it on their hearts; and I will be their God, and they shall be My people." (Jeremiah 31:33 NKJV)

Disciple read, "I will give you a new heart, and I will put a new spirit within you. I will take the stony heart out of your flesh and give you a heart of flesh. I will put my Spirit within you which will cause you to walk in my commandments, and you will keep my just decrees and do them." (Ezekiel 36:26, 27)

Disciple said, "He caused us to be born again and have a new nature that was created after His image in righteousness and true holiness." (Ephesians 4:22-24)

Disciple said, "You've been presenting all of yourself as a living and continuous sacrifice to God, which caused your conduct to be holy and acceptable to Him. By receiving His words into your heart you stopped conforming yourself to the ways of this world, and you have been being transformed by the renewing of your mind." (Romans 12:1, 2)

Chapter 28

Peter said, "I can do all things through Christ, because He is. the one who strengthens me." (Philippians 4:13)

Disciple bowed his head. "Oh Lord, You said that You would keep us in perfect peace as our mind stays steadfast on you." (Isaiah 26:3)

Disciple read, "Why are you cast down and discouraged, Oh my soul? Why are you disturbed within me? Hope in God! For I shall still praise Him for the saving help of His presence." (Psalms 42:11)

Jesus promised to give us His peace. (John 14:27)

Stephen said, "Lord, I do not understand why this tragedy came to our family. Yet Oh Lord, I will not murmur and complain against you, for I know that the things we suffer while on this earth are producing for us an eternal weight of glory which is beyond comparison. Because we do not look at the things which we can see, but to the things which we cannot see. For the things which we can see are only temporary, but the things we cannot see are eternal." (2 Corinthians 4:17, 18)

Jacob prayed, "Even as Job said, even though you slay me, I will still trust you." (Job 13:15)

A song that I feel goes really well with this part of the book is available on YouTube. Go there and do a search on the song: "Though You Slay Me" (featuring John Piper)

Disciple read, "Let us not become weary in doing good, for we will reap in due season, if we don't quit." (Galatians 6:9)

Verse about hope: (Romans 8:24)

Verse on Sovereignty of God: (Romans 8:28)

Chapter 29

Disciple read, "Come to Me, all you who labor and are heavy laden, and I will give you rest. Take My yoke upon you and learn from Me, for I am gentle and lowly in heart, and you will find rest for your souls. For My yoke is easy and My burden is light." (Matthew 11:28-30 NKJV)

Disciple read, "Be humbled under the mighty hand of God, so that He may exalt you in due season, having cast all your care upon Him, because He cares for you." (1 Peter 5:6, 7)

Disciple read, "Fear not, for I am with you; Be not dismayed, for I am your God. I will strengthen you, Yes, I will help you, I will uphold you with My righteous right hand." (Isaiah 41:10 NKJV)

Chapter 30

Verses quoted to the prisoners in the Castle of Despair in order: (Psalms 146:5) (1 Corinthians 15:19) (Titus 2:13) (Jeremiah 29:11)

Disciple said, "I understand completely. It is no longer we that live, but Christ in us." (Galatians 2:20)